# The John Blake Chronicles

Three Square Meals

By

M Tefler

(c) 2017 M Tefler

## Dedicated to:

My loyal fans, whose boundless enthusiasm kept me motivated and for their encouragement to turn what started as a hobby into a professional career.

My team of editors, who've generously dedicated so much of their time to this mammoth story and helped me learn so much.

And to my wife, for all her love and support. Maybe one day, I'll write a story you can tell your parents about!

# Contents

The John Blake Chronicles ....................................................................... 1

   Dedicated to: ........................................................................................ 3

   Three Square Meals Ch. 01 – A Fool's Errand ............................................ 5

   Three Square Meals Ch. 02 – The long journey home ........................... 23

   Three Square Meals Ch. 03 – Pivotal moments ..................................... 39

   Three Square Meals Ch. 04 – The Change ............................................. 60

   Three Square Meals Ch. 05 – Avenging angels ...................................... 88

   Three Square Meals Ch. 06 – The real adventure begins .................... 120

   Three Square Meals Ch. 07 – Breaking in the new ride ...................... 150

   Three Square Meals Ch. 08 – A rescue left unfinished ........................ 183

   Three Square Meals Ch. 09 – Living the dream ................................... 223

   Three Square Meals Ch. 10 – Completing the circle ............................ 259

   Author's Note ..................................................................................... 298

# Three Square Meals Ch. 01 – A Fool's Errand

John suppressed a triumphant smile as the mine owner plugged an auth device into his ship's logging manifest and pressed a couple of buttons to confirm the transaction. Signing over ownership of the ore could be done in the blink of an eye, but John wanted this transaction logged with the Merchant's Guild. There could be absolutely no doubt as to the legitimacy of this deal.

He knew it would take some time before confirmation was routed through the long chain of comm beacons, so he relaxed back in his chair and gazed out the window. The view outside was gloomy and depressing, overlooking the Mortimer Mine compound. John was in a mining colony known as Karron on the edge of the outer rim. It was a vast asteroid that could be better described as a tiny planet, its core slowly being hollowed out by the independent miners extracting the mineral wealth contained within.

Karron's dirty tunnels and squalid hab-zones received no sunlight from the bright red sun it orbited. The only illumination came from faded lighting-strips that were hammered into the rough-hewn walls, casting long forbidding shadows around the mining compound. Huge, six-wheeled trucks rumbled past the manager's office, the blocky vehicles on their way to collect the priceless cargo John had just purchased. They slowly disappeared from sight as they drove around huge piles of waste rock that nearly touched the cavern ceiling. The sombre greys of those granite mounds reminded him of a Trankaran's rocky hide and he cast his mind back to the last time he'd seen one of those aliens, on that eventful day over a month ago.

He'd been back in the Core Worlds having a drink at a local bar, which was well known for its tolerant attitude to the odd and eccentric. Popular amongst alien traders for just that reason, there were a broad selection of

exotic creatures in the bar that night. A hulking slab-faced Trankaran propped up the bar, chatting with the stocky three-armed, three-legged Ornalith it was towering over, the booming sound of its laughter echoing around the establishment. The two silicon-based lifeforms were a rarity that deep in human territory, but both were benign species and welcomed within the Terran Federation.

Returning his attention to his companion that evening, John focused on the drunk deep-spacer he had befriended years before. The gnarled old spacer was called Jonah, or 'Mad Jonah' to the other regulars in the bar, most of whom strongly suspected the poor unfortunate had gone space crazy years ago. John liked the old timer though and would spend hours listening to his wild stories of incredible sights beyond the outer rim. On this particular night, Jonah had recently returned from his latest jaunt into deep space and had been recounting a lurid time spent in a brothel on Karron...

"I tell you John, those worm girls have magic hands! I ain't never felt anything like what these pale-skinned jezebels could do to a fella!" he said, eyes widening as he recalled his misadventures.

"Worms" was slang for the residents of mining colonies, who often received no sunlight for years. Living underground in homes with no direct access to the Sun, meant that its inhabitants were pale-skinned to the point of albinism.

"You should head over there, youngster, and see for yourself. Tell Madame Trixie I say hi!" Jonah said, coupled with a theatrical wink and a guffaw.

John nodded obligingly, having no intention of heading that far out on the rim just to visit a brothel. He had initially objected to being called "youngster", having just hit forty last month, but he supposed everyone must seem young to the octogenarian and let Jonah continue.

"Ah, if only I were a younger man, I would have stayed there longer, but I figured I best skedaddle before those strumpets were the death of me. The ticker isn't quite up to as much exertion as it used to be," Jonah added with a snicker, before taking a long swig of booze.

Suddenly Jonah's alcohol induced stupor seemed to temporarily clear and he leaned into John conspiratorially. The old man's breath was toxic enough to be classified as a bio-hazard.

"It might be worth your while heading there besides those worm gals, youngster," he whispered in a hushed voice, casting a suspicious glance at a passing Yelneg merchant. He waited until the short fungoid creature had drummed past their table on its six stumpy legs before continuing. "One night I was hangin' out in Madame Trixie's parlour and a couple o' them miners came rollin' in havin' drunk up a storm. They were out celebratin' and lookin' to round out the night with some pleasures of the flesh. I got to chattin' with those fellas and seems like they had stumbled on a whole heap of Tyrenium."

At this, John's ears pricked up! John already had pointy ears due to his unusual parentage, but this comment caused them to prick up even further.

Tyrenium was a key component of plasma cores, used to power top-of-the-line military grade ship weaponry. It was sufficiently rare and in such huge demand, that the price for a ton of the element was astronomical to the right buyers. With John's military connections, he knew someone who would be very interested indeed...

John had stayed with Jonah for as long as could be considered polite before bidding him farewell. He sprinted back to the dock where his freighter was parked with his heart hammering in his chest, knowing that he had to move fast on this one. John dashed across the boarding gantry, before quickly tapping the airlock's security access code to gain entry to his ship, the 'Fool's Gold'. Rushing up to the cockpit, his hands shook with

excitement as he searched the Sector Maps for Karron. The moment he found it, he forced himself to take a deep breath to steady himself before he entered the navigation coordinates. There could be no mistakes when plotting his course. The route he was taking would take over a month and travelling this far to the outer rim held many hazards for the unwary...

The mine owner, Seb Mortimer, cleared his throat pointedly. "John?"

Snapped out of his reverie, John gave the man a smile of apology. "Sorry, I was light years away there. Everything okay?"

Seb nodded, a broad grin on his face. "Just got confirmation from the Merchant's Guild. The ore's all yours!"

The deal was now struck and the grinning men shook hands, both of them overjoyed at the completion of the trade. John had ransacked every rainy-day account he had, scraping together every last credit of his life's savings and sinking them into this deal. He was purchasing ten tons of Tyrenium at a ludicrously cheap rate, but it was still expensive enough to bring a huge grin to Seb's face. Two-point-five-million credits was an awful lot of money in a place like Karron.

John realised that being this far out on the borders of known space, Seb was unaware of just how valuable this element could be. Then again, he undoubtedly didn't have the exotic military connections that John did. The Terran Federation military strictly regulated trade in Tyrenium, only allowing its purchase by certain authorised traders... and the military of course. The two men shared an amiable drink of whisky to seal the deal, before John left the mine owner's office to oversee the loading of his cargo.

He strolled over to the waiting trucks that had been loaded with his haul of Tyrenium and nodded to the driver as he climbed up into the cabin of the lead vehicle. The huge truck roared into life and John felt the thrumming of the powerful engine as they pulled away.

Karron was a bleak, ugly, and inhospitable colony, far from the centre of human galactic civilisation. The brief journey from the mine to the starport provided a grim tour of the dark, grubby, and dilapidated slums that had built up in the hollowed out asteroid. They passed a middle-aged woman in a grey, ill-fitting jacket and trousers, tugging a child along behind her. Their faces both had a hard, sullen look to them, which he might have expected in the mother, but to see this beaten expression on such a young boy was sobering.

John felt a surge of relief that he'd be leaving this depressing place in a couple of hours. In fact, he was in such a hurry to leave, he decided to forego a visit to Madame Trixie's brothel. John had a moment of hesitation, as he wondered if the establishment really would live up to his old friend's claims, but then again, Mad Jonah did have more than a few peculiar tastes. In any case, John wasn't in the mood to deal with any potential mishaps that might arise, especially after just making the deal of his life and decided to give the place a pass.

The trucks eventually arrived at the starport and after a quick dialogue with the guards and the deck officer, the industrious miners loaded the cargo of Tyrenium aboard the Fool's Gold. John waved the miners goodbye and sealed the cargo bay doors. After setting the controls in the Cargo Bay for auto-decontamination, he then strode purposefully to the cockpit.

John slumped in the pilot's chair and pressed a button on the comm interface to call Karron Flight Control. After waiting for thirty seconds his call went through.

"Yeah, what?" a bored voice muttered.

John rolled his eyes, knowing this far out on the rim he couldn't expect much in the way of professionalism. "This is John Blake aboard the Fool's Gold. Requesting permission to depart."

"Sure," the man replied, closing the comm channel a second later.

John punched in the course for home, before activating the auto pilot to disembark from the asteroid. The ship's engines roared into life and the old freighter seemed to groan in protest as it took off. It slowly cleared the rough-hewn entrance to the docking bay, cruising out into the blackness of space. John let out a big sigh and was finally able to relax now that the deal was done and the cargo of Tyrenium was safely secured in the ship's hold.

He stared out of the cockpit as the ship turned towards the Nav Beacon. Karron was by far the biggest asteroid in a broad belt of rock, which orbited the giant star in the centre of the Omicron Ceti system. The star cast a blood-red glow over the freighter as it slowly pulled away from the asteroid belt, having to clear the local gravity wells before it was safe to jump out of the system. When he reached the beacon, John hit the button to activate his FTL drive and after a few seconds, the freighter groaned and lurched into hyper-warp.

Surprisingly John still felt twitchy, which he assumed was due to the adrenaline wearing off after the excitement of brokering such a life changing deal. He rose from his pilot's chair and after a good stretch, headed to his cabin to take a much-needed nap.

John unbuckled the harness to his heavy pistol and carefully unholstered it, then removed the magazine and checked the safety before placing it on the weaponry rack in his cabin. When he pressed his thumb to the door-lock, the locker closed with a swish. Deep space could be a dangerous place, with marauding pirates and the occasional misunderstandings with aliens, so it was sensible to be prepared in the case of a hostile boarding action.

The cabin was meticulously clean, courtesy of one of John's personality quirks. He liked to keep his ship obsessively tidy and couldn't abide

leaving mess anywhere. The rooms and corridors of the ship were kept spotless, which was handy with avoiding contamination, but took plenty of hours to maintain. After a soothing shower to clean away the dust and stink of the colony, John collapsed onto the crisp, pristine sheets on his wide bed and fell asleep.

Several hours later, after a nice relaxing sleep, John awoke feeling horny. He was hard as steel and ready for action. This came as quite a surprise, as John had spent years meditating to avoid getting into this kind of state. With his parentage being what it was, he couldn't be too careful. He sat up and assumed a meditative pose, clearing his mind and focusing on being calm and at peace. When the horniness and his erection abated, he got up, got dressed and went about his normal routine.

\*\*\*

A couple of days passed, with John awakening each morning to a rock-hard surprise. Each day it was getting more difficult to maintain his self-control, but he went through his meditation rituals and gradually calmed himself. He had been travelling for four days now, having left Karron far behind and he decided to check on his precious cargo.

The door to the cargo bay opened with a satisfying clank. Even though everything in the cargo hold seemed to be as expected, John still felt on edge. Standing on the gantry overlooking the ship's hold, he felt alert, focused, pensive, wary; he had great instincts and they were all telling him that something was wrong. Backing out of the cargo bay, he hurried to his cabin to collect some weaponry. John grabbed his broad-muzzled auto shotgun, perfect for up close work in the confined quarters of a spacecraft, and slammed in a clip. The autoshot hummed to itself happily for a few seconds as he flipped the power button on the grip and a holographic targeting grid appeared above the weapon. John turned back into the corridor and jogged briskly back to the hold.

Inside the cargo bay, John flicked on infrared on the scope and did a quick sweep of the hold with his shotgun. Looking for any telltale signs of red that signified heat, he saw nothing untoward in the targeting grid but cool shades of blue. He turned to the adjacent wall-mounted panel and cranked the illumination to maximum. He avoided looking at the blinding overhead lights as he searched the room thoroughly. It was not until he returned to the door-panel that he noticed a faint dusty scuff mark outside the door. Having meticulously scrubbed that section of floor in an OCD fury before landing, he knew that someone or something had come aboard with the cargo at Karron.

John resealed the cargo bay and began to sweep the ship. The Fool's Gold was not huge, having only the cockpit, his cabin, the hold, a secondary cabin, his recreation room and the ship's storage. The engine room and equipment room were kept sealed and a quick check confirmed that their locks hadn't been tampered with. He found no signs of life in the cabins or cockpit, and there wasn't anywhere to hide in the recreation room, consisting only of a dining table, a comfy sofa and a small but functional kitchen. That meant his interloper had to be in the storage room.

John took a deep breath and readied himself for action before stepping into the doorway. Raising his weapon, he looked through the scope. Nothing! The targeting grid depicted the room in expected blues, with the occasional red glow from the overhead lights. Turning slowly, he carefully checked any potential hiding places through the scope, until he finally faced a storage compartment near the back of the room. A faint but revealing red glow edged the door to this particular compartment, signifying a warm presence inside.

"I know you're in there, come on out!" John barked at the storage compartment, keeping a wary distance.

He waited pensively to the count of ten, but there was no movement from the mysterious interloper.

"Either you come out in five seconds, or I unload this shotgun and space your corpse!" John shouted at the compartment door.

He heard some kind of squeak from inside the compartment and the storage door swung open slowly. A dirty unkempt figure stepped timidly out of the compartment and into the bright lights of the storage room. It was obviously a miner's kid; some mid-teen boy he guessed by the look of him. He was scrawny and malnourished, wearing shabby grey overalls, a bulky tattered jacket and a cap pulled down low. Frightened eyes in a dirt-smeared face peered warily at John from beneath that dog-eared cap, watching and waiting for his next move.

John sighed and lowered the shotgun. "Oh, for fuck's sake!" he groaned. Thoroughly pissed off, he muttered, "Now I'm going to have to turn right around to drop your ass back at Karron! We're days away from there already!"

This dumbass kid's desire for adventure was going to cost him over a week on a pointless detour.

"Please don't take me back to Karron!" the boy pleaded in an oddly high-pitched voice. Perhaps this kid was younger than he initially thought, John mused.

"Why not?" John demanded. "There's no chance in hell I'm going to risk being done on a 'kidnapping a minor' charge and I don't for a minute think you have any money to pay me for the trouble. What's your name anyway, boy?"

The frightened stowaway looked down, momentarily breaking eye contact with John. "My name's Al."

"Well 'Al', my name's John. It's lovely to meet you," John snarled sarcastically. "Now we've made introductions, you still haven't answered my question. Why shouldn't I just take you straight back to Karron?"

"Maybe I could work for you as crew on the ship?" the grubby figure suggested hopefully.

"Sorry boy, I work alone. Besides, what skills could you have that would be useful on a starship? No, I'm going to have to take you back," John said, as he turned and started to walk out of the storage room.

"No! Wait!" his unwanted passenger pleaded.

As John turned back to look at the urchin, the kid gave a big sigh and seemed to make some kind of decision. Al reached up and pulled the tatty cap off, revealing dirty blonde hair that, with a few quickly removed clips, tumbled down revealing shoulder-length tresses.

"I'm not a boy, I'm a girl and I'm not a minor, I'm eighteen. Maybe there's something else I could do to earn my passage?" Al asked cautiously, but with a clearly suggestive undertone.

Now, in John's defence, under normal circumstances he would have turned her down flat, but his perpetual horniness over the last few days had rapidly eroded his will power. At least his morning surprises were now explained; he must have been reacting subconsciously to her pheromones. Without relief, it was going to be a trying four-day trip back to Karron if he decided to take Al back.

John cast an appraising eye over his passenger, but with the worn, bulky gear, and covered in all that dirt, it was impossible to tell what the newly-revealed girl looked like. Against his better judgement, John slung the shotgun over his shoulder and beckoned his stowaway out from the storage room.

"Follow me, I want you to get cleaned up before I make my decision," John said, as he led the girl to the passenger cabin. "You can use the

shower in there, and leave all the dirty gear in the corridor, including your ID. I want to make some checks."

The girl warily handed him a dog-eared foldout ID, that revealed the mystery passenger's full name to be Alyssa Marant.

Taking the ID, John pointed out the shower tucked into the corner of the passenger cabin, and said, "Thanks 'Alyssa', the shower is back there."

John left Alyssa to clean herself up and walked to the cockpit to scan in the ID. It took a few minutes to make the connection to Galactic-SEC, and he drummed his fingers on the armrest while he waited impatiently. Finally the computer beeped, and the brief readout confirmed the name on the ID, that his new passenger was eighteen and that she was not wanted for any felonies. That information calmed most of his worries; he would be doing nothing illegal in letting Alyssa stay on his ship and any agreements between them would be strictly between consenting adults. He felt himself getting hard again, and his excitement levels rose. Maybe the trip back home didn't have to be so boring after all?

John heard a small cough from the corridor behind him and saw Alyssa peeking around the door to the passenger cabin trying to get his attention.

"I've had a shower and that's all my gear," Alyssa said cautiously, pointing to the heap of filthy clothing piled in the corridor. "What do you want me to wear instead?"

John shuddered as he looked at the garments staining his pristine floors. Turning his attention back to his stowaway, he tilted his head to the same angle as hers, and said, "If you were suggesting what I think you were, then you'll be fine just as you are. Come on out so I can make my decision."

John reached behind him and pushed a button on the console. This activated the internal security cameras and would record their verbal agreement. You can't be too cautious, he figured.

Alyssa blushed, and taking another deep breath, stepped warily out of the cabin. Now that she was scrubbed clean, John could see that she actually had a very pretty face; piercing blue eyes, a cute nose, and full lips that immediately made him think of one thing. The girl was obviously from a mining colony, her ghostly white skin never having had sun exposure. Her hair fell to just beyond shoulder length, but it looked thin and lifeless, matching her unkempt sandy-blonde bush. She was roughly five-foot-two, about a 28A cup, and painfully skinny due to what he could only assume had been borderline starvation on the desolate mining world. He figured a steady diet would do her wonders and there was no time like the present to get started.

"OK. I've made my decision. You can stay; I won't take you back to Karron," he told her.

Alyssa jumped with joy, full of the exuberance of youth. "Oh, thank you John! Thanks so much!"

John smiled at her unexpectedly cheery outburst. Had she forgotten their arrangement already?

"Now that's decided, let's just lay out some ground rules about your duties on the ship," he said carefully.

Alyssa's face fell but she tried to hide it. Bless her, she had forgotten.

"I won't do anything to hurt you, and I won't force you into doing anything weird. I'll make sure you get regular meals, and you can have the passenger cabin as your own, but I expect you to keep everything just as clean as it is now. In exchange, I expect you to service me whenever I ask," he explained, looking into her eyes.

Alyssa was thoughtful after John's little monologue, and after a moment spent considering his terms, she said, "That all sounds reasonable."

"Good," he said with a smile. Glancing at her slim waist, he added, "Finally, are you on birth control?"

Alyssa looked a little bit uncomfortable as she admitted, "No, I'm not."

John shrugged, and said reassuringly, "OK, regular sex is out. I don't plan on knocking you up."

"That's a relief," she said, a playful smile on her lips.

"One last warning though," he said, his voice striking a cautionary note. "I have pretty hefty equipment, and once we've started this, I'll be needing your services several times a day."

"Yeah, I've heard that one before..." Alyssa smirked. "You've got a deal."

John smiled right back, and gestured behind her. "Let's get started. Why don't we reconvene in the rec-room, my balls need emptying."

That wiped the smirk from Alyssa's face, and with a resigned expression on her face, she turned around and walked back down the corridor. Following after her gave John another chance to check her out, but from behind this time. Alyssa had a wiry, toned body from living a hard life on the colony, evidenced by a handful of rough scars marring her skin. John's eyes travelled down her back, past the dimples above her hips to her pert little ass. It was lovely; round and compact, two perfect hemispheres that just needed filling out a little. Her legs looked lean but toned; runner's legs, he mused.

They walked into the rec-room and John strolled over to the sofa, while Alyssa gazed wide-eyed around the unfamiliar room. He took off his T-

shirt and combat trousers, standing naked except for his briefs, that did nothing to hide the size of his bulging package. He turned to face Alyssa, and at six foot two he towered over her petite five foot two form.

"Now, you can probably tell from these that I'm not completely human," John said, tilting his head and touching one of his ears.

Alyssa's bright blue eyes widened, staring at the elongated, pointy tips in fascination.

"That's not the only difference," he continued, nodding towards his groin. "I'm slightly different down there too."

Alyssa had an almost comic look of trepidation on her face, watching spellbound as John inserted his fingers into the waistband of his briefs. He carefully lifted the cotton material over his equipment, then dropped his underwear to the floor, unveiling his cock in all its glory. Alyssa let out a gasp of shock.

"You're fucking huge!" she exclaimed.

Overcoming her initial surprise, she looked closer at this startling revelation. John had an enormous cock, with girth thicker than her delicate wrist. John could see the doubt forming in her mind.

"Don't worry, it will fit," he said reassuringly. Sitting down on the sofa, he spread his legs and motioned her forward. "Kneel there please, Alyssa."

Alyssa took a nervous couple of steps and then sank to her knees. Face-to-face with his enormous cock, she licked her lips nervously, her gaze travelling down its swollen length.

"Holy Fuck!!! You've got four balls!" she gasped, gawping at the cluster of orbs below his burgeoning shaft.

"I did say I'm slightly different. I call them my quad," John explained helpfully.

Alyssa seemed to have overcome her initial surprise and was looking at his balls in fascination. They looked like regular Terran testicles, only there were two pairs, one set in front of the other. Oh, and each was the size of an orange!

Alyssa had a number of questions, but John cut her off as she opened her mouth to speak.

"No more questions Alyssa. It's time to get started," he said firmly. "Now take the head of my cock in your mouth."

With a resigned look on her face, Alyssa tentatively brought her hand forward to hold the base of his enormous cock. Her small hand struggled to surround the impressive girth, and she gasped as she touched his velvety hardness for the first time.

"It's so hot!" she exclaimed, as his cock throbbed in her hand.

She cautiously tilted the turgid member down towards her face, as a gleaming drop of pre-cum began to form on the swollen red crown.

"Open your mouth wide and take in the head," John commanded.

Alyssa leaned forward hesitantly, opening her soft pouty lips, and brushing them over his swollen mushroom head. The big dollop of pre-cum touched her tongue, and spread over her taste buds.

"It tastes sweet!" Alyssa exclaimed in surprise, as she pulled her head back momentarily.

The pretty girl savoured the taste of his pre-cum in her mouth for a moment, licking her full lips to make sure she hadn't missed any, before

moving forward to engulf more of the head this time. John gasped with pleasure, as Alyssa swirled her tongue over the eye of his cock. She had begun to apply gentle suction and was trying to get some more of his tasty pre-cum. John's swollen set of balls were happy to oblige, and provided the eagerly sucking young woman with another small spurt.

John was in heaven feeling Alyssa's hot, wet, silky smooth tongue slide over the head of his cock. It had been so long since he had last been with a woman and he luxuriated in the sensations. John watched enthralled, and he saw the girl's throat move as she swallowed the pre-cum he was feeding her. Alyssa leaned in further, opening her mouth wide to take more of him in. John could only groan with excitement, as her full soft lips stretched enough to finally engulf the whole head of his engorged member.

Alyssa's eyes started to glaze over as she continued to swallow his precum. He had seen this happen before, as it seemed to be a side effect of his unusual parentage. The girl was pushing forward, then pulling back, gradually taking more of his massive cock into her mouth as she bobbed her head. Inch by inch, she was making steady progress down his dick.

"That's a good girl, take me in nice and deep," he muttered, as he gripped the sofa tightly with his hands.

Every fibre of his being urged him to grab her pretty face, and stuff his cock down her gullet, but he knew he had to be patient.

"Mmm!" Alyssa hummed contentedly, as she continued to take him deeper.

Abruptly her progress stopped as the engorged head met the entrance to her throat. The girl gagged for a moment before pausing, pulling back a couple of inches. His fellatrix seemed to visibly relax, and then push her head forward in one long smooth motion, her lips nibbling his shaft as she took him deeper and deeper. John felt a tight pressure around the head of

his dick, before something seemed to give way, and with a loud swallow, Alyssa took him into her throat.

John groaned in ecstasy as the teen's body gripped his cock like a warm, wet, tight-fitting glove. With her throat relaxed, it was easier for her to make progress, and with regular breaks to breathe, she was able to swallow more and more of his tool. In what seemed like no time at all, Alyssa was taking his whole length into her obscenely stuffed throat, her lips stretched taut around his girth. John's long drought played havoc with his control and he had a white-knuckled grip on the armrests of the sofa. He looked down as her chin touched his balls, her nose gently brushing his stomach and couldn't hold back any more. An explosive orgasm started building from deep within him.

"That's right baby, time to fill your belly," John muttered, before throwing his head back as his climax began. His cock seemed to swell even more and his balls churned as they prepared to unload.

"Oh fuck, YES!" he exclaimed, as a massive surge of cum exploded up his shaft.

The thick, heavy cum slid straight down Alyssa's throat, settling in her slim tummy. The girl groaned, and her legs began to tremble violently as she joined him in orgasm. Surge after surge of powerful spurts of spunk rapidly filled her stomach, her belly starting to expand to take the sheer volume of cum. Finally, she was forced to pull back so that just the head was in her mouth, giving the teen a chance to draw in a lungful of air. John continued to blast into the girl's mouth, and she gulped down his thick load, desperately making room for more.

His multiple balls finally emptied, John collapsed back into the sofa. Alyssa let him slip from between her swollen lips as he stopped filling her mouth, using her delicate finger to catch the dribbles of cum that had escaped her lips, swallowing them too. John looked down at the young woman kneeling in front of him. Her mouth was still hanging open as she panted

for breath and he could see that he'd painted the inside white. He could even see his cum dripping from her tonsils where he had hosed down the entrance to her throat.

Alyssa leaned backwards and finally sat up straight. She hadn't lost the glazed look in her eyes, and her hands moved down to stroke her grossly distended belly. She was a thin girl anyway, but the several pints of thick sperm rich spunk he had just fed her, made her look several months pregnant. Numerous drops of cum had dripped from her mouth when she had been blowing him, and Alyssa moaned as her hands glided over her swollen stomach, rubbing his cum into her glistening skin.

After taking a few moments to recover his wits, John rose to his feet and gently scooped Alyssa up in his arms. He carefully carried her back to the passenger cabin, laid her out on the bed, and gently tucked her under the pristine white covers. Alyssa fell asleep the moment her head touched the pillow, so he dimmed the lights and quietly left the room so as not to disturb his new guest.

As he slowly backed into the corridor, John nearly tripped over the pile of soiled gear in the hallway. He quickly scooped up the offending items, and made his way to the airlock, where he blasted the tattered and filthy gear into space. With a shudder of relief, he watched through the airlock window as the sad scraps of clothing sailed off into the black.

Returning to the rec-room he dressed quickly, before collecting cleaning gear to battle the mess in the hallway. He sighed happily as he got to work, enjoying the dull ache in his freshly relieved balls.

# Three Square Meals Ch. 02 – The long journey home

John reclined in the comfortable embrace of the Pilot's chair in the cockpit of the Fool's Gold. He had purchased this chair specifically for its well-designed ergonomics. Knowing how many hours he spent here in the cockpit, he figured that paying top dollar for this marvel of form-fitting handiwork was worth every penny. Considering the fortune in doctor's bills some of his freighter pilot friends had shelled out to fix their bad backs, it had been a wise investment!

He'd spent the morning cleaning and tidying an already pristine storage room, so slumping in the chair was a welcome chance to put his feet up. Checking the Sector Map, he saw that they were just approaching the Mu Lyrae system and were going to slingshot around it to help reduce their travel time. John looked out the cockpit window and watched the bright orange star loom large on their port bow. He knew there were nearly a dozen planets in that system, mostly gas giants, but there were also several nearly habitable planetoids. They were still a long way from civilisation though and the Federation hadn't started Terraforming planets this far from the Core Worlds.

He glanced at the oval display for the long-range scanners, but there was nothing unusual showing. This far out in deep space it was rare to encounter other ships, but in John's experience, those encounters could turn nasty very quickly. Deep space was a lawless and dangerous place, light years away from the commonly travelled space lanes and the accompanying Federation patrols.

John opened the Holonet, and switched to the newsfeed to keep up to date with Galactic events. According to the latest reports, tensions were high between the Terran Federation and the neighbouring Kintark Empire, with reports of numerous border incursions from both sides. Video feed was playing in the corner of the TFNN news report, and the anchorman,

23

Bill Armstrong, had just ended a studious and boring interview with a Terran expert on Terran-Kintark Galactic relations. The anchor started an animated discussion with an exceptionally pretty reporter who caught John's attention. Swiping his finger over the video, it expanded into a full holographic image that hovered over his console and he rewound the segment back to the start.

"My thanks for providing that fascinating insight, Professor Baumann," Bill Armstrong said, with a gleaming - but totally insincere – smile at the camera. "For our next piece, we're lucky enough to have one of the newest members of the TFNN team right in the thick of danger! Here's Jehanna Elani, with a special report right from the heart of contested space!"

"Thanks, Bill!" the exceptionally pretty, dusky-hued young woman replied, focusing on the camera with a lovely smile. "I'm reporting from the Dragon March, in Port Medea, our bastion of power in these far flung reaches of the Federation! With me today is Lieutenant-Commander Mortensen, who has graciously agreed to this TFNN interview."

Jehanna turned her dazzling smile on the uniformed man beside her. They were standing on a balcony overlooking a well-maintained plaza and behind them, squads of troops were marching through the starbase.

"It's my pleasure, Miss Elani," the officer replied, doing his best to keep his eyes on her face, rather than the tantalising glimpse of cleavage showcased by her tight blouse.

"Can you confirm the rumours that the Kintark have been growing increasingly belligerent in recent weeks?" Jehanna asked, her lovely brown eyes fixed on his face.

Mortensen nodded, his expression darkening. "I'm afraid so. We've had to deal with completely unprovoked attacks on Terran merchant shipping by

the Kintark military and just today they've gone so far as to close their borders to Terran vessels!"

Jehanna shook her head with a frown. "Has there been any justification given for these most distressing actions?"

"Pointing the finger at us mostly, that kind of nonsense. I think they never got over ceding the Dragon March to the Federation," Mortensen replied with a helpless shrug. He grinned at her as he added, "But if they want another fight, we're ready to give it to them!"

Jehanna turned back to the camera with a serious expression on her face. "With brave troops like these defending the far reaches of Terran Space, the Kintark should seriously rethink their hostile actions. The Terran Federation never initiates conflicts with our neighbours, but we'll stand strong in the face of terror!"

"Thank you, Jehanna," Bill Armstrong said, smiling at her in gratitude. "Now, we have the results from this week's Zero-G football games..."

John turned off the holo image and stared into space with a worried frown. He was travelling in the opposite direction to the Terran border with the Kintark Empire, but it was still alarming to hear that the Kintark had closed their borders. The Terran media were all favouring the Federation line; that they were responding to unwarranted aggression from the Kintark, but John had enough independent contacts with neutral alien trading partners to know that there were two sides to this story.

He had traded with the Kintark about five years earlier and he found them to be reliable trading partners. There'd been a brief war between the two empires over two centuries earlier, but John had assumed that was all water under the bridge as he'd not run into any trouble in Kintark Space. The reptilian race could be unsettling with their emotionless, sibilant speech, but if you could overcome humanity's instinctive fear of the unknown, they were a straightforward species to deal with.

His mind drifted and he struggled to concentrate on the Holonet story. His thoughts kept returning to his guest and he wondered how she was doing. Alyssa had been asleep for just over fourteen hours since their session in the recreation room, and the last time he had checked in on her, the girl was still slumbering soundly. Just as he had made up his mind to check on her again he heard a faint rustling from the passenger cabin and the pad of feet on the steel deck.

John spun the pilot's chair to face the corridor as Alyssa stepped through the cabin door. She had wrapped herself in the bedsheet in an impromptu toga and was making her way into the cockpit.

"Please could I have some water, I'm feeling really thirsty," Alyssa requested politely as she moved to sit in the co-pilot's seat.

John got up from his chair and went to the water dispenser in the cockpit. He moved to the side so that she could clearly see how he was operating the machine and pressed a couple of buttons. A glass slid out and the dispenser gurgled happily as it filled it up with sparkling clear water. Condensation immediately began to form on the delightfully chilled drink and John handed the glass to his guest before he sat down again. The two sat in silence, studying each other as Alyssa took small sips, soothing her parched throat.

"How are you feeling?" John asked pleasantly, breaking the silence. "Did you sleep ok?"

Alyssa paused a moment, looking thoughtful before answering, "I don't remember the last time I slept that well. How long was I asleep for?"

"You were out for fourteen hours," John explained. "I checked on you a couple of times and you seemed ok."

"Fourteen hours!" Alyssa exclaimed, looking astonished. "I normally only get a couple of hours at a time. Back on Karron, you had to sleep with one eye open..."

He smiled at her and said, "Well, I promise you can sleep safely here with me."

The girl darted him a curious glance, then put her glass down on the console and stretched languidly. "I feel amazing!" she sighed happily. "If only I'd known I'd feel like this after getting a good night sleep!"

As she straightened her back and stretched her arms up over her head, her makeshift outfit suffered a wardrobe malfunction. The sheet around her chest slipped loose, and dropped into a pool in her lap, revealing her slim upper body. Alyssa flinched and hurried to restore her modesty before stopping suddenly, catching John's gaze and leaving the sheet where it was. Her stomach seemed to have reverted back to its normal trim size, her waif-like body absorbing the huge meal he had so enjoyed filling up her belly with yesterday. The girl also seemed to have lost some of the painful skinniness that had defined her ribs so clearly when they first met.

"What happened last night?" Alyssa asked with a puzzled look on her face.

John was quiet for a moment, then countered, "What do you remember?"

"I remember us going to the rec-room and you introducing me to your equipment," she replied, blushing prettily. "I especially remember the 'Quad'," she added, with helpful air quotes. "After that it's all a blur."

"Well... do you want the romanticised, obfuscated version or the brutally honest version?" John asked with a playful smile.

"Give me the brutally honest version please, I'd like to know what I'm dealing with," Alyssa said, looking slightly apprehensive. "Besides, I have no idea what obfuscated means!"

"You sucked my cock like a pro, then I filled that lovely little belly of yours with several pints of cum," John explained, watching her pretty face. "Then I tucked you up in bed to sleep off your meal."

Alyssa blushed deeper, looking shocked and slightly embarrassed... but not as much as he would have expected.

"Don't be embarrassed, honey. You did a great job," John reassured her comfortingly. "I couldn't be happier you decided to stow away on my ship!"

The cute teenager absorbed John's words and seemed to visibly grow in confidence. John saw a teasing smile form on her pretty face, as her eyes dropped to his groin, then back up to look at him.

"I'm feeling hungry John; what have you got for breakfast?" she asked coyly.

John grinned back and unbuckled his trousers. Alyssa stood, leaving the sheet behind on the co-pilot's chair and walked towards him as he dropped his trousers to the floor. His huge cock stood up past his belly button and throbbed expectantly. The petite teen moved between his spread thighs and dropped to her knees.

Alyssa reached out and grasped two of his balls, one in each hand. She cupped them gently, feeling the orange sized orbs in each sack. John watched the girl with interest as she explored his body, curious to see how she would react. Alyssa moved from the front set of balls to the set behind, cupping each in turn and feeling their heavy weight.

"They're just so big!" she exclaimed, glancing up at him in wonder. "How do you even walk with all these between your legs?"

John laughed out loud. He had never been asked that before. "It does get a bit tricky when I'm full up and turned on," he admitted with a smile.

"Well it's good I'm here to help you out then!" Alyssa grinned back at him.

The perky teen leaned forward and swabbed the top of his manhood with her tongue. She moved one of her hands from his balls to caress his turgid shaft, before wrapping her slim fingers around his girth. John watched intently as her ghostly pale hand slid up and down his cock in a smooth rhythm, looking tiny against his massive shaft.

Alyssa leaned forward and her soft lips spread invitingly over the engorged head of his pulsing cock. She maintained eye contact with him as her tongue danced over him, warm, wet and silky smooth. The petite girl had managed to take the entire head in her mouth, her lips spreading obscenely wide to welcome him into her. He looked deeply into her brilliant blue eyes as she sucked on him, finding it impossible to break that piercing cerulean gaze.

"Oh my God! That's so good!" he groaned, as he watched her enraptured.

The corner of Alyssa's mouth seemed to twitch, wanting to smile. There was just no way to do so with his massive tool spreading her lips so wide. John's balls seemed to throb contentedly, as if they knew there was a receptive female happy to provide a new home for their contents. Alyssa was sucking strongly on the head of his cock and John began feeding her pre-cum as his excitement levels rose.

The pretty teen's eyelids began to get heavy, and that sharp, perceptive gaze began to lose focus. Alyssa closed her eyes and she started taking more of his meat into her mouth. Her head began to move in a smooth bobbing motion, matching the same rhythm of her hand. The teen was on

a mission now, fully intent on taking his whole cock into her throat, her saliva filled mouth making debauched sounds as she blew him.

Looking down, John watched as the blonde-haired girl took more and more of him into her mouth. Alyssa paused with the head of his swollen cock at the entrance to her throat, and took a deep breath before sliding forward, enveloping him in the tight warm confines of her body. Staring intently, he cradled her head and guided her forward, as her throat relaxed and accepted his whole length in one long, smooth motion.

John moaned, unable to form coherent words at the incredible sensations he felt along his shaft. Alyssa's tongue glided along the underside of his cock as she withdrew, then plunged forward again, easing his passage in and out of her body, and heightening his pleasure. John was only able to groan in appreciation when the girl took in his whole length, her dancing tongue snaking out to lap at the top of his balls. He marvelled that she was able to take him so deep in such easy, fluid motions.

The couple maintained this lustful rhythm, Alyssa kneeling submissively and stroking his cock with her talented mouth. She swallowed occasionally, clearing the saliva from her mouth and massaging his cock with the strong muscles in her throat. John could only moan appreciatively as the talented girl deep throated him time after time, only pulling clear to take the occasional deep breath. This blowjob was amazing, even better than last night. John recalled a vision of Alyssa stroking her swollen belly yesterday and struggled valiantly not to explode too soon.

Alyssa seemed to be reading his body perfectly, sensing the rising ecstasy growing in the man she was servicing with such incredible skill. Her throat gripped him in a comforting sheath as he throbbed in her mouth, her lips soft, yet insistent as they travelled down to his root time and time again. Subconsciously sensing that he was ready, the girl drew back, clearing her windpipe and allowing her to take a deep lungful of air. Her body

rejuvenated, she slid right back down his length again, her body promising him relief.

The change in sensation was too much for John and he seized the armrests of his chair in a fierce grip as he threw his head back and exploded. "Oh, fuck me! I'm coming!" he bellowed, as his quad prepared for action.

Spurt after spurt of gloriously rich spunk blasted up his shaft and into the welcoming pit of Alyssa's stomach. John's hips thrust forward in rapid reflexive motions, as he desperately unloaded his cum into the willing girl kneeling submissively before him. Alyssa's soft full lips cushioned his thrusts as she leaned forward, eagerly sucking on him and taking his huge load.

The pretty teen's slim belly soon began to round out, as John filled her with heavy spunk. Alyssa's throat throbbed in sync with his cock as his jism raced up his huge shaft and pulsed into her body. The young woman's body trembled as she joined him in mindless orgasm, her body revelling in being used so completely.

Eventually, John's mind-blowing orgasm abated. Alyssa pulled back, letting his cock slip from the tight confines of her throat until only his head remained in her mouth. He could only shudder as she sucked powerfully on him one last time and his spent balls desperately tried to feed her more cum. When she finally let him go and sat back on her haunches, she had a self-satisfied smile on her lovely face as she stared ahead of her in a daze.

John sighed with relief, and smiled as he said, "You look like the cat that got the cream."

Speaking of which, his cream had filled out her tummy nicely. The petite waif was stroking another bellyful of the rich cum that had settled in the welcoming new home of her stomach. The massive load had given her

another swollen belly, just as large as that of the previous night. On her slim body it looked obscene.

Alyssa's eyes were heavy-lidded and still glazed over, so John got up, scooped the slim girl up in his arms and carried her back to the passenger cabin. She sighed contentedly into his chest as he walked back to her room. He marvelled at her light weight, and despite the extra load he'd just added to her rounded midriff, was able to carry her effortlessly. John gently laid her on the bed, returning a moment later to cover her slim form with the sheet. He paused at the door and smiled at her slumbering form, dimming the lights again before he left.

John busied himself with routine maintenance around the ship. After relieving his baser urges, he was now able to concentrate again, and he hummed happily to himself as went about his various chores. Some power cabling resealed here, an overhead light fixed there; time seemed to disappear as he worked on the ship. He'd had a strong work ethic nurtured in him during his youth and it had never left him. Several hours passed and John had just finished cleaning the recreation room when a noise behind him brought him back to full awareness.

"Ahem!" Alyssa cleared her throat, announcing her presence. When he turned to face her, she demanded, "What did you do to my tummy?"

Alyssa stood, hands on hips, in the entrance to the rec-room. As she strode towards him, he saw that the object of her indignation had reduced in size somewhat from when he had initially filled her up. Unfortunately, her body had not had enough time to absorb the heavy, protein-rich spunk and the petite girl still looked several months pregnant.

"You look amazing, Alyssa," John reassured the girl as he moved towards her, momentarily regretting his pledge not to knock her up.

He gathered her smoothly in his arms, leaning down to kiss the surprised teen full on the lips. She sighed a breathy moan as her soft, pouting lips

parted to let him push in his tongue. They kissed passionately for several moments, her own tongue moving to duel his in her mouth. John moved to the sofa, gathering the girl in his lap as he sat down, maintaining their kiss and fierce embrace.

They paused for breath and leaned back, studying each other. John moved his strong hand to the teens stuffed belly and stroked her gently. Her stomach felt firm and full where his heavy spunk had blown out her waistline, forcing her slim tummy to accommodate his load. He thought about the millions of sperm swimming around inside her, desperate in their futile task to impregnate the slim teenager and he felt a stirring in his loins.

"I explained that I fed you several pints of cum last night. This is what it looks like," John said, caressing Alyssa's engorged belly pointedly.

"I thought you were exaggerating," Alyssa mumbled, flushing with embarrassment.

"Don't worry, your body will absorb it all and you'll be back to normal in no time," John reassured the worried girl, while gently stroking her tummy.

She placed her hand on his as he caressed her and lightly brushed her thumb over his fingers. She looked at him in fascination and asked, "How do you know? Have you done this before?"

John smiled at her and replied, "Yes, I've been with a woman before."

"What about the memory loss then, the blackouts?" Alyssa persisted.

"Yes, that's normally what happens." John confirmed, his tone soothing. "I cum, the girl gets a huge belly, and is comatose for a while. She wakes up after a good long sleep, none-the-wiser and feeling great, then we happily part ways."

Alyssa looked thoughtful for a moment, then gave him a look filled with sympathy. "No long-term relationships then? That sounds lonely."

John was taken aback by the abrupt shift in conversation topic, and he blinked at her in surprise. "Well, yes, I guess," he stammered, unprepared for this line of questioning. "Considering I'm not exactly normal, I figured it was probably for the best."

Alyssa now wore a caring, understanding look on her face. She looked at him intently then reached up to stroke the side of his face in a gentle caress. Pulling his head down, she kissed him again, her soft lips feeling amazing against his own. They kissed and made out like teenagers, which was not all that surprising, considering one of them was actually only eighteen.

The kissing grew more passionate and John ran his hands over Alyssa's nubile form. His hand slid over her swollen stomach, slipping down between the girl's thighs. Her teenage skin felt so soft and smooth under his fevered touch and Alyssa spread her legs as his hand moved further between them. John could feel how turned on the girl was when his hand moved higher and his finger slipped between the lips of her pussy. She was slick and inviting as he cupped her pussy and slid his finger deeper inside.

Alyssa gasped, as his questing finger burrowed in.

 John finger fucked the moaning girl for a few moments, enjoying the exquisite warmth and tightness. He could only imagine what it would feel like to penetrate her young body with his massive cock. He maintained the forceful thrusting of his finger inside her, delighting as she moaned responsively.

"Oh fuck, that feels good!" Alyssa gasped.

John undid his trousers with his free hand as he pleasured her with the other. Lifting her easily, he placed her in his lap, each cheek of her pert little ass resting on either side of his reawakened cock. Alyssa's wonderfully firm round bottom felt amazing pressed to his groin and the slippery fluids from her excited little pussy added plenty of lubrication to his cock. He rocked her up and down on his shaft, enjoying the tight firmness of her cheeks, whilst maintaining his finger's insistent stroking in and out of her snug young pussy.

Moving the other hand down, John began to stroke the girl's swollen clit as he added a second finger to her deliciously tight pussy. Alyssa squealed as the second finger slid in against the first, widening her young hole and increasing the intensity of her sensations. John curled his fingers up, looking for her G-Spot and then began to rub the sensitive little area in sync with the stroking he was giving her clit with the other hand.

"Holy fuck!" Alyssa wailed, as her body arched and thighs spasmed.

The trembling teen came long and hard, her pussy rewarding his fingers with a delightful massaging sensation. John revelled in the sound of the teenager's breathy cries and gasps and just as she was calming down, he massaged her body hard and fast, forcing another toe curling orgasm from the primed girl.

"Good, she's multi-orgasmic," he thought to himself, her body convulsing hard from the intense pleasure she was experiencing.

Finally having mercy, he pulled his soaked fingers from Alyssa's pussy and held her in a warm embrace as she calmed down and relaxed against him.

"That was amazing!" Alyssa gasped, turning to look up at him in amazement. Gazing at him with shining eyes, she exclaimed breathily, "I've never come twice like that before! I didn't know it was possible!"

John just nodded agreeably as he held the teenager's hips in his hands. He was rocking her gently on his pussy-slicked cock, and her firm little ass felt incredible straddling his length. Her tight little pussy was warm, wet, and only a few tempting inches away. John fought an ever-increasing internal struggle not to lift the petite teen up and slide her snug little body onto his eagerly awaiting rod. As if sensing she was only moments away from potential motherhood, Alyssa slipped out of John's grasp and slid to her knees in front of the sofa.

"Let me take care of that for you." she purred seductively, opening her mouth wide, and covering the swollen mushroom-head of his cock.

This time John felt no resistance at all as the petite girl smoothly swallowed his engorged girth into her throat, and engulfed his entire length in one ball-trembling move. It was like her mouth and throat were a warm, wet, massaging tunnel that had been custom-designed to empty his balls whenever needed. He groaned ecstatically as the teenager took his full length time and time again.

John had never experienced pleasure like this before and he lost track of time as Alyssa worked him closer towards his climax. He was suddenly overcome by the unstoppable urge to unload, and he grasped Alyssa's blonde head, as he exploded down her throat. Her tongue massaged the underside of his cock, coaxing out each blast of spunk and welcoming it into her body. Even though Alyssa's full lips were already tightly encircled around the root of his shaft, with her nose rubbing his stomach, his hips still thrust forward mechanically, trying to force himself deeper.

Surge after surge of heavy cum was added to the previous load that she had swallowed and her tummy gurgled contentedly as it expanded yet again to house his essence. The teenager's distended belly touched the floor as the girl leant over, eagerly sucking down every last spurt of cum.

Eventually he was spent, and Alyssa slid John's cock out of her throat and mouth. The heady pheromones from the potent load she had just

ingested rendered Alyssa insensate. She leaned forward and rested her exhausted head on his thigh as she breathed deeply. Her thighs were splayed wide to accommodate her semen-packed belly that now rested comfortably on the floor.

John soon recovered and, just like last time, fell into what had become their routine. He scooped up the wiped-out girl, cradling her in his arms as she mumbled incoherently into his chest, carried her to the passenger cabin and tucked her into bed. As the teenager rolled onto her side, facing him, he could see a slight movement under the covers that he realised was her stroking her overloaded stomach in her sleep.

"Well, she won't ever need to go hungry again," he thought to himself, with a smile of contentment.

His shoulders and arms popped gratifyingly as he stretched his broad back, before he looked down at the slumbering girl. John enjoyed the feelings of protectiveness and satisfaction that he felt when looking at his young charge and congratulated himself on his decision to let her stay on board.

He was quiet as he left the passenger cabin, only humming to himself contentedly when he strolled into the cockpit and settled into the pilot's chair. Glancing at the long-range scanner, there was nothing unusual highlighted on the screen, just the vast blackness of space and the occasional hunk of uninhabited rock. Even at the incredible speeds possible in hyper-warp, it was still going to take them over three more weeks until they reached his intended destination.

The Fool's Gold was an ex-navy auxiliary ship and while he'd kept it pretty well maintained, it was still an old and outdated vessel and in need of a good service. The FTL drive was hardly state of the art, and the fifty-metre-long freighter wasn't even sporting any weapons, but she'd kept him out of trouble all these years and he was quite fond of the old girl.

Once he'd been able to shift his cargo of Tyrenium, he could do something about all that and make some real improvements.

John sighed contentedly, and folding his arms behind his head, he relaxed back into the comfy chair. At least with his eager new companion, the trip back home would be a whole lot more interesting than the painfully dull journey he'd made getting all the way here to the outer rim. A little bit of excitement sounded like just what he needed right now and he found himself looking forward to Alyssa waking up from her nap.

# Three Square Meals Ch. 03 – Pivotal moments

The water cascaded over John's face in a soothing waterfall, washing the sweat and grime from his body. He stood still for a moment, face tilted upwards, enjoying the hot streams from the shower splashing over his head. He had just spent the last several hours cleaning out one of the engine filtration units and the caked-up layers of dirt were now swirling down the plug in the shower floor. He really hated cleaning out the carbon build up in the filter because there was no way of avoiding getting absolutely filthy. Still, it had to be done, and in his euphoric post-orgasmic state he hadn't really minded so much.

A light tapping on the shower door brought John out of his soothing reverie. The door opened tentatively and Alyssa's tousled blonde head appeared through the steam.

"Mind if I join you?" she asked with a mischievous grin.

"Be my guest!" John replied, greeting her with a smile and pushing the door open wider to let her in.

The young girl stepped into the roomy shower, the steam swirling in her wake as the door swung closed behind her. She moved closer, invading his personal space but not actually touching him, their bodies only an inch or so apart. Alyssa's pretty face was tilted upwards to look at him. The playful smile that had never left her lips was now joined by a raised eyebrow that seemed to challenge him to initiate contact between them.

John laughed and brought his arms around the petite girl in a welcoming hug. Alyssa's giggles were muffled in his chest, but the lovely melodic sounds of female laughter reverberated around the shower when he tickled her for her cheekiness. He eventually had mercy, and Alyssa's arms encircled his ribs returning his hug and resting her head on his chest. They

stood like that for several moments, both enjoying the closeness and physical intimacy.

"Well, we better get you cleaned up," John said to the teenage shower intruder.

Moving one of his arms from behind her back, he cupped his hand under the cleaning gel dispenser. A dollop of soapy gel automatically dropped into his waiting hand, prompted by the device's sensor. John stepped back from his young guest and lathered up both hands, before bringing them forward to glide over her shoulders. Her skin felt delightfully soft and warm under his heavy hands. He massaged her shoulders briefly before moving to her neck. Alyssa tilted her head back to keep her hair out of his way, exposing her throat to him, a look of trust in her blue-eyed gaze.

John cupped the back of her head with one hand, as he stroked the soapy gel down her slender neck with the other. With her head tilted backwards, it was easy for them to maintain eye contact and an unspoken conversation seemed to pass between them.

"My cock belongs in here," his gently massaging hand implied.

"Yes, whenever you want," her eyes confirmed.

John's cock rose to full firmness, like a sleeping behemoth awakening from its slumbers.

Still supporting Alyssa's head with one hand as she gazed up at him, John brought his other hand lower, gliding down over the girl's chest. He enjoyed the feel of the soft flesh of her tiny breasts, and the pert hardness of her erect nipples as his hand explored her upper body. It might have been a trick of the light in the shower, but her skin didn't seem to be quite so ghostly-pale any more, having adopted a much healthier pinkish hue. As his hand glided teasingly over her erect nipples,

he figured it was probably just her skin reacting to the warmth of the shower.

His curious fingers slid lower, skating over her ribs. Her body no longer felt like the emaciated waif he had initially met. Alyssa felt firmer, more youthful, and full of vitality. Stroking her slim tummy, which had now reverted back to its normal size, he admired the expanse of perfect, blemish-free skin.

"Now it's time to do your back," he murmured, as he rotated the teenager away from him to face the wall.

Alyssa looked over her shoulder at him, her gaze heavy with lust. Turning away from him, she placed both hands against the wall, spread her legs slightly and waited expectantly.

John lathered up both hands again as he loomed over the submissively postured teen before him; their difference in physical size quite pronounced. He placed both hands on her shoulder blades, before running his hands down her back, following the path of her spine. The comfortably warm gel let his hands glide effortlessly over her body, as he gently massaged her soothingly.

Sinking to his haunches behind her, John brought his face level to the girl's lower back. Alyssa's bottom seemed to have also filled out nicely, forming two perfectly spherical globes that sat proudly above her toned thighs. The water cascading from the shower ran down her back, over her dimples of Venus, and then slid between her two wonderfully pert cheeks. John reached out to take one in each hand, feeling the firm, pliant flesh beneath his fingers. He massaged her with his strong hands, eliciting contented sighs from his young companion. The sighs turned to an excited gasp as John spread those delicious cheeks apart, exposing her to his greedy eyes.

The girl's nether hole was tightly closed, looking pink and virginal as he gazed at her lustily. Below, the neat labia of her pussy had parted slightly, looking wet and inviting. He was sure that wetness was not just from the shower.

John relaxed his strong grip on her cheeks, letting them move back into place and obscuring the tantalising view. He let each hand slide out and then down, following the outer contours of her body. Alyssa's legs had filled out too. They felt wonderfully muscled and firm under his exploring touch and the skin of her creamy pink thighs felt incredibly smooth under his sensitive fingers. He finally reached the end of those legs, his hands moulding over her shapely calves. He could see her tiny feet shift underneath her, her toes gripping the shower floor to try and retain her balance under the sensory overload of his touch.

John raised himself back up to full height again before moving slightly around to the girl's side. Alyssa tilted her head to her left to watch his face, as his right hand cupped her bottom again, while the left hand slid around and over her tummy.

"Yesss!" the teenager hissed as his left hand slid lower, his finger parting the lips of her pussy. He brushed her clit with the base of his index finger triggering a gasp from the girl. John massaged the lips of her pussy, 'accidentally' gliding over her clit from time to time.

Alyssa moaned as John's right hand slid down from her trembling buttocks and between her legs, to place a finger in her tight young pussy. John began to strike up a steady rhythm of in and out strokes with the finger of his right hand, whilst circling and gently rubbing her clit with his left.

The trembling in her nubile young body grew more and more pronounced as he worked her to fever pitch, until she finally threw back her head, her slender back arched in a graceful curve. Her eyes were squeezed tightly shut as she screamed explosively, coming hard for him as she writhed to his touch.

John supported her in his arms as the trembling girl gasped out her pleasure. He enjoyed the feeling of her body grasping his finger tightly as her pussy convulsed around him. Slowly withdrawing that finger from her snug hole, he moved it an inch higher, and began gently encircling the teen's rosebud.

The unfamiliar sensation roused the blonde girl from her post-orgasmic high and Alyssa looked up at him nervously. "I've never..." she blurted out between laboured breaths.

"Shhh, it's ok, I'm not going to hurt you," he replied reassuringly.

When Alyssa gave him permission with a tentative nod, John began to massage the entrance to her back passage. He started to apply gentle but insistent pressure to her anus, and with the help of the unctuous lubrication from her pussy, he was able to part the tight muscles of her sphincter and slide in the tip of his finger.

"Fuck!" she gasped, clenching up around his probing digit.

The girl's body was rigid with anticipation, so he stroked her clit again, and whispered to her comfortingly, "There we go, just relax, I'm not going to hurt you".

The tension immediately dissipated from her rigid shoulders and back, as she made a visible effort to relax by focusing on his soothing voice. John maintained the distracting stroking of her sensitive clit and the girl began to moan again in pleasure. Taking that as a good sign, John applied a little more pressure with his right hand and slid his finger an inch deeper into her body.

"Ohhh," Alyssa gasped, feeling him invade her unplundered depths.

"Is that ok?" John asked.

"Yes, it just feels a bit... weird," Alyssa panted, her young body distracted by the smooth rubbing of her nubbin.

Sliding his left hand further under her, John slipped his index finger into her now vacant pussy. Alyssa's eyes bugged out as she felt her body being double-penetrated for the first time. John's two fingers provided a steady unrelenting rhythm that the teenager was helpless to resist, and he brushed her sensitive, swollen clit as the finger of his right hand pushed well past the second knuckle into her ass. Alyssa's legs were trembling violently as he stroked his fingers in and out of her primed young body.

"Oh my God!" she shrieked, as the thrusting fingers brought her to an explosive orgasm.

John allowed her laboured breathing to return to normal as she recovered from cumming so hard, before gently removing his fingers from the secret places in her body. Holding her in a comforting embrace, he stroked her back gently enjoying the quiet intimacy of the moment.

"That was amazing! I've never felt anything like that before," Alyssa sighed happily into his chest. She tilted her head back and parted her full lips invitingly for a kiss. John was happy to oblige and the two kissed passionately under the unrelenting flow of water.

"Come on, we better get out of here before we turn into prunes," John said, as he smiled down at the happy girl.

Reluctantly breaking their embrace, they left the shower and the autosensing jets turned off behind them. John took two luxuriously soft, fluffy towels out of the warming-locker beside the shower, and they wrapped themselves up in their downy softness as they moved into John's cabin and dried themselves off.

Alyssa sat on the bed drying her hair, while John finished drying his legs. She watched him with a soft smile on her face, as he finished drying himself, straightened, and placed the towel back in the heating locker. He turned to face her, his massive cock untended and forgotten, still throbbing with need.

"Oh John, I'm so sorry!" Alyssa gasped. "You made me feel so good, I forgot all about you." She gave him a coy smile and added, "Let me make it up to you now..."

John smiled back, and had just started walking towards the bed when a shrill alarm filled the cabin. The two of them both jumped at the grating sound, before John's face twisted in alarm and he darted out of the door to run for the cockpit. He'd barely made it into the corridor when there was a loud crash and the freighter juddered violently, knocking him to the floor and tipping Alyssa out of bed with a thump.

"Ow!" she gasped as she landed on her knees on the cold metal decking. "What the fuck?!"

"We hit something!" John exclaimed, as he staggered to his feet, the ship still vibrating. "It knocked us out of hyper-warp!"

He rushed into the cockpit and checked the sensors to see what had happened. Alyssa limped in after him a few seconds later, a frightened look on her face. "What did we hit?"

"Debris, from some kind of wreck..." he muttered, glaring at the sensors. "It must have been recent, the Nav charts haven't been updated with the hazard. It looks like a freighter got blown to bits!"

"Was it some kind of accident?" Alyssa asked, her eyes wide at the thought of the Fool's Gold spontaneously exploding mid-journey.

John tapped a few buttons on his console and a holographic image appeared a few moments later, revealing what had once been a large ship of some kind, which had broken up into charred chunks. It was surrounded by a sea of metallic fragments of various sizes that were spread out in a wide arc around the derelict vessel.

"That was an Atlas-class freighter," John said, grimacing as he stared at the wreck. He pointed to several melted holes on the flanks of one of the larger sections of tattered hull. "They were shot at by Laser Cannons. Whoever was doing the shooting probably hit something nasty like the Power Core and the explosion scattered all this debris all over the place."

"Then we sailed right through all that shit..." Alyssa said in a hushed voice, looking at the field of metal fragments.

John nodded, glancing back at her. "Yeah, exactly."

She saw the worry in his eyes and asked nervously. "How bad is it?"

He threw another quick glance at his console, then shrugged helplessly. "The Fool's Gold doesn't have sophisticated damage control systems. All I know is the FTL drive is damaged. I'll have to go out there and take a look..."

"You're going out into space?!" Alyssa blurted out, looking very afraid.

When he saw how frightened she was, John felt a sharp pang of sympathy for the young woman. He turned away from the console and pulled her into his arms. "Don't be scared, I won't be gone long. I'll just go for a quick spacewalk on the hull to check out the damage, okay?"

Alyssa didn't pull away, she just tilted her head up to look at him. "What if whoever did the shooting comes back?"

"Like I said, I'll be quick," John replied, leaning down to give her a reassuring kiss.

She reluctantly let him go and John strode back into their cabin to grab a form-fitting jumpsuit from his wardrobe and pull it on. As soon as he was dressed, he walked over to the wall and hit a button that was circled in red and white chevrons. The wall panel opened up, revealing a spacesuit hanging inside the unobtrusive closet.

Alyssa watched him dress in silence, a thousand questions running through her mind. She realised that asking them wouldn't help them out of this mess any faster, so she just nibbled anxiously on a nail, wondering what was going to happen if they were marooned. "Is there anything I can do to help?" she finally asked, desperate to make herself useful.

"Go to the cockpit and just wait for me to call. You know how the comm system works?" he asked in a rush as he clipped a toolbelt around his waist.

Alyssa bit her lip and shook her head.

"Okay, come with me," he said, grabbing the helmet for his spacesuit and striding out of the cabin.

She followed after him in a rush, then stood by the co-pilot's chair as John leaned over to point at the console.

"You see that button?" he asked, pointing to a circular one near the top of a panel containing more than twenty. When Alyssa nodded, he continued, "When it flashes green, push it. That'll be me calling you."

"Okay, got it," she replied, taking the seat.

John clipped the collar of his spacesuit into place, then pulled the helmet over his head, the seals locking in place with a hiss. He gave the girl a

comforting pat on the shoulder, then strode away down the corridor and through the door into the Cargo Bay. Activating the inner airlock door, John stepped through into the decompression chamber inside the airlock. He'd been putting on a brave face for Alyssa, but they were in really big trouble. If the FTL drive had been destroyed, they were stuck out here in deep space, marooned and helpless until they could flag down a passing ship.

This far out on the frontier, there wasn't much in the way of traffic and it could be weeks before they spotted anyone. Even then, activating a distress signal was probably too risky. He was sure it had been pirates that had destroyed the freighter and it must have happened within the last week. The pirates might be the closest ship in this part of space and sending out a distress call would draw them in like a bear to honey.

Even if the FTL drive had only been damaged, he wasn't an engineer and only really knew the basics for ship maintenance and repair. The chance of him being able to repair any significant damage was slim to none. Still, telling Alyssa any of that wouldn't have helped the situation and would have just scared her even more.

Pressing the button to decompress the airlock, John waited until the light went green, then pressed the button to open the outer airlock door. After a three second wait, it spun open, giving him an unrestricted view of the stars. They were as beautiful as always, a glittering array of a million tiny lights, shining bright against the black void of space.

Unfortunately he had no time for star gazing and he activated the magnetic grips on his boots and carefully headed outside. It took a bit of careful manoeuvring to walk out onto the hull but soon he was standing upright on the frame of the airlock door. He'd had a lot of experience with walking in mag-boots and he strode across the metallic surface of the ship, using the odd-looking gait necessary to quickly lock and unlock magnetic boots from the hull.

The Fool's Gold was only fifty metres long and the airlock was positioned half-way down the hull. That meant it only took him two minutes to reach the hyper-warp initiator on the spine of the freighter. There was a nasty trough cut through the ship's armour, where the offending piece of debris had gouged its way into his ship. The sight of that deep trench did little to buoy up his confidence.

Approaching the hyper-warp initiator itself, he saw that a chunk of the external armour plating was badly buckled and something had punched its way inside. With a sinking feeling in his chest, John removed a multi-tool from his belt and crouched down next to the warped maintenance panel. He began to twist the mag-bolts free, dreading whatever he was going to find...

\*\*\*

Alyssa waited anxiously in the cockpit, suddenly feeling very scared and very alone. This wasn't like being back on Karron. True, the asteroid was a wretched dump, but it was a dump she knew like the back of her hand. Whenever she got in too much trouble, she'd always been able to bolt, losing any pursuers in the rabbit warren of abandoned tunnels.

Stuck here in this ship she felt horribly exposed, knowing there was nowhere she could hide and no way she could run if trouble came looking for them. Sitting there naked didn't help, so she rushed back into the cabin and returned a minute later wrapped in the bedsheet like a toga. When she returned to the cockpit, she saw the comm light was flashing and she lunged forward to press the button, feeling guilty for having left, however briefly she'd been gone.

John's laughter echoed eerily around the cockpit as she opened the comm channel and for a moment she worried that he'd gone space crazy. "What happened? Is everything okay?" she asked, her voice shaking with nerves.

"We're fine!" he replied, sounding tremendously relieved. "The debris just sheared through a power cable knocking out the FTL drive! The hyper-warp initiator is fine!"

Feeling a bright surge of hope, Alyssa grinned as she said, "Will it take long to fix?"

"I've already patched it up, I'm on my way back now," John replied, chuckling again. "I just had to re-splice the power cable, it only took a minute to repair."

"I'll see you soon!" she replied, feeling equally happy.

She didn't have to wait long and she soon heard his heavy boots clomping along the decking as John returned to the cockpit, his helmet tucked under one arm. He grinned at her and she ran over to greet him.

"My hero!" Alyssa exclaimed, showering him in kisses.

John laughed and gathered her in his arms, attempting to return the flurry of affection.

Finally Alyssa pulled away and gave him a smouldering look. "I'll be waiting for you in the cabin..." she purred, before sauntering out of the cockpit, giving him a mesmerising look over her shoulder.

He watched her leave in awe, amazed at her raw sexuality, only snapping himself out of his lust-fuelled daze when the blonde disappeared from sight. Turning back to the pilot's chair, he checked their flight path on the Nav-computer then activated the FTL drive. When they were safely back in hyper-warp again, he hurried into the cabin after his young companion.

She was waiting on the bed for him, artfully posed with the sheet around her, revealing tantalising glimpses of her body. Her cerulean eyes watched his every move as he quickly stripped off his spacesuit and left it casually

discarded in a pile on the floor. Making a come-hither motion with her finger, Alyssa beckoned him over to join her as she moved backwards on his big bed, making room for him to join her. Grinning like a man who knows he is on to a sure thing, John settled down comfortably, folded his arms behind his head and spread his legs to clear a space for his teenage companion.

Alyssa slid smoothly over to kneel between his muscular thighs, before throwing him a mocking salute, and saying, "Ship's cum bucket reporting for duty, Sir!"

John doubled over with laughter and Alyssa's musical laugh joined his own. She eventually pushed him back so he was leaning against the pillows again. Joking around was fun, but now it was time for serious business. She leaned forward, grasped his mighty shaft with her delicate hand, and tilted it towards her mouth. Her plush lips opened invitingly and enveloped his broad head.

"Your mouth feels so good," John sighed in contentment, tangling his hands up in her hair and stroking her gently.

His quad ached after the extended foreplay in the shower and then the rude interruption of the emergency repairs to his ship. However, Alyssa made no move to take him any deeper, her tongue swirling slowly over the powerful maleness filling her mouth. Focusing on the sensitive head of his cock, she alternated between licking and sucking, while maintaining eye contact so she could watch his reaction to her oral attentions.

Gearing up for action, John's well-primed balls helpfully provided the young girl with a sweet-tasting surge of pre-cum. Alyssa's throat bobbed as she swallowed it down, and she savoured the sweet tingling aftertaste on her tongue. Her lovely blue eyes glazed over, and began to hide behind her eyelids which started to feel unbearably heavy.

Suddenly she leant back, releasing his throbbing scarlet crown from her mouth, and shook her head furiously - as if to clear the fogginess from her mind. Her blonde locks made a soft swishing motion around her face, and she smiled at John before moving back to envelop him again in the warm, wet confines of her mouth. Her piercing blue eyes transfixed his own eyes hypnotically, watching for his reactions to her lips and tongue.

"This is new!" John realised with a shocked start. He couldn't ever recall any other girl shrugging off the irresistible effect of his pre-cum like that before.

Alyssa momentarily closed her eyes, breaking eye contact as she tilted forward and swallowed his entire length in one long, smooth motion. Her eyes suddenly flew wide open, and she tried to stare at the root of his cock, which was being softly massaged by her own pouty lips. This resulted in a hilarious cross-eyed expression, which would have caused John to laugh out loud, if she hadn't rocked back on her heels, causing his cock to swiftly abandon the comforting sheath of her throat.

"What the fuck!" Alyssa gasped loudly, a look of puzzled amazement on her young face. She eyed his cock suspiciously as she added, "I've never been able to deep throat before! My gag reflex was too strong, but now I'm able to suck down this monster effortlessly!"

John's appendage throbbed angrily in front of her, annoyed at the cessation of activity.

"Erm... muscle memory maybe?" John stumbled for an explanation, having never really thought about this before. "You had no trouble the last few times, maybe your body remembered how?"

Alyssa stroked her neck with her free hand, a thoughtful expression on her face. She leaned forward, her cherubic lips opening in a perfect oval, before she engulfed him to the balls in one long fluid move. She massaged his whole length wonderfully in her throat's snug embrace as her lips

kissed his groin. John watched as her hand moved to touch her neck, feeling where his swollen girth had forced her throat to stretch wide to accommodate him. She slowly drew back, savouring every mouth-stretching millimetre of him.

"That was awesome!" she grinned ecstatically. With a mischievous smirk, she added, "No wonder you were happy to have me aboard!"

"Yeah, no complaints from me there," he agreed with a pained expression, his quad throbbing with need.

"Does every girl you've been with end up 'sucking your cock like a pro'?" she asked, her lips forming an obviously fake pout as she quoted his comment from that morning back at him.

"Can we discuss this later please?" John pleaded. "I'm finding it hard to concentrate at the moment!"

Alyssa nodded agreeably. She reached out to gently stroke his painfully swollen balls, and purred to them, "I'm sorry boys, you were waiting to give me dinner and I rudely interrupted." Looking at John with a lust-filled expression on her face, she continued, "After all, that's what I'm here for isn't it? To keep you drained dry?"

He could only nod in wide-eyed amazement.

"You want to fill my tiny belly up again, don't you? Force me to swallow down a huge load of cum?" Alyssa enquired her blue eyes sparkling with her excitement.

John could only nod again mutely, struck dumb by the new level of confidence in the excited teen kneeling before him. Alyssa moved forward to put her new-found skill to good use. Moments later he was sliding deep into the silky-smooth, snug embrace of her throat. Her tongue massaged

him on the way down with its wet velvet caress, promising ecstasy at the end of his journey.

"Oh Fuck!" John groaned helplessly as the teenager massaged his whole length in the muscular grip of her throat.

She had been quite correct earlier. All girls who gave him blowjobs had been able to eventually deep throat him before he fed them his cum. However, this was wildly different! All the other girls had felt great, but there was a comfortingly familiar sameness to their blowjobs. Alyssa had shrugged off the dazing effects of his pre-cum and was now an active participant. The sensations he was receiving from the eagerly sucking girl felt wonderfully new, unpredictable and intense.

Alyssa rocked back a bit and John found himself going from half sheathed to fully embedded over and over again. He was literally face-fucking her, whilst just lying there having to do nothing other than enjoy the exquisitely tight grip around his cock. His incredible fellatrix paused on the top of her backstroke to look him in the eyes again. Even though her pouting lips were stretched obscenely wide around his girth, she was still able to provide an incredibly insistent sucking action.

Alyssa's eyes were lusty and inviting. He could sense her hunger, her eagerness to see him cum... How could he resist such a siren call?

"Aahhh!" He bellowed, as his back arched and his orgasm blasted out of him.

If the pretty teen wanted to drain his balls dry, they were happy to accept the invitation - and kicked into overdrive. Long, heavy spurts of cum shot out of his balls, up his shaft and down the sucking teen's throat. Alyssa could feel each blast pass her lips, as his urethra expanded with each rapid evacuation of his balls. His spunk felt warm and filling as it settled in her stomach, quickly giving her the feeling of having eaten a huge meal as she swallowed what seemed like an endless explosion of cum.

Alyssa moaned excitedly, her throat stuffed with his cock. Her hand moved down to feel her rounded stomach as she felt her body making room for his enormous load. Her steadily inflating belly edged her hand lower, so that her fingers brushed her clit. It felt like she was on a hair trigger as she joined him in orgasm, her body trembling in ecstasy as he filled her up.

Finally, John's orgasm abated and he collapsed back on to the bed, struggling for breath. He had never cum that hard before, not even close. Alyssa let his deflating cock slip from her mouth with a wet plop, a string of cum temporarily extending the link between his glans and her lips.

"Wow!" Alyssa gasped with wonder, as she stroked her hugely inflated belly.

It looked like the girl had swallowed a beach ball. Her slim waistline had been blown out so much, a casual observer would be forgiven for thinking she was nine months pregnant and rapidly approaching her due date. Her soft fingers traced the beautiful gracing arc of her swollen stomach down to her belly button. She was astounded to find it had popped out, as her teenage tummy had expanded to house his rich spunk and run out of room.

John opened his arms invitingly, rendered speechless in the afterglow of such a stupendous orgasm. Alyssa waddled forward, weighed down by her taut cum bloated belly, before lying down carefully beside him and laying her head on his shoulder. John rolled them both so he was spooned up behind her, his strong hand stroking her engorged abdomen possessively and protectively. Alyssa breathed a long sigh of previously unknown contentment as she lay comfortably in his arms.

They lay like that for a long while just enjoying the peaceful silence, before Alyssa rolled on to her back and looked up at him with her piercing

blue eyes. "John, would you tell me a little more about yourself please?" she asked tentatively.

"Sure," he replied, a warm smile on his lips. With a playful glance at her heavily rounded tummy he added, "I think you've earned it."

Alyssa grinned as she looked up at him and then waited patiently for him to begin.

"Well I'm currently working as a trader," he began. "I bought this freighter, the Fool's Gold, a good while ago with the intention of exploring the galaxy and it's been my home ever since."

"Have you been anywhere exciting?" she asked, gazing at him with interest. Her voice was tinged with regret as she added, "Before I snuck on board, I'd never left Karron before."

"Sure, lots of places," John replied with a smile. He spoke animatedly as he continued, "I've traded with all the major races in the Galactic League and visited quite a few of their homeworlds. The galaxy is an amazing place with lots of incredible things to see out there."

"That sounds amazing," she agreed, sounding wistful.

With a gentle smile, he teased her playfully, "You seemed strongly opposed to going back to Karron, so there's nothing stopping you from doing some exploring of your own."

"Maybe," Alyssa said, looking thoughtful. Rubbing her tummy where she carried his heavy load, she smirked as she added, "I've certainly been enjoying my first trip into space."

"I've been enjoying it too," he grinned, continuing with his comforting caresses.

The blonde girl smiled at him, but she seemed a little pensive, as though wanting to ask something else.

"Go ahead and ask," John said with a chuckle.

"You said you were 'currently' working as a trader," Alyssa asked him. "What did you do before that?"

"I was in the Terran Federation military for quite a while," John replied, as he looked into her eyes. "I was a Marine officer before I finally retired."

"I thought only really old people retired?" Alyssa asked innocently. She gave him a speculative look, then with an impish grin, she added, "You don't look quite that ancient; you're early sixties, right? Still a few years to go until retirement?"

"Ouch! That hurts!" John replied with an answering grin.

Alyssa laughed mischievously before leaning up to give him a quick kiss on the lips. Her bright blue eyes twinkled as she asked, "So, why did you retire from the military, old timer?"

A haunted look flashed over John's face for a moment, making her instantly regret asking.

"Sorry John, I didn't mean to dredge up bad memories," she apologised, stroking his arm.

"It's okay," he said with a sad smile. "I was in the military for a long time and fought in a lot of battles. In the end I just didn't want to lose any more friends, so I thought it was probably past time for me to move on to something new."

Alyssa reached up with her delicate hand and tenderly caressed his face, which he found strangely comforting.

"Sorry for getting all maudlin on you," he apologised, giving her a self-conscious smile.

"It's okay, it's been good getting to know more about you," the teenager replied with a fond smile.

He studied her lovely face, and asked, "Perhaps you can tell me a little bit more about yourself too?"

"Maybe next time, if you're lucky!" Alyssa replied with a nervous laugh.

Sensing that the young woman was trying to deflect his questioning with humour, John let it go. He stretched languidly before sitting up.

"I'm just going to check the long-range sensors," he explained. "I won't be long if you want to just stay here and rest." he said, eyeing her heavily rounded stomach.

"Thanks. I'll take you up on that!" Alyssa grinned as she relaxed into the bed.

John climbed off the bed and shrugged on some trousers, before strolling out of his cabin and heading into the cockpit. He sat in the comfortable pilot's chair and had a good look at the view screen for the long-range scanners.

There didn't seem to be anything active out there, but the scanners were picking up quite a few more wreck sites in this sector. Breakdowns and other accidents were not uncommon occurrences for space farers, but this many wrecks reinforced his earlier suspicions about pirates. He'd come through the sector unscathed on his way to Karron, but now he was starting to worry that was pure luck rather than anything else. Just to be on the safe side, he double-checked the long-range scanner to make sure that the alarm was still active.

Finding everything operating correctly, he was about to leave the cockpit when he stopped and glanced back at the brightly lit pilot's console. He began to power down all unessential sub-systems, leaving the Fool's Gold running on minimal energy and making it much harder to pick up with sensors. You can never be too careful in deep space, he thought to himself, before giving the room one final check.

John walked back to his cabin and stripped off before climbing into bed again. Alyssa had rolled over and was sleeping angelically, so he snuggled in behind her, wrapping her up in his arms and soon fell into a deep, restful slumber himself.

# Three Square Meals Ch. 04 – The Change

John slowly opened his eyes, as the fog of the night's sleep began to fade from his mind. He was about to perform his normal stretching routine when he felt a strange weight on his left side. He looked down to see a mass of blonde hair resting against his shoulder, and the previous night's events came flooding back to him. He half-turned, careful not to wake his sleeping companion as he wrapped his arm around her again. This was a new experience for him and he savoured the feeling of protectiveness he felt for his young bed-mate.

John's hand began to gently and carefully explore the nubile girl's body. Alyssa's tummy had shrunk back to normal again, her body voraciously consuming the high-protein feast he had fed the pretty teenager the evening before. The gloriously smooth skin on her toned stomach felt incredible to his sensitive fingertips. His fingers roamed upwards, cupping one of her breasts which nearly filled his hand with warm, pliant flesh. He decided not to do any more exploring for fear of waking her, so he settled down for a nice lie-in and waited for the young girl to wake on her own.

John didn't have to wait for long, as a mere ten minutes later Alyssa stirred as well. She seemed to flinch initially when she felt another body surrounding her, but as she regained full consciousness she sighed happily and snuggled into his embrace. She raised her hand to brush the wayward blonde locks from her face, and twisted in his arms to look up at him. John studied her lovely fresh young face and realised he would have to stop thinking of her as pretty, and more accurately describe her as beautiful. Alyssa's skin seemed to be glowing this morning and she looked radiant. Her piercing blue eyes were sharp and focused, watching his every movement intently. The wide, full smile on her face lifted his spirits and he felt a strange feeling of contentment and happiness that was most unusual for him.

"Do you know what I'd like to do today?" she asked him quizzically.

"I'm fascinated to find out," John replied, genuinely interested.

"Have breakfast in bed!" the exuberant teen answered, before ducking below the covers.

John could only moan appreciatively as the eager girl zeroed in on his stiffening shaft and engulfed him in the warm, wet softness of her mouth. He leaned back, fingers interlocked behind his head, as he enjoyed the insistent sucking sensation that felt so wonderful on his cock. He could see no sign of Alyssa, just the bobbing mound under the covers, but he could hear the delightfully debauched sounds of her slick mouth as she slid up and down his length.

He lost track of time as his enthusiastic companion worked her magic on him and before he knew it, he was gasping in pleasure as his balls gave up their sweet tasting reward. He came long and hard, serving the teenage girl her first meal of the day. Alyssa appeared from under the covers when he was finally done, licking her flushed lips suggestively.

"Mmmm, that was a hearty breakfast," she purred contentedly, as she sat up and stroked her convex tummy.

John sat up and kissed the beautiful young woman squarely on the lips. "That was a hell of a way to start the day! Thanks, beautiful."

"You're welcum!" she replied.

"I am indeed!" John riposted, as he strode into the shower with the swagger of a man who'd just emptied his balls.

He stepped into the roomy cubicle, Alyssa's laughter drowned out by the autosensing shower spraying him with jets of water. When they began their rhythmic pitter-patter, John relaxed under their hot caress, his body feeling invigorated and ready to start the day. He finished his shower

uninterrupted, which left him feeling a slight sense of disappointment, as he'd hoped his lovely companion would join him.

He reached for a towel as he left the shower, the hamper opening automatically. His mind wandered over the various tasks he needed to complete for the day, starting with making breakfast for himself and his lovely shipmate, while smiling to himself at his recent good fortune. He shook his head while rubbing himself dry as he walked back into his cabin. The sight before him stopped him in his tracks. He almost had to pinch himself to check if he was dreaming as he marvelled at the sight before him.

His bed was a vision of orderly perfection. While he'd been in the shower, Alyssa had made his bed for him, taking painstaking effort to copy the way he usually did it. He took in the crisp clear lines, the smoothed-out pillows, even the eight-inch strip of sheet folded back over the cover.

"That's how you like it, right?" she asked cautiously.

John picked the young woman up in a tight hug before swirling her in a circle around him. She laughed gaily, delighted at his reaction. He planted a big smacking kiss on her lips, before placing her down lightly on her feet again and helping to steady her, with her rounded tummy upsetting her balance.

"Thanks honey, that was very thoughtful," he said, giving her an appreciative smile. The girl basked in his praise and grinned up at him. John considered getting dressed, but then decided to embrace the new 'clothing optional' dress code aboard his ship.

"Is there anything else I can do to help around here?" Alyssa asked enthusiastically.

"If you could bring me some breakfast, and meet me in the cockpit, that would be fantastic," John replied, thinking how useful having a crewmate was turning out to be.

Alyssa nodded eagerly and bounded out of the cabin, or attempted to with the heavy load in her belly. John watched her leave and realised that if he was being honest with himself, then it was her company and the companionship that he really relished. Lost in his thoughts, he followed the teenager out the door, but turned right instead, heading into the cockpit.

John checked the ship's performance readouts and the long-range scanner for any activity. He then moved on to track the progress the ship was making on the route home. He was so engrossed in the system charts that he didn't notice when Alyssa returned and placed an assortment of food carefully on the console. She sat quietly in the co-pilot's chair, watching him in fascination as he checked their projected path through the holographic representation of the upcoming star systems.

"Which system are we travelling through now?" the inquisitive girl asked, snapping him out of his preoccupied thoughts.

"This is Carilan-Prime," John said, pointing at the glowing red orb in the centre of the holo-display. His hand made a slight sweeping gesture and the display moved on to centre on a fiery orange orb surrounded by the arcs of its orbiting planets. "And this is Iridani-Major, we'll be travelling through here next," he said, his finger tracing the blue path of their intended course.

"I like learning about stars. Stars are pretty!" Alyssa chirped, her face a picture of wide eyed innocence.

John looked at her incredulously, before her expression broke suddenly and she dissolved into peals of laughter. "You had me going there for a minute..."

"I'm sorry, John" the teenager said, her cerulean eyes twinkling. She reached out and touched his arm. "Please continue, I'd love to know more."

John launched into a beginner's guide to Astro-Navigation. Alyssa was a remarkably quick study and was able to rapidly grasp the concepts of gravity wells, flight vectors, and directed thrust. He soon found himself moving on to more complex topics, and was pleasantly surprised that she was able to process and understand those too. They spent a few hours covering as much as he could recall off the top of his head, before he turned her loose to practice using the ship's navigation system. He was delighted with her progress as she plotted a potential course through a sector, using a slingshot manoeuvre around a gas giant to increase the ship's velocity.

"That was excellent, Alyssa! Are you sure you never received any kind of training on this before?" he asked her, quite amazed.

The girl shook her head, beaming at the praise.

"Keep this up and we'll make a first-class navigator out of you in no time!" John said, grinning with encouragement and waving her back to the console to continue practicing what he had just taught her.

In his eagerness to teach Alyssa about astro-navigation, he'd completely forgotten about the food she'd brought him. His stomach hadn't though and rumbled indignantly. He frowned at the protein bars and reached for the apple instead, taking a bite of the fresh-tasting fruit. Alyssa tore her eyes away from the console and gave him, or more specifically the apple, a curious glance.

Intuitively, he asked her, "Have you even eaten an apple before?"

Alyssa gave him a small, sad smile and shook her head. "It was best not to ask too many questions about most of the food I scavenged. Those protein bars would have been considered a luxury," she replied, glancing at the untouched packets on the console. "I've never really seen any fresh fruit, let alone tried any."

John handed her the apple to her and did his best to mask the feeling of sympathy he felt for the young woman, not wanting her to feel like he was pitying her. "Go head, give it a try."

She took an experimental bite, her face lighting up in surprise and delight at the sweet refreshing taste. "This is amazing!" she gasped, before giving him a wicked smile. "Almost as good as your cum!"

He laughed and rose from his chair. "You can finish it, I'll go and get another."

John left her happily munching on the fruit as she continued learning about astro-navigation. He strolled into his rec-room and glanced thoughtfully at the kitchen. Now there was more than just him on the ship, he was tempted to make an effort with cooking again. He couldn't help grinning when he remembered that he'd still effectively just be cooking for himself, with his beautiful companion's dietary requirements already well taken care of. He grabbed a fresh apple and a banana, then returned to the cockpit, where he sat down in the pilot's chair to eat his lunch and watch his enthusiastic new student.

Alyssa cycled through the stellar charts, experimenting with navigation routes and flight trajectories. John was forced to re-evaluate his young companion, realising that Alyssa had a remarkably quick and agile mind. For her to have grown up in such a bleak environment as Karron was a tragic waste and he sighed, thinking about how many other bright young lives had their potential squandered in such a manner.

She seemed to sense the change in his mood and looked over at the downcast expression on his face. "Did I do something wrong?" Alyssa asked, worried that she had upset him somehow.

"No, no, of course not, you've been doing great!" John replied quickly, snapping out of his dark introspection. "Sorry, my mind just wandered a bit."

"Maybe I can help distract you," Alyssa replied, as she rose from her chair and walked towards him.

The sultry young woman held the back of his chair and gracefully swung her shapely leg over his thighs, before carefully lowering herself to sit in his lap facing him. It was a move John had seen exotic dancers perform before and Alyssa executed it perfectly. She cupped his face in her hands and then moved in to press her full lips against his. They shared a number of tender kisses before the girl's mouth parted and she delicately licked his lips with the tip of her tongue. Her tongue brushed over his lips as it darted into his mouth and she intensified the passion of their embrace. She kissed him fiercely, then moaned in excitement as he duelled her darting tongue with his own.

John's body responded accordingly and his manhood grew thick and hard as the teenager seduced him. Her small breasts grazed over his chest, her pink nipples excited and erect. He moved his hands to hold her fantastically firm ass cheeks causing the girl to moan into his mouth. He lifted her slightly, then repositioned her, so that her labia were centred over the shaft of his burgeoning cock.

"Ooohhhhh!" she gasped, as he rocked her body along his length, her lubrication easing the way.

Alyssa opened her eyes and stared intently into his matching gaze. Her mouth was slightly parted, her lips glistening after their kiss. John's strong hands held her firmly and he stroked the teen's body along the underside

of his cock, the warm wet velvety touch feeling amazing. She moaned breathily, her face mere inches from his own as he rocked her in his lap.

The girl's clit was in constant contact with the firm heat of his shaft and her thighs began to tremble as her body revelled in the stimulation. Alyssa threw her head back, her long hair billowing out behind her as she rode him to climax.

"I'm coming!" she wailed, as her body reacted to the overwhelming sensations to her clit.

She arched her back, her tummy pressed against him as she came hard, her hips making tiny rocking movements as she thrust against him. She rode out her orgasm, before collapsing forward to rest on his chest. He stroked her back comfortingly as her panting breath tickled his neck. Eventually her breathing returned to normal as she sat up and thanked him with a soft, tender kiss.

Alyssa lifted herself off his lap, smoothly dismounting and standing to his side. He'd already begun to miss the silky smoothness of her body where she had straddled him. She turned towards the doorway, looking over her shoulder with a lust filled, heavy lidded glance, and held out her hand for him to take. John rose behind her and reached out to take her small hand in his much larger one. The beautiful young woman turned back towards the door, and led him back to his cabin. He could only follow mutely, transfixed by the hypnotic movement of her hips and the way her perfectly rounded ass cheeks seemed to sway enticingly.

They entered his room and Alyssa let her hand slip from his. She turned to look at him coyly over her shoulder, as she climbed on to the bed, arching her back suggestively. She waited patiently as his roaming eyes drank in the delicious curves of her body, before he locked eyes with her again. Never dropping eye contact, she smoothly rotated her body so that she was lying down on her back, her head towards him. Alyssa let her eyes drift closed, then moved back just enough so that her shoulders were

resting near the end of the bed, her head tilted slightly backwards. Her mouth slowly opened, her full succulent lips forming a welcoming oval. Her pink tongue darted out to lick her top lip suggestively, before waiting for him invitingly.

John realised he'd been holding his breath, transfixed as he was by the erotic and sensual display. He took a deep breath to steady himself, before walking towards the supine girl in front of him. She was offering him her body to use for his pleasure, and after feeling her spasming along his length only a short while back, he was desperate for his own release.

He hefted his massive cock, bringing the swollen mushroom head to rest on Alyssa's wonderfully soft lips. Her tongue snaked out, licking daintily at the tip, leaving him glistening in its wake. He saw her chest rise, her lungs filling with air as she took a deep breath, before she opened her mouth wider and engulfed the throbbing head of his dick. John leaned over the girl, placing his hands on either side of her torso, his body dwarfing hers.

The urge to thrust forward was irresistible and his hips pushed forward. His mighty cock slid smoothly to the back of Alyssa's mouth, before finding the familiar entrance to her throat. He stopped to savour the warmth of her hot little mouth surrounding him, as she sucked eagerly, beckoning him deeper. Taking the hint, he drove forward, impaling the teenager’s welcoming body until his balls rested over her nose. It was fascinating to watch her slim neck bulge outwards as his invading tool forced her tight throat to accommodate his girth.

He gasped in relief, feeling the warm, snug grip as he was embedded to his full length again. Alyssa moaned contentedly, the vibrations feeling incredible as she sucked him, with him resting deep in her gullet. His balls ached for release and he could feel them trembling with anticipation. He slowly and cautiously withdrew the entirety of his male sword from her velvet sheath, until the head cleared the wanton teen’s lips. He paused for a moment, his heavy tool throbbing forebodingly above the teenager’s head as she leaned up to plant soft sensuous kisses along his shaft.

Alyssa's mouth opened again into that inviting oval and he took up that invitation, gliding into her proffered throat with one long, satisfying thrust. He began to drive his cock into her encouraging and welcoming mouth, truly face fucking the beautiful girl for the first time.

Alyssa revelled in being pinned to the bed under him as he pounded her mouth and throat. She used her lips to maintain a tight seal around him and sucked encouragingly whenever he paused in his smooth thrusting action. She looked up in fascination at his four swollen balls as they swayed back and forth above her face. Soon their contents would be blasting into her slim young belly, forcing her body to expand and house their delicious cream. She could hardly wait.

John drove forward again and again, his breathing becoming laboured as he got closer to his peak. He pulled out completely so that Alyssa could breathe, but she grabbed his ass and pulled him back into her enticing throat. Her clear excitement and lust triggered his climax and his body spasmed powerfully as his balls raised up to deliver their cargo.

He bellowed with relief as the orgasm washed over him, thick heavy spunk blasting out of his cock to fill the waiting girl below. He could only stare at her rapidly moving throat, as she sucked eagerly to get every last drop of his cum. Surge after surge of semen filled the young girl's stomach as her tummy desperately tried to house the warm, heavy meal. John watched in awe as her belly rounded out and rapidly inflated as he unloaded his spunk into her.

"Mmmph!" Alyssa moaned out her own orgasm as her thighs trembled in time with John's.

The powerful pulses of cum eventually subsided and John pulled his spent cock from the girl's lovely lips. He pitched forward and collapsed on the bed to her side as he laboured for breath. Alyssa bathed in the afterglow of her orgasm and stroked her swollen midriff contentedly, loving the

fantastically full feeling. She covered John with the sheet where he lay comatose on the bed and snuggled in behind him, hugging the broad expanse of his back. She sighed happily as she waited for him to return to the land of the living.

John gradually recovered from the explosive orgasm, his balls feeling satisfyingly numb after energetically delivering their load. He turned to face Alyssa, where she was lying behind him and kissed her softly.

"That was amazing!" he thanked her appreciatively.

Alyssa returned his kiss, then rubbed the tip of her nose against his in an Eskimo kiss, before smiling broadly.

"Help me up would you handsome?" the teenager requested holding out one of her hands, while the other rested on top of her sperm-bloated belly.

"Sure thing, beautiful," John replied, as he gallantly took her hand, assisting the unbalanced girl to her feet.

Alyssa looked hesitant for a moment. "Is it okay if I continue learning about astro-navigation?" she asked shyly.

"Go right ahead," John answered, pleased that she was so keen to learn. "Just let me know if you see anything on the long-range scanner."

His enthusiastic student nodded eagerly and set off to the cockpit, humming happily to herself. John worked through a mental checklist of maintenance chores that needed completing, before coming up with a number of tasks that would keep him busy for a few hours.

This developed into a pattern for the next week, with John working on various jobs around the ship, while his young guest spent her hours learning as much as she could absorb. They met up regularly for

mealtimes before he would send her on her way with a nicely rounded out tummy.

John woke on one particular morning, slowly opening his eyes to see Alyssa's excited face watching him closely.

"Oh goodie, you're finally awake!" she grinned exuberantly. "Come on, I want to show you something!" the perky teenage bubbled, her excitement contagious.

"What is it?" John asked, sounding groggy, still not quite fully awake. The beautiful young woman swung lithely over him before pivoting gracefully and landing nimbly on her feet.

"Come and see!" she called to him over her shoulder, as she skipped out of the room.

John roused himself and followed the girl out of his cabin, bemused at her excitement. He strolled into the cockpit and sat down in the pilot's chair, spinning it to face her. Alyssa suddenly seemed nervous, as though she was apprehensive about revealing her surprise now that he was there and waiting.

"I plotted a new course to the core worlds," she said, a nervous tremor to her voice. "Please take a look, and see what you think."

John nodded agreeably and turned to the holo-display, curious to see what his protégé had been up to. The display sprung up before him, clearly showing their current path through the upcoming star systems highlighted in blue. As he expected, the computer helpfully displayed an ETA of fifteen days next to his blue course. Alyssa reached over and her fingers flickered, summoning up the overlay showing her proposed course highlighted in green. He looked over at the summary for the green course, wondering how Alyssa had got on and was shocked to see the result... ten days.

"There must be some kind of mistake," John thought to himself, as he double checked the summary. No, the course was definitely plotted from their current location to his intended core world system. He began to zoom in to the system charts, looking at the route in more detail as it wove its way from star to star.

He was able to follow the calculations for a while, before some things didn't look right. He was about to point out what he believed to be several mistakes, when he suddenly remembered that the Navi-computer had confirmed the girl's course was valid. He turned to look at his young companion and saw that she was nibbling on one of her nails nervously, awaiting his verdict.

"This is absolutely incredible Alyssa!" he smiled at her in wonder, shaking his head in disbelief. A huge grin of relief broke out on the beautiful young woman's face.

"I must admit I couldn't follow what you did here," John pointed to a key location on the course.

"I did some research and tried something new! It's called warp tunnelling!" she answered animatedly. "You can create the effect by oscillating the hyper-wake...." Alyssa launched into a complicated explanation of Astrophysics that went way beyond his layman's understanding of the subject.

John turned and pushed a button on the console, confirming that her newly plotted course should be laid in for the ship.

"I'm in awe honey, you seem to have surpassed my navigation skills," he admitted honestly. "I'll let you plot our course from now on."

"Yay!!" Alyssa clapped excitedly.

The teenager was suddenly nervous again as she reached behind her and picked up her ID. She passed it over to him, a pensive look on her face.

"What is it Alyssa, are you ok?" John asked, surprised by her abrupt change in mood.

"Please scan it," Alyssa requested cautiously.

"Your ID? I don't understand..." John replied, somewhat confused. He turned to the console again and scanned in the girl's ID. He waited a moment for the readout to confirm her details.

"Alyssa Marant"
"Age 18"
"No outstanding warrants"
"Navigator First Class"

John blinked twice before reading the display again. The glowing green text confirmed it for him: Navigator First Class.

"What...? How did you...?" he blurted out, truly astounded. These IDs were not forgeable, at least not without millions of credits worth of very illegal equipment.

"I've been staying up late and studying. I took the Astro-Navigation exam last night when you were asleep," his young ward explained cautiously, her face wary as she watched for his reaction. "You aren't mad, are you?"

John's mind whirled, trying to process this astonishing turn of events. One week! The girl must be some kind of genius to have mastered this subject so quickly. It normally took months of intensive study and years of practical experience to qualify at that high a grade. With a First Class Navigator's license, Alyssa would be able to command a hefty salary with a wide choice of ships clamouring for her skills. She really did have a

blazingly bright future ahead of her. John had a catch in his throat and he had difficulty speaking.

"This is amazing, I'm so proud of you!" he congratulated her, his voice thick with emotion.

Alyssa had been waiting for his reaction with trepidation. When he spoke, he saw her eyes well up with tears. She got up and sat in his lap, hugging him tightly. So many times in her young life her hopes had been cruelly dashed, so to finally succeed at something and make John proud of her was an overwhelming experience. There were so many ways he could have reacted, but to see his open admiration and respect filled her heart with joy.

They sat like that for a few minutes, overcome with the heady emotions. John stroked the young girl's back reassuringly before she released him from her fierce hug and pulled his face down to kiss his lips tenderly. Their kisses grew more passionate, before John stood suddenly, scooping up the young girl in his arms.

"Let's move this to our cabin, It's time for a proper reward," he said, as he smiled down at her.

John might not have picked up on his subtle renaming of his cabin from 'my' to 'our', but Alyssa noted it straight away. She smiled back at him, feeling a giddy lightness in her chest. She couldn't remember ever feeling this happy before.

John spread the beautiful young woman on his bed and then mounted the bed himself, hovering over her. He leaned down and gently kissed the swooning girl on her full, sensuous lips which she returned passionately. He moved from her welcoming mouth, trailing kisses along her well-defined jaw-line, before moving up to plant more along the outside of her left ear.

"Oh God! That feels so good!" Alyssa moaned as shivers ran down the length of her body.

She arched her back, tilting her head and exposing her throat for his gentle exploration. Her graceful neck received more kisses as he worked his way over her sternum to her firm, proud breasts. They stood up from her chest, full, round and luscious, her soft pink nipples pointed upwards and demanding his attention. He took each one into his mouth in turn, gently sucking as her body reacted to his touch.

Alyssa moaned again louder and longer, as he ran his nails around the tender, sensitive skin on the soft side swell of her breasts. Her tits felt wonderful as he cupped them in his strong hands. They were each just slightly larger than his eager hands could hold, and her flesh felt warm and firm under his excited touch. Something tickled at the back of John's mind, but he ignored it to focus completely on the writhing teenager beneath him.

John moved lower, planting gentle kisses along the girl's skin, her chest thrust upwards as she gasped for breath. The top of her stomach formed a perfect arch where it met her ribs and he admired the incredible curves of the female form. He moved further down, his lips parting slightly so his tongue could flicker out to taste the wonderfully soft skin of her stomach. His hands moved down, following her contours, from her narrow, slim waist to her flared hips.

Alyssa parted her legs wide to give him plenty of room to kneel in front of her. His questing lips kissed lower over her abdomen, before veering to the side to take playful, gentle nips at the silky-smooth skin of her spread thighs. He copied the movement on the other leg, avoiding her pussy and causing the gasping girl to arch her back with need.

Finally having mercy, John moved back to her centre and began to carefully kiss around the outside of her pussy. As he kissed along the side of her labia, he noticed that Alyssa's blonde downy hair was missing and

she was now completely exposed to him. Liking the new look, he took advantage of her exposure to kiss and explore her body. Her skin felt supple and wonderfully soft, like she had been waxed completely smooth without leaving even a trace of stubble. He began to lap at her pussy, licking either side of her lips before moving forward with his tongue to seek out her clit. He gazed up over the toned, tanned skin of her slim tummy to watch Alyssa's reaction, but with her back arched and the perfect spheres of her firm breasts pointing upwards, he couldn't see her face.

Again, John's mind seem to itch, as it struggled to grasp hold of something. The slippery thought proved elusive however, so John concentrated on giving the girl pleasure.

His strong hands slid under the girl's back, feeling the toned muscles beneath his fingers, before he moved them lower to cup her pert ass cheeks. Alyssa moaned again as he worked on her clit, just focusing on licking the sensitive little organ with the tip of his tongue. He alternated between that and long sensuous licks using the flat top of his tongue and the varying sensations drove the teenager wild with lust. Her thighs trembled violently as she got closer to climax, and the gyrating girl gasped as he lapped away at her pussy. Her breathy cries sounded amazing, and his massively swollen cock was a testament to how turned on he was.

Working the beautiful young woman to a crescendo, he captured her clit in his mouth, sucking at her, before stroking her with his tongue. This was the trigger that finally allowed her to cum, and Alyssa exploded in orgasm, her body twisting and turning as though to escape his eager mouth. John kept the helpless girl pinned in place and licked, nibbled and sucked her to three escalating orgasms before he finally released her.

John watched the girl's chest heave as she struggled for air, her gasps and moans having left her quite breathless. He moved to her side and laid a trail of soft kisses over her stomach, between her pert breasts and finally

planted a gentle kiss on her mouth. Alyssa's eyes opened slowly and she kissed him back, her lips moving in silent gratitude.

The beautiful teenager took a long breath, which she let out with a sigh. John rested comfortably beside her as she rolled over on her tummy, her head resting on the pillow, her piercing blue eyes heavy with lust as she gazed languidly at him.

He reached out to caress her shoulder, gently brushing aside her lustrous blonde mane. His hand followed the sculpted muscles of her back as his fingers brushed down her spine. He coasted over the lower part of her back, feeling the slight dimples above her bottom. He then moved that hand lower, to cup and stroke her lovely derriere. Her ass was pert, the muscles taut under the probing touch of his fingers. He massaged one cheek and then the other, admiring its rounded firmness.

"I often think back to that time in the shower," Alyssa purred suggestively as John explored her body. She watched and waited for his reaction.

John smiled as he recalled the lustful memory and let his hand slip lower between her cheeks. The girl spread her thighs a little, to let his searching fingers collect moisture from her soaked pussy. He moved his finger back upwards and caressed her rosebud again, re-enacting the moves from his memory.

"Mmm, that feels good," Alyssa sighed, encouraging him to continue.

John applied some gentle but insistent pressure and he was able to slide his lubricated finger into the wonderfully tight hole. Her snug little anus gripped his finger tightly, only letting him push in past the first knuckle. He paused for a moment, letting her adjust to the intrusion. The young girl closed her eyes and moaned softly.

"Do you like that, beautiful?" he whispered in her ear, as her body relaxed and let him push in further, this time past the second knuckle.

"Mmm-hmm," she moaned back seductively. "But it feels like I need something bigger..."

John slowly withdrew his finger to get a second digit well lubricated in her pussy. He added that finger to the first and then gently pushed the pair at her now slippery nether hole.

Alyssa gasped as he stretched her tight ass wider than before, his fingers sliding inside her. She managed to stay relaxed and her body was able to welcome the full length of both fingers as he slowly and carefully penetrated her.

"That's a lot better," she purred. Her body seemed to grasp his fingers in a hot, tight embrace as her hips rocked back and forth a few millimetres at a time. "It feels like I need something bigger though... Something hot, hard, and long."

Barely able to believe his ears, John eased his fingers from the girl's tight embrace and then knelt in front of her, his engorged cock leading the way. Alyssa opened her eyes when she felt his heat at her lips and looked up at him lustily.

"That looks perfect," the girl said, before licking his throbbing crown. "Now let's make sure he's wet enough to slide right in."

She parted her lips and took in his head, sucking strongly at him to urge him in further. John cupped her blonde mane in his hand, and then stuffed inch after inch of his wide girthed length down her throat. He stopped pushing forward when he felt her nose against his stomach and her chin resting against his balls. Alyssa's throat seemed to massage his whole cock before he slowly withdrew, her slick tongue making sure he was well lubricated with saliva.

She kissed the end, then lay her head down on the pillow again, waiting expectantly. John moved down the bed, so that he was straddling the prostrate girl. His gaze moved down her smooth, muscled back until it fell on her perfectly round ass cheeks. The cleft between the rounded spheres was dark and inviting, hiding the treasures within.

Supporting his weight with one hand and guiding his throbbing cock with the other, he brought the swollen head up to nudge between her pert globes. The girl reached back with both hands to spread her cheeks, exposing the pink, tight little knot of muscle to his burning gaze. He nuzzled up against it with the broad head of his shaft, blocking it completely from sight.

John pushed forwards with his hips, applying insistent pressure. The tight ring tried its best to refuse him entry, but eventually the lubrication and the undeniable pressure proved to be its undoing.

Alyssa groaned as her anus unfurled, the heavy, blunt head of John's cock forcing its way inside. The tight ring was stretched wide open, enveloping him like a second skin. For a moment Alyssa panicked that he was too big and that her ring would tear, but then it snapped tightly over the rim of the mushroom head, offering her slight relief.

"Oh God that's big," the exposed girl moaned through gritted teeth as she tried to relax and accommodate the huge invader.

John held still, to let the quivering teenager adapt to the stretching her body was experiencing. He waited until the tension left her arms and she looked over her shoulder at him. Her gaze was heavy lidded with lust, as she nodded imperceptibly at him to continue. Supporting his weight with his arms, he began to flex his hips slightly, pushing a few more millimetres of his burgeoning length deeper into the compliant young woman. The slick saliva eased his way into her hot tight passage and he was able to push further in, until half his cock was buried in the girl's ass.

Alyssa hands tried to spread her quivering buttocks further apart, to ease the way for his thrusting shaft. John was able to push even deeper, her rectum stretched wide by his huge girth. Alyssa moaned and panted with every inch he gained inside her until her snug anus was wrapped tightly around the base of his cock. Her firm cheeks were pressed right up against his groin and their trembling felt magnificent as he rested, fully embedded inside her.

"So full..." Alyssa groaned, feeling his turgid weight deep in her belly.

"That's a good girl, you took my whole length," John whispered in Alyssa's ear comfortingly.

His swollen balls were pressed up against her pussy and he could feel her excited heat beneath him.

"Can you feel my heavy balls resting on you?" he enquired. The girl could only nod that she could. "They're packed full of cum... and where does that cum belong?" he asked.

"In... my tummy!" she gasped, her senses overloaded.

"Yes, that's right," he crooned in her ear. "Such a good girl."

John began to slowly pull back, leaving her bowels feeling vacant and empty as he withdrew. Alyssa hissed at the bizarre feeling of being voided in this way. He pulled his hips back until just the head was still inside her, her tight anus refusing to give up its clenching grip under the helm of his cock. Reversing direction, John pushed back into her, his passage much easier this time.

"Ufff!" Alyssa gasped out loud as she was suddenly shoved full of meat again. She had never felt this stuffed before, her internal organs having to rearrange themselves to find room to fit this enormous intruder.

John began to establish a steady rhythm, sliding his broad cock deep into her ass time and time again. The girl could only grunt and groan as he stroked into the snug fit of her clenching body. He rested on her back, kneeling to either side of her legs, her smaller body completely covered by his own. Taking a firm grip on the end of the bed, he rocked back and forth, fucking her smoothly in the ass.

The teenager had arched her back, her skin glistening with perspiration. Her head was thrown back, resting against his shoulder and her eyes were squeezed tightly closed. The beautiful teen's mouth hung open as she gasped with pleasure, her lips swollen with passion. Alyssa's hands came forward to cover his own, and they interlaced their fingers, gripping each other tightly.

"That's it baby, you're so fucking hot!" John hissed in her ear, as he pounded her firm taut cheeks under his hips.

"Do it harder!" she grunted in reply. "Show me who's boss!"

John kissed the panting teenager fiercely, which she returned with passion.  Her sweat-slicked hair flew around her face as he rutted into the clenching grip of her ass, fucking her furiously. He couldn't remember ever feeling this turned on before, his body surrendering to pure animalistic lust as he buggered the beautiful teenager splayed out beneath him. Eventually the vice like tightness of her anal passage milked him to the point of release, and he thrust hard into her as his balls exploded in climax. John was seeing spots before his eyes as cum rocketed out of his cock and blasted into the teen's bowels.

"Ohh! I can feel it inside me.... It's so hot!" Alyssa gasped as he gave her a cum enema.

She joined him in climax, her excited young body bucking and convulsing beneath him as he rode out his long explosive orgasm. With his weight

pinning her in place, she was forced to accept each long surge of spunk, her stomach rounding out beneath her as he filled up her tummy.

"Ohh fuck!" she groaned helplessly, as her waistline expanded to house his thick, heavy cum.

"That's it baby, got to fill your belly," John grunted, as his balls lurched again and again.

They stayed locked in place with his cock balls-deep up her ass, his hips driving her into the bed and trying to force his spunk as far inside her as it would go. Alyssa could only hold on tight as the firm, supple skin of her tummy stretched to house all that cum. His jism felt warm and heavy as it filled her up, comforting her as he used her ripe young body.

Eventually John's orgasm abated and he rolled over to the girl's side so that he wouldn't squash her with his weight. His deflating cock slithered from her ass, which sealed up tight behind him. They cuddled together as they both panted for breath, and he gently stroked her cum packed abdomen.

"Oh John, that was amazing! I felt so submissive, so helpless, like I had surrendered all control," the satiated young woman sighed contentedly. "It felt so... intense."

John could only nod mutely in agreement, not able to speak quite yet.

Their breathing eventually returned to normal as they relaxed in the afterglow of a truly tremendous climax. Suddenly Alyssa lurched upright, a funny look on her face, before she dashed to the bathroom. She returned a few minutes later blushing cutely, her tummy now returned to its normal size. John didn't comment and just opened his arms, inviting her back to his embrace. They relaxed together, enjoying the comfortable silence, until John's stomach protested loudly and broke the moment.

Alyssa laughed, the melodic sound filling his cabin. "You poor man! Let me go fix you some breakfast," she volunteered, giving him a peck on the cheek as she climbed off the bed.

He watched entranced at the alluring sway of her hips as she padded out of the cabin and headed towards the rec room. John could only marvel at his wondrous good fortune.

"What could I have possibly done in a previous life to have got this lucky?" he thought to himself as he closed his eyes with a big grin on his face, and waited for Alyssa to return.

He was missing something important however and the unknown mystery tingled in his mind, dancing tantalisingly out of reach. He was developing strong feelings for his young shipmate and they were clouding his reasoning.

John sat up and adopted his meditative pose. He breathed long deep breaths for several minutes, calming himself, and trying to centre his being. The rapid blur of events over the last couple of weeks seemed to fade away and he felt sharp and in control once again.

A few minutes passed before his keen ears picked up the soft measured tread of Alyssa's feet as she walked back to their cabin. The beautiful young woman stepped smoothly into view, carrying a tray in her hands that supported a varied selection of fruit, some pastries, and a couple of chilled glasses of water. She posed her shapely body for him coquettishly, before her lithe long legs carried her into the room.

Alyssa sat at the end of the bed and placed the tray between them, giving him a glorious smile that revealed her sparkling white teeth. "Breakfast is served!"

John was amazed at how hungry he was as he devoured the fruit and pastries in no time. Alyssa watched him eat, just plucking the occasional

grape from the bunch and popping it between her succulent lips. He eventually finished the morning feast, feeling contentedly full and replenished.

His newfound clarity let him drink in the appearance of his breakfast companion for seemingly the first time, the fog shrouding his mind finally clearing. He couldn't believe the huge transformation she had undergone in such a relatively short period of time. He had a sudden brainwave and rose to his feet.

"Thanks for a wonderful morning," he said, thanking the beautiful young woman before leaning in for a kiss.

Alyssa beamed up at him happily before she began to tidy up their room. John strode purposefully to the cockpit and sat in the pilot's chair before rotating to face the console. He pressed a couple of buttons, searching for the recording he had made a couple of weeks before. He found it a few moments later and reviewed the footage.

The video camera reinforced what he had suspected, but his mind had oddly seemed to ignore. The ghostly white girl in the footage was about five feet, two inches tall, a 28A cup if he guessed correctly, and painfully skinny, suffering from malnutrition.

John hit the record button on the internal cameras and turned to the doorway, then called to the cabin, "Alyssa, could you come here a moment please?"

She came into view a moment later, her slinky walk reminding him of a catwalk model as she glided over to see him.

"What's up John?" Alyssa enquired politely as she sat in the co-pilot's chair, her posture erect and self-assured.

His eyes lingered over her succulent form before he tore his gaze back to the console. He pressed a couple of buttons causing a nearby monitor to blaze into life and play back the newly recorded footage.

The beautiful teen sauntered into view on the screen, before he paused the recording. The stunningly attractive girl filling the image was about five foot eight inches tall, her 32D breasts appearing huge on her slim athletic build. Her tanned, flawless skin seemed to glow and her hourglass curves were the epitome of feminine allure. Golden blonde hair cascaded down past her shoulders, thick and lustrous, framing her exquisitely beautiful face perfectly.

Alyssa cast her eyes towards the monitor, intrigued by the image. "Wow, she's gorgeous John! Who is that, an ex-girlfriend?" the teenager teased him playfully.

"It's not just me under this spell," John mused to himself.

"Look again, honey," John said quietly, as he hit a couple more buttons. The adjacent monitor flickered to life showing a still of the previous recording. The stark comparison between the pale, skinny waif and the tanned vibrant beauty could not be more glaring.

Alyssa pouted when she saw the picture of herself. "Hey, that's harsh. We can't all be as beautiful as this mysterious goddess," she said, pointing at the other image, her feelings hurt.

"You are the goddess, sweetheart," John said, smiling at her reassuringly.

"That's nice of you to say," Alyssa mumbled, clearly not understanding, and thinking he was just being kind.

John laughed, this wasn't getting them anywhere. "Come here," he commanded, holding his arms open in a clear invitation for her to sit in his lap.

Alyssa got up and then sat down obediently, still not understanding the situation and feeling a little dejected.

John reached around the confused girl and cupped her round, firm breasts. This evoked a contented sigh from the teenager as she enjoyed his tender touch.

"Look at the pictures again, honey," he whispered in her ear, as he gently squeezed the taut flesh of her pert chest. "Which of those girls has delicious breasts just like these?"

John watched the girl's face as shocked understanding suddenly hit her.

"Holy fuck!" she swore animatedly, leaping to her feet with her hands moving up to cup her breasts. The stunned girl gawked at the proud tits filling her hands and then back at the image on the screen.

"What... I... How is this possible?!" she gasped.

"I'm not sure," John replied honestly. "I've never seen or heard of anything like this before."

Alyssa seemed to be trying to look at the monitor and examine her body at the same time, a look of stunned disbelief on her face. He waited patiently and let her acclimatise to her ravishing new form.

The lovely teenager eventually sat down demurely in the co-pilots chair, her head tilted to the side as she scrutinised the two images in front of her. He could almost see her mind whirring as she processed this change.

"You said you had never had any long-term girlfriends before?" she asked, her eyes darting to his face. "Were they all one night stands?"

John nodded tentatively. "Yes. With my unusual parentage, I figured it was probably for the best," he answered, repeating his earlier explanation.

"So, you've never fed this amount of your cum to a girl before?" Alyssa probed him.

"No, never."

Alyssa sat, studying him shrewdly for a few minutes, her mind turning over possibilities, constructing theories. Eventually she seemed to make her mind up on something and a big beaming smile formed on her luscious lips.

"Well thanks for choosing me as your test subject!" she giggled.

John laughed along with her. "You're welcum!" he joked, eliciting peals of laughter from the girl.

She came over to him and kissed him soundly. "I mean it John. Ever since I was a little girl I wanted boobs and it looked like I was never going to get them." She hefted her impressive rack in both hands and gave him a broad grin. "These are awesome!"

"They really are!" John grinned back, her enthusiasm contagious.

The happy moment was suddenly cut short by a klaxon wail from the console, causing the couple to jump in surprise. There was something on the long-range scanner!

# Three Square Meals Ch. 05 – Avenging angels

"What was that?" Alyssa gasped, her head snapping around to look at the console.

"We're picking up an emergency distress beacon," John replied over the din of the klaxon, quickly pressing a button to reduce the volume to a much more subdued level. He studied the monitor, his eyes searching for any useful information. "It looks like it's a freighter experiencing engine trouble. They probably need a tow or spare parts."

"Are we going to help them?" Alyssa asked, excited at this unexpected turn of events.

John frowned. "It could be a trap."

"They might be genuine though!" Alyssa replied, eager to ride to the rescue.

John tapped his chin with a finger, looking thoughtful. "Okay, but let's be cautious. We can approach under minimal power, so we shouldn't appear on scanners. If everything looks legit we can help, if not, we pass them by."

Alyssa's eyes shone with excitement. "This is such a rush!"

John smiled at her and arched an eyebrow as he looked at the delightfully nude teenager. "We can't have you strolling in there naked though. We need to sort you out an outfit."

"Unfortunately, someone blasted my clothes into deep space!" she retorted with a playful frown.

John admired her pert bust and shapely curves. "I doubt they would have fitted you any more anyway, not since your recent growth spurt."

Alyssa arched her back and thrust her chest out, her perfect D-cup breasts standing high and proud with no sag whatsoever. "I think you might be right," she said with a flirtatious smile, enjoying the attention.

They had a look through John's spare gear. Most of his outfits were much too large for her, sized as they were for his broad-shouldered six-foot-two frame. They eventually found a form fitting body sleeve, that he would normally wear under a space suit. It hugged the contours of Alyssa's body in very interesting ways, but at least she wouldn't be completely naked.

John then turned toward his weapon locker. "Have you had any experience with firearms, Alyssa?" he asked the nubile young woman.

"I've never fired one before. Sorry," the teenager replied, shaking her head.

He pressed his thumb to the lock and the locker door rolled backwards to reveal the racks of weaponry. There was a broad selection of weapons there, ranging from pistols to rifles and John looked through the guns, trying to decide what would be the most sensible to give to her. He eventually settled on the auto shotgun, where accuracy was less of an issue, and made sure it was unloaded before handing it to the girl.

Pressing a couple of buttons on the grip, John increased the strength of the auto-damper, which would limit the effects of weapon recoil. "It's still going to kick if you fire quickly," he warned her. "So be very careful!"

Alyssa nodded, her eyes wide as she gazed at the broad-muzzled shotgun in her hands. Her full lips lifted into a playful smile as she said, "I much prefer holding this monster instead of staring down the barrel!"

"Yeah, I bet," John replied wryly, remembering their first encounter. His expression turned serious as he reached out to place a hand on her shoulder. "Normally, I'd never even consider exposing a civilian with no weapons training to combat, but you'll be in just as much danger if I left you behind. When we dock, I can't protect my ship and board that freighter at the same time, so you better come with me. That means I'll need to give you a crash course in firearms."

She looked up at him, her expression sombre and attentive as she responded to his firm tone. "Okay, I'm listening."

They went through reloading and clearing jams, the best way to hold the weapon and how to use the infrared scope. Alyssa was an eager student and after an hour of intensive training, John felt reasonably confident that she wouldn't shoot him by accident.

John grabbed a dangerous looking assault rifle and loaded the bullpup magazine with hollow point ammo. You had to be extremely careful firing weapons inside spacecraft, as one stray round punching through the hull could depressurise the ship. Using armour piercing ammunition was asking for trouble, so he hoped they didn't come across anyone unfriendly in tactical armour. He held the high-tech weapon to his shoulder and looked through the integrated scope to check everything was fully operational.

He donned his own combat gear which consisted of a polymer-weave jumpsuit with ceramic composite plates to protect his limbs and chest. Once he was happy with the fit, he grabbed some spare magazines for his rifle and slotted them into pouches on his belt.

They headed back to the cockpit and powered down almost all the ship's subsystems to keep as low an energy profile as possible. John let Alyssa plot the course and the darkened ship crept towards the source of the distress beacon.

An hour later and they were close enough for visual contact of the ship transmitting the distress signal. A large old freighter filled the viewscreen, but it seemed that John and Alyssa were not the only ones to respond to the signal. They could see a sleek grey warship had docked with the troubled freighter, a corvette class vessel by the size of the spacecraft. The emblem of a winged sword pointing to a star was proudly emblazoned on its hull, the emblem identifying it as a Terran Federation ship.

"Oh, they beat us to it," said Alyssa, sounding deflated.

John frowned, his eyes narrowing in suspicion as he took in the scenario in front of them. "Something isn't right over there."

His finely tuned senses and years of ship to ship combat experience were all warning him that there was danger ahead. John had learned to trust these instincts, as it was usually his subconscious picking up tiny details that all pointed to something being wrong. As he studied the scene, he realised what had been bothering him.

Pointing towards the front of the corvette, he said, "Do you see the navigation lights set for that docking manoeuvre?"

Alyssa peered through the cockpit window, then looked back at him with a frown. "No, what lights?"

"Exactly," he said, his expression darkening. "Most Federation Captains are real sticklers for protocol. There's no way they'd dock with that freighter without following standard Terran Federation docking procedures."

"What does that mean?" the blonde asked, holding her breath as she stared at the corvette.

John grimaced and said quietly, "That they're in trouble."

In exchange for some very useful privileges, he had a certain number of obligations to the Terran Federation, like intervening in exactly this kind of scenario. Unfortunately, that left him with very few options.

He blew out a deep breath in a long sigh. "OK. We're going to have to investigate." He studied the two ships for a long moment, trying to plan his best approach. Remembering he had a newly-qualified First-Class Navigator with him, John pointed to the airlock on the closest flank of the Federation warship. "Can you bring us in nice and easy, then dock with the corvette? On the opposite side to that freighter…"

His young shipmate nodded in reply and propped her auto-shotgun against the wall, then sat in the co-pilot's chair. Her slender fingers darted over the controls as she set up a docking solution to connect with the corvette's closest airlock. The Fool's Gold slid silently into position, guided in by her expert use of retro-thrusters until she made contact with the docking collar, magnetic clamps holding it in place. The sleek Federation warship was now sandwiched between the two bulky freighters.

"That's it, we're docked," Alyssa said with satisfaction, rising from her chair and gingerly retrieving her shotgun. She paused, looking curiously at John, who was staring intently at a holographic schematic. "What're you up to?"

"That's a Marlin-class freighter," he replied, nodding towards the holo-image. He lifted his left arm, showing her the computer built into his armoured vambrace. "I'm just uploading the deck plans to this."

"Oh, I see," she replied, her voice quiet and worried.

John turned to look at her and saw Alyssa's apprehensive expression. He clasped her hand and squeezed it gently. "Don't worry, we'll be okay. Just stick close behind me and I'll keep you safe."

He led his young companion down to the cargo bay which housed his freighter's airlock. The airlock followed the same standard conventions used in all Terran vessels, allowing the most modern of warships to dock with ancient hulks. There were two sets of doors on either side of a small pressurisation chamber, so that crewmen in spacesuits could exit the vessel without depressurising the interior of the ship.

They performed a final weapons check and John pressed a button opening the inner airlock door. Once they had stepped inside the airlock chamber, he sealed the door behind him, then checked the nearby console to make sure they were safely connected to the corvette. The readings showed a secure connection to a pressurised ship, so he pressed another button, opening the outer airlock door. It slid open, revealing the door of the corvette. The grey door of the military ship looked brand new, with the words "TFN Griffon" stamped right in the centre.

John produced a small chrome device from a holster on his belt. He hooked up the device to the corvette's airlock door and it hummed happily to itself. After a few moments, there was a dull "Thunk" and the Griffon's sturdy airlock door rotated upwards, granting access to the corvette. He retrieved the device and stashed it back on his belt.

"Let's go," he said softly, raising his rifle and cautiously entering the warship.

He recognised the faint but distinctive aroma that assaulted his nose; a smell that he was all too familiar with. It was a rank and pungent smell that was mixed with a sickening sweetness. Leading the way deeper into the corvette, it didn't take them long to find the first corpse. Sprawled on the deck was a Federation marine, who had been shot several times in a firefight in the adjacent corridor. Rigor Mortis had set in and the young man's face was frozen, contorted in fear and pain.

"The Griffon must've been captured some time ago," John whispered to his young companion.

She nodded, a grim frown on her face. "Yeah, to smell like that, he must've been dead a while." When she saw his look of surprise, she added, "I grew up on Karron. Believe me, I know what a corpse smells like."

They stepped carefully over the body and headed further into the Griffon. A corvette was the smallest class of hyper-warp capable warships in the Terran Federation military, with a relatively compact and functional interior, consisting of only a dozen rooms. It took John and Alyssa ten minutes to finish their sweep of the ship, finding fourteen more dead crewmen and evidence of looting in most rooms. It appeared obvious to John that the crew had been caught by surprise and most of them had been killed during a hostile boarding action.

The only really interesting find was the ship's armoury. This room was sealed behind robust locked doors, which were scarred with the evidence of a number of attempts to blast them open. Once they had finished their sweep of the ship, John led Alyssa back to the reinforced doors and retrieved the chrome device from his belt. He hooked it up to the locking mechanism on the doorframe and after a few moments of contented humming, the door rose smoothly into the ceiling. Uncoupling the device from the opened portal, he packed it away on his belt again.

Alyssa looked on with a raised eyebrow, then asked in a hushed whisper, "Breaking into a high-security door? How much did that thing cost you on the black market?"

"It's legit, I promise!" John murmured defensively, before leading her into the armoury and locking the door behind them.

A quick glance through the contents provided some interesting results. They found a number of suits of standard issue Federation body armour, which the crew had not had time to equip. John searched through the suits until he found one in the right size and had Alyssa don the protective

gear. He also found some grenades which he carefully loaded on his combat webbing as she struggled to put on the unfamiliar body armour.

When she was finished she turned around, looking self-conscious as she modelled it for him. "What do you think?"

Made from similar ceramic plating to John's armour, her new armour protected her limbs and torso with moulded pieces of armour plating, that were attached to a polymer-weave combat suit. The armour was in Terran Federation grey, which wasn't particularly inspired, but did feel comfortingly familiar to John.

"Much better!" he replied, greatly relieved to see her protected by body armour. "That'll keep you safe from most low calibre rounds." He turned to leave the room, hitting the button beside the door to open it again.

Alyssa smiled, touched by his concern for her safety, then followed after him as he left the armoury. John covered the corridors with his rifle, then headed towards the front of the corvette.

"Where are we going now?" she asked, following his purposeful stride.

"To the cockpit," John replied, his sharp ears straining for the slightest hint of enemies. "We need to find the ship's roster and the Captain's log. They might be able to give us some more clues as to what had happened."

Unfortunately, the cockpit had been badly damaged in a fire-fight. The grenade that killed the Captain and the pilot had also ripped through the command console, rendering it a broken charred wreck. They backtracked to the ship's medical bay, Alyssa following closely behind him.

"Why are we going to Medical?" she asked curiously.

John stopped by one of the computers in the medical bay and began tapping away at the keyboard. "Well, if I'm lucky.... Yes! I've found the

crew's medical logs. This will give us a list of actively serving crew members."

The personnel roster confirmed his fears. There were eighteen serving crewmen aboard this corvette, which meant that three were missing. Almost all the dead Federation crew they had found were men and after a quick scan of the crew listings, he confirmed that the missing crewmembers were all women.

John turned to his young companion. "It looks like they captured three of the women," he said, his grim tone matching the look on his face. "I've seen what happens in these kind of scenarios and it isn't pretty. Are you up for mounting a rescue operation?"

Alyssa looked up at him with wide eyes and she nodded her head vigorously.

"This could get very dangerous, so follow all my instructions to the letter," he ordered, his voice stern.

The young girl threw him a quick salute, her face set in a determined expression.

"OK, let's move out," he said, gesturing for her to follow. "Stay behind me and cover our backs. If you see anyone, try and let me know before you start shooting..."

"Will do," she agreed, hefting her shotgun in readiness.

They left the medical bay and moved quickly and quietly to the airlock on the other side of the Corvette, the one that was connected to the much bigger freighter. The connecting doors had been left unsealed, leaving the way into the grubby interior of the other ship yawning wide open. The battered freighter was in a terrible state of disrepair, with wall panels discarded on the floor and exposed power cables showing evidence of

crude patching efforts. The corridors were filthy, which made John's lip curl with disgust.

He moved forward, carefully checking each intersection as they moved further inwards. This Freighter was old and battered, but it was also big and it would be easy to get lost in here. The main overhead lighting was out in this part of the ship and the crew had jerry-rigged flickering festoon lighting along the passageways. John motioned Alyssa to hug the wall a moment and the two crouched in the shadows. He tapped at the computer built into the vambrace on his left arm and the schematic of the freighter he'd uploaded earlier popped up on the screen. With a few more clicks he marked their current position and the route they would need to follow to leave. John nodded to his young companion and they set off again.

They had still not encountered anybody yet and John was beginning to wonder where everyone was, when he began to hear the sounds of some kind of commotion up ahead. They moved closer, listening to the sounds of many raised voices shouting raucously. John turned a corner and saw that the corridor to his right opened out onto the top level of a large cargo bay. He could see dozens of dark figures on the overhead gantries, all of them leaning over railings to look at some scene below. These men were clearly pirates and the baying mob were drinking booze and laughing raucously at the evening's entertainment.

John held his hand palm upright to Alyssa indicating for her to stay right there, before he turned and crept closer to the cargo bay. As he approached the entrance to the room, he was eventually able to see through the transparent gantry floor. The dim flickering from the overhead lights illuminated a hellish scene below.

There were two naked bodies on the deck below, both corpses broken and horribly violated. Towering over the dead crewwomen, a brutish hulk of a creature lurched around the cargo bay, its back to him. He watched for a moment as the massive shape moved to the side and a much smaller

figure came into view. The young woman was clearly terrified, desperately trying to ward off the monstrous beast with a short metal pole she was using as a makeshift spear.

John instantly recognised the creature stalking its prey. It was a Largath; a very strong and powerful alien humanoid that often worked for pirates and slavers to keep their merchandise under control. The Largath slobbered with anticipation as it circled the last crewwoman, trying to herd her into a corner of the cargo bay. It reared backwards and roared, its rippling muscles flexing in its shoulders as it was cheered on by the pirates watching from above. Its roar revealed that the creature was naked; a burgeoning, bright red, two-foot-long cock jutted out angrily from its groin, clearly intended for its next unfortunate victim.

John darted back to Alyssa, his presence unnoticed by the distracted pirates. "Two of the women are dead," he briefed her rapidly. "We have to move fast if we want to save the last one!"

Alyssa nodded but stayed silent, awaiting his orders.

"I'll use flash grenades to stun the pirates on the gantries, then I'll take out anyone still moving," he said, quickly outlining his plan. "Keep your eyes closed until you hear the explosions, then I want you to shoot the beast below with your shotgun. It's a big target so should be easy to hit, but watch out for the woman!"

The teenager raised her weapon to her shoulder indicating she was ready and John turned back to face the cargo bay again. They approached quickly in a crouch and he let his assault rifle dangle on its strap around his neck as he grabbed a flash grenade in each hand. He depressed the timer on each grenade before rolling one along the gantry to the left and another to the right. He had just enough time to grab a third grenade which he lobbed in a graceful arc to land on the gantry opposite.

The pair ducked down, closing their eyes tightly as the three grenades seemed to detonate simultaneously. The room was suddenly filled with different sounding screams as the men reacted to the searing light from the flash grenades. John took in the chaotic scene before him. Two pirates had stumbled over the barriers and had fallen the thirty-foot drop to the cargo bay floor below, while a third was desperately hanging on to the railing to avoid a similar fate. Most of the rest were rolling around on the gantries, clutching their faces and screaming in pain. However one was still standing, a burly looking guy who seemed to be unaffected by the grenades. When his head whipped around, John was able to see why. The brawny man had a pair of crude cybernetic eyes, both of which flared with a red light when he spotted John.

"You're fucking dead!" the cyborg roared, raising an ugly looking, heavy-calibre pistol in John's direction.

John had already levelled his own weapon at the big pirate and he squeezed the trigger, both of them shooting at the same time. The assault rifle chattered and John's three-round-burst hit the cyborg square in the chest, red fountains of blood spraying out behind him. The pirate keeled over on his back, screaming in pain as he landed on the gantry with a loud crash. The answering slug from the pirate's pistol hit John in the arm, staggering him slightly. The round didn't penetrate his armour, but the impact left a big dent in the plating and he knew he'd be left with a nasty bruise. John heard the bark of the shotgun from behind him as his young companion announced her presence.

Alyssa had kept her head down, waiting anxiously for the sound of explosions, just as John had instructed earlier. After the grenades went off, she darted forward to look for her target, spotting it only seconds later when she reached the gantry. The Largath was roaring in defiance, its four red eyes blinking rapidly to try and shrug off the sudden searing blindness.

She looked through the shotgun's infrared scope, picking out the cowering form of the woman they were trying to save. Huddled in the corner of the cargo bay, the crewwoman frantically rubbed at her eyes, reeling from the effects of the flash grenades. Alyssa focused her attention back on the Largath, seeing the creature's two foot phallus blazing bright red in her heat sensitive scope.

In the excitement of combat, Alyssa made a rookie mistake. Holding down the trigger on the shotgun, she unloaded the entire magazine on her target, the recoil making the broad muzzle climb and sending half the shells sailing harmlessly over the Largath's head. Unfortunately for the hulking creature, the first few rounds had been viciously accurate and its groin was now a mangled mess, gouting blood across the decking. The brutish creature keeled over on its front, squealing in agony.

John shot two more pirates as they struggled to regain their footing, the hollow point rounds painting the walls with copious amounts of blood. He looked over the railing and made eye contact with the terrified Federation crew woman who was squinting up at the gantry.

Pointing to a stepladder built into the wall beside her, he barked, "Move! Get out of there!"

She managed to gather her wits enough to stumble over to the ladder. Dropping her crude spear, the crewwoman fumbled for the rungs, groaning in pain as she began to climb.

The pirates were also shrugging off the effects of the flash grenades. Several of them had drawn pistols and were firing wildly in the rescuer's direction, sending bullets zipping over John's head. He dropped to his knee, taking careful aim before punching the tickets of three more of the brigands. The last he dropped with a headshot, the man's decapitated body crumpling backwards as his head exploded.

Alyssa watched the woman struggling with the torturous climb, exhaustion and injuries taking their toll. She was about to climb down to help, when she saw that the Largath had stopped its mad thrashing on the floor and was struggling to stand. Its four eyes focused on the climbing crew-woman, both sets narrowing with hate.

The scared teenager popped out her shotgun's spent magazine and slapped in another with shaking hands. She realised that if she didn't do something, the crewwoman had no chance. She leaned precariously over the railing, making sure she had a clear line of sight on the furious beast below. The Largath bellowed as it stomped over towards the wall, its heavily muscled arms reaching up as it attempted to grasp the climbing woman's leg. Alyssa took careful aim at the creature's head and pulled the trigger. Its narrowed eyes exploded under a rain of shotgun shells and the beast tottered over to the side, nothing left of its ruined head but a shattered pulpy mess.

Unfortunately Alyssa's jubilation was short-lived as she was hit in the chest by a slug from the pirates. The round deflected off the armour, but the blossoming pain from the impact was enough to make her lose balance and she began to topple over the railing. Just when she thought she was doomed, she felt a firm grip on her shoulder and she was hauled to safety. As she rolled backwards, she saw John firing his assault rifle one handed at her assailant. The wild spray of bullets caught the pirate across the chest and he was flipped backwards by the impact.

Hearing laboured panting coming from just below where she lay on the gantry, Alyssa reached over to grab the exhausted crewwoman. She pulled her up and over the ledge on to the gantry, the woman groaning in pain.

"Help her back to the ship!" John ordered from somewhere above her. "I'll cover you." He crouched at her side, loading a fresh magazine into his rifle.

The trip back to the ship was the stuff of nightmares. The crewwoman was exhausted and badly injured, which meant that Alyssa had to heavily support her as they staggered back along their previous route. Alyssa tucked her head under the woman's arm and offered her words of encouragement as they shuffled back to the Griffon. She paused at one junction, lost in the maze of dilapidated corridors.

While the crewwoman groaned pitifully beside her, Alyssa glanced back at yelled, "Which way? All these passages look the same!"

John fired off several bursts back down the passageway at their pursuers, catching one furious pirate in the chest and sending him spinning backwards, spraying gouts of blood all over the walls. The rest of the pirates ducked back into cover, giving John and the girls some momentary respite.

"Turn left, then the next right!" he called back to her. "You should see the airlock then!"

She nodded and was about to set off, when a another burly pirate came barrelling around the corner, blocking their line of retreat. The surprised pirate raised his heavy-bore pistol, a sneer of hatred on his face, but Alyssa moved faster. She raised her shotgun at the man and fired it in one motion, blowing off his leg above the knee. He pitched over screaming in pain, and was silenced a second later as John shot him in the face.

"Keep going!" John yelled, whirling around to fire off a couple of shots behind them to keep their pursuers suppressed.

They set off again, while being hounded by the furious pirates and John had to pause at each corridor intersection to temporarily hold them back with bursts from his rifle. Stray rounds from the pirates ricocheted down the hallways making hugging the walls a deadly mistake.

They eventually reached the corvette and John sealed the airlock door with a solid-sounding thunk. "That should hold them for a few minutes," he said, before turning back to Alyssa and the crewwoman, who was leaning against the wall, labouring for breath and wincing with the pain of her injuries.

John studied the woman they had just rescued for a moment. She was a young Latina, with dark brown hair that was plastered to her head with sweat. Her navy fatigues were torn and she was favouring her left side, making him think she might have some broken ribs. While she was obviously in a lot of pain, he was impressed by her quiet stoicism.

"Come on, we need some supplies from medical," he stated, before moving forward to gently scoop up the crewwoman in his arms.

She moaned into his chest as they headed to the medical bay at a brisk walk and he held her gingerly, trying not to jostle her injuries.

Alyssa darted into the medical bay ahead of them and gave him a quizzical look. "What do you need?"

John glanced around the room, then felt a surge of relief when he saw the stack of red boxes, just where he'd remembered them. "Grab one of those trauma kits please, Alyssa," he asked the blonde girl.

She darted over to grab the satchel of medical supplies, which she slung over her shoulder. She also grabbed a half-opened doctor's bag in her free hand, while carrying the shotgun in the other.

John led the way back to the Fool's Gold and they had just arrived at the interconnecting airlock when the dull rumble of an explosion reached their ears.

"They must have blown the other airlock," he guessed. "Time to leave."

The trio entered his freighter and he set the wounded crewwoman on her feet, steadying her with one arm. He hit the button on the airlock to seal the door before turning to Alyssa. "Help her to the passenger cabin. I need to get us out of here!"

Alyssa rushed forward to support the woman, who was start to sway unsteadily, while John raced off to the cockpit. He stabbed the button that would disengage the docking clamps and their freighter drifted free, uncoupled from the corvette. Ramping up the engine power as he turned the Fool's Gold, his freighter began to pull away into the blackness of space, keeping the corvette between them in case the freighter was armed. As soon as he was far enough away from the doomed corvette and the pirate freighter, he activated his ship's FTL drive. The ten second wait was interminable, but when they finally lurched into hyper-warp, he let himself relax, feeling the tension and adrenaline draining away.

John strode into the passenger cabin to see what he could do to help the injured woman. She was sitting on the edge of the bed in a daze, being supported by Alyssa, so he moved closer to see the extent of her injuries.

The olive-toned skin on her back had been horribly flayed, the shockingly deep lacerations from some kind of vicious whip. He gently touched the side of her torso, causing her to gasp in pain, confirming his suspicions about the broken ribs. Finally, she had a broken nose and two newly forming black eyes where some evil pirate had smashed her in the face.

John crouched in front of the woman, looking under her shroud of dark hair into her pain-dulled brown eyes. "My name's John, this is Alyssa," he said, nodding to his blonde companion. "You're safe now, no-one will hurt you again."

The woman began to weep softly, overcome with emotion.

"What's your name?" he asked gently.

"Second Lieutenant...Fernandez..." the woman replied between broken sobs.

Alyssa carefully brushed the woman's hair from her face. "What's your first name, honey?"

"It's... Calara," the brunette murmured, wavering unsteadily.

"Okay Calara, we'll clean you up and treat these injuries," John explained, his voice quiet and soothing. "I'll give you something for the pain, alright?"

The traumatised young woman could only nod her acceptance. She didn't react when John pressed a hypo-syringe to her arm and gave her a shot of painkillers.

John and Alyssa worked on Calara for the next hour, stripping off her torn clothing then cleaning and disinfecting her many wounds. When they were done, John gave her a strong sedative that put the woman into a deep, restful slumber. They left her sleeping on her right side, cushioned by pillows, and backed quietly out of the room.

"She needs serious medical treatment and I'm only really qualified in combat first aid," John whispered to Alyssa as they stood in the doorway. "We need to get Calara to a Terran Federation facility. If I give you the location, could you plot the course?"

"Of course," Alyssa replied without a hint of doubt.

They walked into the cockpit and she plotted the route to Port Heracles in the Nerus system. The Nav-computer provided an ETA of two days.

The exhausted pair then headed to their cabin to strip off their gear and get cleaned up. John unloaded the rifle and shotgun, before replacing the weapons in the secure locker. While he was busy doing that, Alyssa

carefully removed her body armour, leaving it in a neat pile on the floor before she headed into the shower. When their guns were safely stowed away, John unbuckled and unzipped his own armour, then followed the teenager into the shower cubicle. He found her standing under the hot shower, her arms around her shoulders as she shivered violently.

"It's your body reacting to the adrenaline," John explained, as he wrapped his arms around the beautiful young woman. He held her comfortingly and the pair let the soothing streams of water wash over them, cleansing them of the day's events.

"Why are men such utter bastards?" the troubled teenager asked, looking up at him and searching for answers in his calm gaze.

"Some are sick monsters and need to be put down," he agreed, his voice quiet and reflective. "But not all men are like that."

"I know," Alyssa said, smiling affectionately at him. She reached up to stroke his face with a delicate hand before giving him a tender kiss.

They left the shower, dried themselves off and collapsed on the big bed. After what happened today, neither of them was feeling at all amorous, so they soon dropped off into a comforting sleep.

John checked on his injured passenger a couple of times during the night, but she slept on under the blissful haze of the sedative. He eventually awoke to find his head resting on Alyssa's lovely, yielding chest, her skin feeling soft and smooth against his cheek. She ran her fingers through his hair, stroking his head comfortingly. He lay there for a while, listening to her strong heartbeat and getting an up-close view of the bruise on her chest where she had taken the hit from the pirate's bullet. It looked like it hadn't been as bad as he feared, the light purple bruising already beginning to fade.

He leaned up on one elbow so that he was looking down over the young beauty sharing his bed. Her beautiful face looked up at him from the golden halo spread on the pillow, her lovely blue eyes watching his face. He leaned down to kiss her, feeling her lips form a smile before she kissed him back.

"You were brilliant out there yesterday," he commended the teenager, sincere admiration ringing in his voice. "I've seen people buckle under the stress of combat, but you handled yourself like a pro. We saved that woman's life and you should feel very proud of yourself".

Alyssa grinned at him, glowing with his praise. "It feels awesome knowing we helped someone like that."

John moved in for another kiss and they made out for a couple of minutes, before her small hands pushed him insistently on to his back. Alyssa rolled with him until she was straddling him, looking down imperiously from her high perch. She leaned down to kiss him again, her full round breasts feeling warm and firm as they touched his chest. John returned the kisses from the beautiful young woman, enjoying the feel of her lustrous blonde hair as it gently brushed his cheeks.

She moved her head to the side so that her full lips were only millimetres from his ear. He could feel her soft breath tickling him, which sent shivers down his body.

"You saved my life yesterday as well, John. In some cultures that means you own me now..." she whispered to him seductively. "What can I do to please my new master?"

John's arms encircled her youthful, toned body as he tilted his head towards her, searching for her lips. Alyssa moved her head back so that she was directly above him again and locked eyes with his as they kissed passionately. It felt like he was looking into her soul, as those piercing blue eyes held his gaze. The girl's dilated pupils were like two black holes

and they pulled him in with their inescapable grasp. He had never felt this connected to another person before and the feeling was intense, even if slightly unsettling.

She eventually had mercy, blinking slowly and breaking that connection. She moved downwards, trailing kisses along his jawline. He tilted his head back, exposing his throat trustingly, and was rewarded with more gentle kisses along his neck. She moved further down his body, kissing his broad chest, her tongue flickering out now and again to taste his skin. John's body felt hyper-sensitive as he awaited each kiss on her exploratory journey.

The beautiful teenager trailed kisses across his stomach down to his groin, her silky blonde hair brushing over his body as it followed in her wake. Alyssa began to kiss and then lick each of his balls in turn, each one feeling full and primed. Her soft lips promised sweet relief to his swollen orbs and he could only groan in pleasure as her tongue gently massaged each bloated sphere.

Those lovely lips began to plant kisses at the base of his shaft, before working their way up to the head. Her lips parted and her tongue darted out to swab the throbbing crown. Pre-cum had begun to build up and the beautiful girl sucked and licked him to try and obtain more, until she eventually opened her mouth into a wide oval and enveloped his head. John could only stare wide-eyed as her velvety smooth tongue glided over him, easing the way for her to take the rest of him inside her throat.

Alyssa was extremely well acquainted with his equipment by now and her lips were soon encircling the base of his cock as her slender neck massaged his length in a tight grip. She began to swallow repeatedly, the muscles rippling along his cock, feeling like he was being stroked by a dozen eager young hands. John grasped the beautiful girl's head, groaning at the unexpected and incredible sensations he was experiencing. She moaned in satisfaction, enjoying the feeling of being controlled by him.

John could only gasp and writhe as the young woman's throat rippled around him, her heated moans adding more vibrations to the coaxing massage. Eventually it became too much for him to resist and his body trembled with anticipation as his balls trembled in preparation to deliver their cargo.

With a wordless grunt, his ball-shaking orgasm overtook him. A long, heavy spurt of cum blasted up his shaft and then down into the kneeling girl's belly. This was rapidly joined by dozens more protein-rich surges of spunk, all settling in the welcoming home of Alyssa's stomach. The submissive teenager's waiting tummy soon rounded out, the strong muscles in her abdomen unable to prevent her belly from expanding from the gut-busting meal John was feeding her. This triggered a matching orgasm in the quivering teenager and her pussy spasmed strongly as she came hard.

Eventually he was spent and he lolled back on the bed, sighing with deep satisfaction. Alyssa sat up and stroked her bloated stomach, with a happy, contented grin on her face. The heavy, sperm laden meal in her belly felt warm and filling, and she loved seeing the look of happiness on John's face. Alyssa noticed movement by the doorway out of the corner of her eye and turned to look at their silent observer.

Calara had awoken from her long sleep and hearing noises had come to investigate. When she saw the beautiful blonde pleasuring her handsome partner, she turned away from the doorway to give them their privacy. Something drew her back however and she couldn't help but peek around the corner to watch the explosive climax.

Alyssa made eye contact with the voyeuristic Latina, who blushed furiously when she realised she had been spotted. Alyssa smiled reassuringly at her, before the brunette was overcome with embarrassment and darted back to the passenger cabin. The blonde giggled to herself quietly before lying down next to John.

"I think I heard Calara stirring," the mischievous teenager said. "Do you want me to go check on her?"

"No, it's okay, I'll do it," John offered. "You just relax. You earned it, that was sexy as hell!" He kissed the grinning girl enthusiastically before getting dressed in combat trousers and a t-shirt.

"Okay, relaxing..." she purred, reclining on the bed and running her hands over her hugely swollen tummy.

John left the cabin with a lightness in his step, not just from emptying the heavy load in his balls into the receptive teen's belly. He strolled into the passenger cabin and found the Latina lying on her side facing away from him.

"Ah, you're awake," he said to Calara. "I just want to quickly check your wounds. Is that okay?"

Calara was too embarrassed to look John in the eye, so she just nodded.

He touched her shoulder gently as he looked at the vicious weals and lacerations on her olive-toned back. "Those look very painful. Would you like another painkiller and sedative to help you sleep?" he asked the injured woman, his tone kind and sympathetic.

"I would, thank you," she murmured quietly in reply.

John filled up a glass with chilled, ice cold water from the nearby dispenser and then gathered a couple of strong painkillers from the trauma kit. "There you go," he said, as he handed over the drink and meds.

Calara sat upright, wincing at the sharp pain in her ribs and the dull throb from her back. Even her face hurt from the brutal beating that pirate had given her, when all she'd done was try to plead for the lives of her friends.

A bleak sadness descended on the young woman as she remembered all the horrible things that had happened, her eyes welling up with tears at the awful memories. She quickly swallowed the painkillers with the aid of the chilled water, seeking the merciful oblivion of sleep. The cool drink sent shivers down her spine as it soothed her parched throat and she finished off the rest of the glass, realising just how thirsty she had been.

John took the empty glass from her unresisting hand. "We're taking you to the medical facility in Port Heracles. We should only be a couple of days and then you'll be able to get some proper treatment for your injuries. Hang in there, it won't be long."

She was already starting to get drowsy, the quick-acting painkillers lulling her to sleep. Calara nodded her understanding and curled up on the bed, lying on her side to avoid putting pressure on her back or ribs. John left the young woman to rest and headed towards the cockpit to check on their progress to Port Heracles. Calara was asleep before he left the passenger cabin.

The next day was uneventful, with John showing Alyssa how to clean and check over their combat gear, which they had been too tired to do the night before. Calara slept for the rest of their journey and only stirred when they had docked at the Terran Starport and the medical team from Port Heracles were moving her to a stretcher. Her eyes flickered open as she was fastened to the anti-grav sled and she looked up at her two rescuers.

"Thank you for saving me..." she said quietly as she looked at Alyssa and John in turn.

John smiled back reassuringly and Alyssa leaned forward to plant a kiss on her cheek "You're welcome!" the beautiful blonde said with a dazzling smile, her perfect white teeth sparkling in the light.

The medical team whisked Calara away to intensive care, leaving John and Alyssa to watch them depart.

"I hope she'll be ok," Alyssa said, worrying about the young woman.

"They have excellent medical facilities here," John said reassuringly. "You can stay in contact with her via vid-feed as well if you want."

Alyssa leaned up to plant a warm kiss on his lips and walked back to their cabin, an alluring sway to her hips. She paused at the doorway and looked over her shoulder to make sure she had his full attention, before running her hands over her hips and posing her deliciously firm ass invitingly. She strutted into their room as if daring him to follow.

John realised his mouth was hanging open and he closed it self-consciously. He walked down the corridor to their room, anticipation rising in time with his rapidly growing cock. He paused for a moment to steady his breathing before he stepped into the cabin to see what the adventurous young woman had in store for him now.

Alyssa had wasted no time, stripping out of the bodysuit which lay in a crumpled pile on the floor. She was kneeling on the edge of the bed, looking over her right shoulder at him, her knees spread wide and her back arched.

"Fancy taking me for a ride?" she challenged him, her eyes glancing down over her shoulder to her uptilted ass.

John followed that glance and saw that between the perfectly rounded spheres of her bottom, her waiting rosebud was glistening where she had spread lubricant. The prepared teenager watched him with a knowing smile on her face as he strode forward purposefully, stripping off his clothes.

112

He moved up to the bed, her delightfully presented rear waiting at just the right height as she knelt before him. Reaching forward to gather her tousled blonde mane in his left hand, he rested his heavy right hand on the taut rounded flesh of her right buttock. He held her firmly in place as he tilted his hips, the blunt head of his throbbing tool sliding between the tanned cheeks of her ass. The passage was made easier with the slippery lubricant and he nudged up against her tightly clenched rosebud.

"There's a good girl," he said, as though calming a fine thoroughbred.

The beautiful teenager deliberately relaxed her tense posture, letting her body yield to the insistent pressure she felt against her ass. She bit her lower lip, her eyes closed in concentration as John used his unrelenting grip on her hip to pull her on to him. The tight ring of her anus was forced wide open as he pushed his broad mushroom head inside her body.

"That's right, you're doing so well," he said in encouragement, using that same soothing tone.

John's hips flexed forward as he used his tight purchase on her body to pull her back towards his groin. The slippery lubricant let him glide forward, inch after inch sliding deeper into her yielding body until her tight little hole was gripping the base of his shaft.

"Yes!" Alyssa hissed as he impaled her with his entire length.

She gasped as he clenched her hair tightly in his fist and used it to pull her head back towards his chest, arching her back into a beautiful curve.

"That's a good girl," he whispered in her ear, as his cock flexed deep inside her tightly stretched ass. "Let's ride you hard and see if we can burn off some of that energy."

Alyssa gasped with excitement, which then turned into a long drawn out moan of pleasure as he slowly withdrew his cock until only the head was

left inside her. He then thrust forward again, burying his full throbbing hardness into her luscious body, while holding her firmly in place with the heavy grip of his right hand.

John picked up the pace, driving his rock-hard shaft in and out of the girls clutching ass as her rounded buttocks shook with the impact. His broad girth had spread her tightly-clutching ring wide open and she felt exposed and stuffed full at the same time.

She grunted with each thrust, feeling his cock penetrating deep inside her. John was being so dominant and the relentless pounding of her firm young body was driving her crazy with passion.

Suddenly John stopped his thrusting and paused, fully impaled up to the balls in the panting girl.

"Now hold on there a minute! This steed isn't bearing my brand!" he declared, while tenderly caressing the soft smooth skin of her right buttock with his hand.

"Yessss! Do it!" she urged, looking back at him over her shoulder her face wild with lust.

John brought back his right arm before swinging it down in a powerful arc. The sound of the ringing slap as it landed on her rump echoed loudly around the room.

"Oh fuck!" Alyssa shrieked as she came explosively, the tingling skin where he had spanked her overloading her senses.

John held her tight as her body convulsed underneath him, her ass clenching around the length of his cock in rhythmic contractions. Pulling her back against his chest, he could feel her trembling against him. He stroked her sensitive right buttock as the glowing red hand print formed on her beautiful rounded cheek.

"That's much better. Now everyone knows who owns this fine filly..."

Alyssa could only groan in response as he began to flex his hips again, his swollen cock inching back and forth inside her ass.

"A gallop to the finish ought to do it!" he declared, before increasing the length of his backstroke and thrusting powerfully into the gasping young woman.

John played a lustful tune using Alyssa's body as his instrument. Her grunts and moans accompanied the steady beat of her buttocks slapping against his groin. He fucked her hard and long, drawing out a series of gut wrenching orgasms from her before he finally pulled her tight to his chest. The girl's back was arched towards him like a taut bow as he pummelled her toned ass cheeks.

Unable to hold back any longer, he cried out with his explosive climax. His painfully swollen balls blasted a long, powerful spurt of cum into the tight confines of her bowels. Alyssa screamed as she felt the hot cum blasting into her belly, joining him in orgasm.

John's right hand moved upwards, instinctively resting on Alyssa's stomach as his driving cock pumped his cum into her. He could feel each surge of spunk as it was forced into her trembling tummy, her slim waistline quickly expanding to make room for the burgeoning weight of his load. Eventually his mighty climax abated and John held Alyssa in a tight embrace, preventing the nearly comatose teenager from collapsing. His cock began to deflate and he eased out of her slippery passage, her sphincter closing up tightly behind him, holding in her precious cargo. He laid her gently on the bed and flopped down behind her, too exhausted to do anything except draw breath.

Alyssa gradually regained full consciousness and rolled over onto her back, moving carefully with the weight of her spunk bloated belly. She

grinned at him as she glanced down at her tummy, running her hands over the enormous rounded curve. "I look like I'm about to have a foal!"

John laughed loudly in response, Alyssa giggling along with him. "I'll be back in a minute," she said with a smirk, as she got up and headed to the bathroom.

He watched her as she walked away, enjoying seeing the toned muscles in her back, her skin glistening with perspiration. You would never know she carried such a gravid weight in front of her from looking at her svelte figure from behind. She turned to look at him before disappearing from view, her side profile looking obscene with her hugely bloated belly leading the way.

The gorgeous teenager eventually reappeared and she prowled gracefully towards him before joining him on the bed, cuddling up at his side now her stomach was back to normal. As he held her in his arms, he looked down to see his glowing hand print emblazoned on her otherwise perfect ass cheek. His body immediately tensed in response.

Alyssa felt his reaction and followed his gaze down to her bottom. "Hey, relax! It's okay, that was fucking hot!" she calmed him reassuringly. Placing a gentle kiss on his cheek, she gave him a contented smile. "Besides, I like bearing your mark."

John shook his head in disbelief. "You're an amazing woman Alyssa, do I ever tell you that?"

"Usually a couple of times a day, " the beautiful teenager replied. "...but it's always lovely to hear!" She leaned over him to look him in the eyes, her hair brushing softly across his chest as she gave him a tender kiss in gratitude.

The following week passed swiftly. Alyssa seemed to be spending more and more time in John's company and he couldn't recall ever getting on so

well with another person before. They worked together on any tasks he deemed necessary, the enthusiastic young girl perfectly in sync with him. Their normal activities were only broken by mealtimes, which usually meant the beautiful teenager on her knees between his legs, sucking eagerly on his cock. He lost count of the times he rounded out her lovely toned belly, but she savoured every meal, licking her lips and stroking her full stomach contentedly.

Calara contacted them by vid-feed after a couple of days and after some initial shyness, she chattered away with Alyssa as though the two were best friends. The Port Heracles medical team had decided that she didn't need surgery, but she was recovering in hospital there under their careful supervision.

The troubled young woman admitted that she had been having trouble sleeping, her dreams quickly turning into nightmares as she relived the traumatic events of her capture. She seemed to be making good progress with her physical recovery, but it was clear to John that Calara was suffering from PTSD. Alyssa and John did their best to cheer her up and promised to speak regularly. Vid-feed calls soon became part of their routine and they spoke frequently in the final leg of their journey.

Eventually the Fool's Gold arrived at Alpha Centauri, home of Olympus Shipyard and John's final destination after all this time. The Olympus shipyard was the centre of Terran Federation power, the dry docks there constructing the biggest and most powerful spacecraft in this quadrant of the galaxy. This mighty spaceport sat in high orbit around Alpha Centauri B, or the planet Gravitus as it was known to locals.

A squadron of fighters raced by, performing active scans on all new arrivals into the system. Alpha Centauri was a hive of activity, with hundreds of spacecraft approaching or leaving the enormous shipyard. John turned the Fool's Gold to join the stream of bulk freighters, corvettes, destroyers, and cruisers that were heading towards Olympus, while Alyssa gaped at the size of the Terran base.

"Want to take us in?" he asked kindly, turning to smile at his blonde companion.

She nodded eagerly. "Yes please!" she exclaimed, leaning forward and placing her graceful, slender hands on the co-pilot's console.

John sat in the pilot's chair as he watched Alyssa plot their approach to the Olympus shipyard. He couldn't believe their journey together was nearly over. He studied the girl who had stowed away on his ship four weeks ago.

The stunningly attractive teenager was concentrating intensely on the console in front of her, her head tilted slightly to the side. He looked up and down her gorgeous body, drinking in every exquisite detail of the ravishing young beauty before him. She wasn't just the most physically beautiful woman he had ever met; he also loved her intelligence, her fun personality, her enthusiasm and her zest for life.

Yes, he did love her, he suddenly realised. How was he ever going to let her go? His heart caught in his throat at the thought of this incredible young woman walking out of his life. He realised he would be bereft without her.

Then there was the age gap; he was old enough to be her father for god's sake! John bitterly berated himself. The girl was a genius with a blazingly bright future ahead of her. The First Class Navigator's license that she had earned so effortlessly was her ticket to a comfortable life filled with adventure. He couldn't be so selfish as to deprive the young girl of that. A black depression took hold of him as he realised he loved her too much to hold her back.

The abrupt realisation that he had to do the right thing brought tears to John's eyes. He turned to the girl he now realised was his soul-mate and tried to mentally prepare himself to let her go.

It was the hardest thing he had ever had to do.

# Three Square Meals Ch. 06 – The real adventure begins

Alyssa sat in the co-pilot's chair, plotting the course to Olympus shipyard. Her mind was in a spin as she reflected on the astonishing recent turn of events. Of course, there was all that business with her body changing so dramatically, her impressive new breasts being a constant source of delight. However, there was something else that she had been finding far more surreal. She had begun to hear voices...

It had started off innocuously enough, a week or so after she had been forced to escape from Karron and John had found her aboard his ship. He had asked her to become a Navigator First Class in a roundabout sort of a way, so she had thrown herself into his request with gusto. She had been studying in her free time and then meeting up for "mealtimes" with the handsome Captain.

She loved kneeling in front of him, servicing his massive cock and encouraging him to unload his sweet tasting cum into her eagerly awaiting stomach. Alyssa had grown to adore his "quad" and the way he filled her to the brim after every orgasm. She hadn't felt hungry once since they had made their agreement and for someone who had lived on the borderline of starvation for most of her life, that was a big deal. She did wonder if she should vary her nutrition a bit, but she felt charged with energy and her body seemed to be thriving on the high-protein diet.

As well as the contentedly full feeling in her stomach, she almost seemed to sense his pleasure when he exploded in her mouth. At first, she had dismissed it, but she had then become so in tune with the man that his orgasms would trigger her own. Eventually, she had started to pick up other emotions as well, not just on the occasions she was pleasuring him. When she had shown John her newly acquired Navigators ID, the bewildering onslaught of emotions she had sensed from him had been almost overwhelming.

Just after they had rescued Calara she had begun to hear the voices. Well more specifically, one voice. It was like hearing little snippets of conversation at random times. At first, she had wondered if she was going mad, but the voice was calm and kind which put her at ease. Most of the time the disembodied voice was saying lovely things about her and that was when she first noticed that she only heard it when John was exploring her body with his eyes. She had put two and two together and with some bewilderment, realised it was his inner voice she was tuning in to.

Alyssa sighed happily. It felt amazing to be so lusted after by the handsome man. She had entered their agreement with a certain amount of bitterness and resentment to start, but unsurprised at her predicament. However, to her amazement, he was so kind and gentle with her that her cynicism and distrust fell away and she started to develop strong feelings for him. When he told her he was proud of her, it felt like her heart would burst she had been so overjoyed. She found herself doing little things to please him any chance she could and his earnest gratitude was tremendously rewarding.

She had spent the last week trying to spend as much time with him as possible, surreptitiously listening in to his inner monologue whenever she could. It was difficult not to react to some of the things he thought, but she was developing quite the poker face. She figured it was prudent to keep this little secret to herself... Besides, what woman wouldn't want to be able read her man's thoughts without him knowing it!

Sitting in the cockpit when they arrived in the Alpha Centauri system, she had been awed by the sheer numbers of spacecraft hurrying about the system. Karron only saw a new spacecraft arrive once every few weeks, so to see hundreds of ships filling up the System Map had come as a shock. She quickly recovered, then plotted their course to Olympus Shipyard. It had only taken her a few seconds to set the Fool's Gold on its new course, so she pretended to be focused on the console, seizing the opportunity to tune into John's thoughts once again. Alyssa tilted her head slightly to the side and heard his inner voice fill her mind.

*She's so beautiful,* John thought happily. *It's not just that she's totally gorgeous, I love that she's so intelligent and fun to be with...*

Alyssa had to fight hard not to grin like an idiot to be held in such high regard. She darted a furtive glance in his direction and watched his face as he gazed distractedly out of the freighter's cockpit window at a squadron of destroyers in formation around a light carrier.

John's eyes widened as he suddenly realised, *I'm in love with her!*

Alyssa's heart sang and she wanted to leap into his arms and declare how much she returned his feelings.

Unfortunately, his thoughts suddenly took a dark turn.

*I'm old enough to be her father for god's sake!* John berated himself.

Old enough to be her father? Alyssa wondered. He only looked to be around thirty or so, which got Alyssa curious to know exactly how old he was.

*She's a genius with a Navigator First Class license. She's got a bright future ahead of her, you can't ruin that by trying to get her to stay,* John lamented, getting increasingly depressed.

Now he was thinking about getting her to leave his ship for her own good?! Didn't he understand she had only been half joking when she said that he owned her? Any thought of being away from him felt gut-wrenchingly miserable and her mind shied away from it instinctively. No, she needed to nip this shit in the bud right now!

John turned towards Alyssa, his face set in a grim expression, his eyes welling with tears. He opened his mouth to speak, but she cut him off abruptly.

"Well, our journey is nearly at an end, perhaps we should have a chat about our arrangement?" Alyssa suggested, smiling warmly at him.

"Of course," John replied, his face a mask of barely concealed pain. "With your new qualification, you'll have your choice of ships you could sign up with."

Her musical laughter filled the cockpit. "Other ships? Why would I want to leave? I've never been happier!" Her full lips formed an outrageous pout. "Unless you don't want me here any more?"

"No, of course I do, you're amazing!" John blurted out, reacting instinctively before remembering he was trying to be noble. "You have your whole life ahead of you though. Why would you want to saddle yourself with an older guy like me?"

Alyssa slowly rose and walked gracefully towards him before sitting in his lap. She cupped his face in her hands and looked deep into his eyes. "I feel safe, valued, and cared for... and that's all thanks to you." She paused to watch the hope spreading across his face. "I love you and I can't imagine us being apart!"

John encased the earnest teenager in a fierce hug. "I love you too!" he declared, all thoughts of being noble abandoned.

The couple kissed passionately, losing track of time. Revealing the extent of their feelings for each other was such a relief and they revelled in their new-found sense of contentment. They eventually separated to gaze at each other, drinking in each other's happiness, huge grins on their faces.

"I would like a promotion though..." Alyssa said offhandedly, a mischievous twinkle in her bright blue eyes.

John smiled back, intrigued. "Oh really, what did you have in mind?"

"I think I've outgrown the cumbucket role. I'd like something that will stretch me more..." She informed him, arching an eyebrow and giving him a coy smile.

John laughed at her lewd comments. "I do enjoy stretching you," he agreed wholeheartedly. "What did you have in mind?"

"I was thinking 'Executive Officer'," Alyssa replied, giving him a sparkling smile. "The XO is second-in-command and helps lighten the Commander's load, so he can focus on all the important things."

John doubled over with laughter. "You're hired!"

"You won't regret it," Alyssa purred seductively, moving smoothly to her knees between his legs.

John gasped as the beautiful teenager began to show him just how seriously she took her new role. He looked down at the poised and elegant young woman as she tilted forward, inch after inch of his throbbing cock disappearing into her mouth, until she finally touched her nose to his stomach. Her movements were fluid and graceful as she stroked him back and forth, massaging his length with the muscular grip of her tight throat. Her full lips seemed to be kissing him as they sucked at the base of his shaft, her mouth spread obscenely wide by his girth. He could only marvel at the incredible control she had over her body.

This was his life from now on, John suddenly realised. This stunningly gorgeous young woman was his to use whenever he wanted. He really was the luckiest son of a bitch in the galaxy! Alyssa looked up at him lovingly as she used every trick she possessed to heighten his pleasure. Her velvety soft tongue seemed to dance along the base of his cock, licking and caressing, coaxing him closer to climax.

She closed her eyes and just bobbed her head in his lap, keeping up a relentless sucking rhythm. John held her blonde head in his hands as his hips made tiny thrusting movements as though trying to fit more of his length down her throat. He was already fully sheathed however, so he was just thrusting away at her soft pliant lips.

John moaned in ecstasy as he fucked her beautiful face. The warm suckling sensation surrounding his cock was relentless and irresistible and eventually he could only succumb to her talents. With a final cry of relief, the titanic climax washed over him, overwhelming his senses with pleasure. His balls seem to clench then flex powerfully as the cum blasted out of his cock to reward the girl for her efforts.

Alyssa's eyes flew open when her tongue felt the first long spurt of cum rocketing down his shaft, his length jerking in her throat. She could feel her stomach rapidly filling up, blowing outwards as she provided a warm home for his eager legion of sperm. Through it all, she'd been able to feel John's delight at her loving ministrations, his arousal building until she'd brought him to a mind-blowing orgasm.

She was already moaning with lust and his sudden rush of ecstasy triggered her own climax, Alyssa's squeal of pleasure muffled by the mighty cock throbbing in her throat. Her pussy flexed and her thighs trembled uncontrollably as she joined him with an explosive climax.

John sank back in his chair, all tension having left his body. His balls felt satisfyingly numb and his satiated cock slid out of Alyssa's mouth, receiving a farewell kiss as it left her lips.

*Ah, I love blowjobs,* they both thought at the same time, sharing similar sighs of contentment. Alyssa had to use every ounce of willpower not to giggle uncontrollably.

John offered her a hand and the ravishing young blonde rose effortlessly to her feet, before snuggling into his lap. The movement of her proud firm

breasts rising and falling as she took in deep breaths, was hypnotising and he gazed at the stunning perfection of her beautiful body. He took in the acres of tanned unblemished skin on her spunk swollen stomach, marvelling that her malleable body could handle such a prodigious load.

Her gravid form made him think to the future and he suddenly knew instinctively that this gorgeous young woman would someday be carrying his baby in her belly. John stroked her tummy possessively, his strong hand tracing gentle circles over her nubile body, until Alyssa's delicate hand moved up to rest lightly on his. He sighed happily as he looked at the beautiful teenager's face, her expression doe-eyed as she met his gaze. They cuddled together, enjoying the serene moment and watching the glittering stars in the endless blackness spread out before them.

The blissfully happy couple relaxed for a few hours, enjoying the peaceful tranquillity as the Fool's Gold made its inexorable progress to Olympus Shipyard. Eventually the insistent buzz of the intercom broke their reverie and John pushed a button on the console to receive the communication.

"Incoming freighter, please identify yourself and your business at Olympus," a military communications officer requested politely.

"John Blake on the Fool's Gold to see Captain Harris."

There followed a drawn out pause before the officer replied, "Please approach docking bay forty-seven Commander, Vice Admiral Harris will meet you there."

"Well okay then!" John replied, grinning at Alyssa.

She smiled back at him, delighting in his buoyant and happy mood. The two retired to their cabin to shower and get dressed.

Alyssa zipped herself into the body suit that John had loaned her, while he got dressed in his standard combat trousers and T-shirt. He admired her

beautiful curves, the bodysuit not leaving much to the imagination. Turning to his wardrobe he reached inside and pulled out his flight jacket before throwing it to her. She caught it deftly and raised an eyebrow.

"I don't want to have to fight off the station's complement of randy marines!" he joked.

Alyssa laughed and posed for him, the jacket doing little to hide her lovely toned legs and pert rounded ass.

He tore his eyes away from her statuesque figure and met her playful gaze. "I think a shopping trip might be in order..."

Alyssa bounded up to him, her face alight with excitement. "Really?! We can go shopping on the station?"

"There's not much at the station, but the planet below has loads of retail zones," he clarified.

Alyssa practically skipped at his side as they went back to the cockpit, John smiling at her boundless enthusiasm. They sat waiting patiently as they began the final approach to the Olympus Shipyard and their designated docking bay. On the way into the port, they passed massive carriers and battleships, their freighter appearing tiny and insignificant next to these titans of interstellar space.

Alyssa stared at them in awe. She had never dreamed that anything man-made could be so vast... The gun barrels on some of those cannons were bigger than their ship!

"Impressive, aren't they?" John said, pointing towards the pride of the Terran Federation fleet.

She could only nod her agreement.

He paused, suddenly overcome with memories from what seemed like a lifetime ago. His voice was quiet and distant as he murmured, "It doesn't feel quite the same when something that size is trying to kill you though..."

Fear, pain, loss... emotions spiralled over their empathic link and Alyssa quickly moved to John's side, leaning down to kiss him. Her distracting presence broke through his introspection and his mood lifted immediately. He kissed her back, losing himself in the softness of her full lips. He only noticed that the ship was approaching the docking bay when she peeled away from him and returned to her seat. She darted him a loving smile, before she guided the freighter towards the centre of the vast docking area, a tremor running through the ship as it landed at the shipyard.

John rose from his chair and offered his young shipmate a hand. "We better get going, we don't want to leave our welcoming committee waiting!"

They held hands as they walked quickly to the cargo bay, with John enjoying the feel of her slender fingers intertwined with his. He pressed a button on the wall-mounted console and the airlock spiralled open, the servos in the door whirring in eagerness to perform their task. The couple stepped out of the freighter into the huge cargo bay, the extensive floor lighting illuminating their surroundings in a warm glow.

A young naval officer was waiting for them outside the Fool's Gold and he approached them at a brisk pace then snapped to attention as he saluted John. "Commander Blake, I am Lieutenant Victor Adams, ADC to Vice Admiral Harris. The Vice Admiral sends his apologies. He's in a meeting at the moment, but if you would like to follow me, I'll lead you to his office."

John nodded his assent and they followed the navy officer – a fresh minted lieutenant by the new rank insignia on his smart uniform - as he led them through a series of corridors. It took a few minutes to stroll

along all the long corridors in the shipyard, but eventually their guide ushered them into a reception room.

The young lieutenant strode over to a desk and pushed a button on the intercom. "Vice Admiral, the Commander is here to see you."

There was no reply, but a door on the other side of the room opened a few seconds later. A uniformed figure strolled over to meet them and Alyssa studied him as he approached. She guessed the spry man was in his mid-to-late fifties, his stern face sporting a bushy grey moustache.

John saluted the older officer, a wry grin on his face. "Vice Admiral..."

The man's stern face relaxed as he laughed and returned the salute. "Commander Blake! It's good to see you, how long's it been?"

"Retired eleven years now," John replied, vigorously shaking his old friend's hand.

"Sorry I couldn't come to meet you personally, damnable meeting overran," the Vice Admiral apologised with a frown. The older man's hawk-like eyes locked on Alyssa next."... and who is this lovely young lady?"

"This is Alyssa Marant, my Executive Officer," John said, introducing her with a happy grin. He turned to his beautiful companion. "This is Vice Admiral Charles Harris, we served together a long time ago."

John's old colleague shook Alyssa's hand, smiling at her cordially. "Call me Charles, please."

"Nice to meet you, Charles," the slightly intimidated teenager replied.

The perceptive older man looked at his friend speculatively. "Civilian life seems to be treating you well, John..."

"I've got no complaints," John replied with a broad smile.

Charles gestured towards the open door behind him. "Come join me in my office and let's catch up."

He led the way and they followed him into his office, then sat down in comfortable leather seats surrounding a coffee table. The seats were placed in a semi-circle facing a huge window that overlooked the incoming and outgoing traffic from the enormous shipyard.

"That's one hell of a view Charles," John said, watching a massive Terran Federation Carrier as it slowly made its way to the Nav beacon.

"Isn't it just," Charles agreed with a smile. "Now, tell me John, what brings you to see me after all this time? I can't imagine you came all this way just to relive old war stories."

John turned to look back at his old friend. "Tyrenium... ten tons of it."

Charles looked startled before he whistled appreciatively. "Civilian life really has been good to you John!"

John glanced at Alyssa, before nodding emphatically.

Charles tapped his chin looking thoughtful. "I'll take the whole cargo if you're willing, just name your price."

"Two-hundred-and-fifty million credits," John replied without pause.

"Holy fuck!" Alyssa squeaked.

Charles ignored the teenager's outburst and studied John shrewdly. "Done. You know very well this conflict with the Kintark has the T-Fed over a barrel, don't you?"

John smiled and shrugged his shoulders, his hands spread, palms outward. "A man's got to make a living."

Charles laughed, shaking his head. The two men shook hands to seal the deal. "Congratulations John, you can retire for real now," Charles said, genuinely pleased to see an old war buddy do so well for himself. John grinned back at his old friend.

Meanwhile Alyssa sat wide eyed, stunned at the insane sums of money these two men were discussing so casually. She thought back to her previous life of abject poverty, the years of scraping around for the odd couple of credits here or there.... All the horrible things she'd been forced to do, just to get by. Now here she was, listening to a deal for a few tons of rock that was worth more than the whole hollowed out asteroid she had grown up in. For this kind of money, you could buy the entire place and still have enough pocket change to feed its inhabitants for a lifetime!

John and Charles chatted amiably for a while, leaving Alyssa lost in her thoughts.

"How do you want the money John?" Charles asked. "Credit transfer okay I presume?"

John nodded agreeably as he finished the glass of whiskey his old commanding officer had poured for him. The two men stood to shake hands once more, making promises to stay in touch.

Placing his hand on Alyssa's shoulder, John gently roused her from her thoughts. "Time to go," he said quietly.

Alyssa nodded absent-mindedly and rose to join him, the pair turning to leave the office.

"Before you go, John..." Charles called out from behind him. "I've got something you might be interested in. The Invictus has been decommissioned, I'll be putting her up for auction soon."

John froze, half-turned towards his old friend.

"She'd make one hell of a fine ship for a wealthy young trader," Charles suggested with a knowing smile. "It'd be nice to see the old girl staying in the family so to speak."

"What's the Invictus?" Alyssa asked her handsome lover, puzzled that it should stir up such strong emotions in the man.

John was lost in his thoughts, his mind turning over the possibilities.

Seeing that John was distracted, Charles answered for him. "It's our old ship, Alyssa. I was transferred to the bridge crew back in oh... 2748. John joined the Ship's Marine company nine years later. I eventually made Captain and John retired after ten years service on the Invictus."

Alyssa nodded her thanks for his explanation.

"Why is she being decommissioned?" John asked, sounding intrigued.

"T-Fed Navy has changed its doctrines since you served, John. It's all about dropships on carriers now," Charles replied, rolling his eyes. "There's no place for assault cruisers in the new Fleet."

John was shaking his head. "She's too big, what am I going to do with all that space? Besides, there's only the two of us, how could we crew her?"

Charles waved his friend over to his desk as he pushed a couple of buttons on his console. The lights in the office dimmed and a large holographic display of a spacecraft sprung into being in the centre of the room.

The Invictus was a sleek and ferocious looking ship. Alyssa shivered slightly at its intimidating profile, the top deck bristling with weaponry. Charles zoomed in the display so that now they were looking at the ship's internals. From what she could tell, this assault cruiser was easily ten times bigger than John's current freighter.

"You could upgrade the engines and FTL drive, using this extra space here," the admiral enthused, pointing animatedly at the rear of the ship. "You also won't need the barracks, so you could turn this area of the ship into a cargo bay..." He gestured excitedly at the holographic map. "I'd keep the docking bay for a shuttle, just in case you need to land somewhere the Invictus is too big to dock at."

John slowly nodded, his interest piqued.

"You're still on the books right?" Charles asked.

John glanced Alyssa's way before he returned his attention to his friend. "Yes, I'm still listed."

"Great!" Charles exclaimed, looking delighted. "That means we can keep the gun decks unchanged!"

Alyssa suddenly realised this was a pet project for Charles. Perhaps he had speculated on what he would do with the ship if he had ever been in John's current situation. It was funny to see the mid-fifties Vice Admiral behaving like an enthusiastic schoolboy, but she managed to keep a straight face.

"What about crew?" John asked.

Charles waved his hand dismissively. "Automation will take care of that."

"Okay, I might be interested," John replied, keeping his tone non-committal. "Just how much does a Terran Federation assault cruiser go for nowadays?"

"Well, I can pull a few strings for an old friend," Charles replied with a grin. He leaned in closer and added in a conspiratorial whisper, "Not having to decommission all those weapons will save the shipyard a fortune! I can pass that on as a discount..."

John waited patiently and raised an eyebrow.

"Call it one-hundred-and-fifty million," Charles declared. "Most of that will be covering the new parts and retrofitting costs."

John's face spread into a big grin, matching that of the Vice Admiral.

"Wow! He's actually going for it," Alyssa thought to herself. She smiled, unable to resist rolling her eyes when John and Charles shook hands vigorously, the pair of them grinning like maniacs. "Boys and their toys!"

They left the office, John bouncing along with a spring in his step as they walked back to the Fool's Gold. Charles had volunteered to start the retrofitting work immediately and had promised they would get everything completed in a week.

The navy munitions team had already unloaded the Tyrenium, starting work the moment the deal had been struck. When John and Alyssa boarded the freighter, it seemed strange to see the cargo hold looking so empty. The couple entered the cockpit, taking their usual seats. John hummed happily to himself as he went through his pre-flight checks and activated various displays and subsystems.

Alyssa rotated her co-pilot's chair to face him. "So what's the plan now?" she asked, enjoying seeing him looking so relaxed.

"I did promise you a shopping trip," John said, smiling at her as he entered the course to take them down to Gravitus, the planet they were currently orbiting.

The freighter's engines ignited with a shudder and the ship lifted off.

Alyssa clapped her hands excitedly. "I doubt I can top your spending spree though... one-hundred-and-fifty million credits in just one morning! That's got to be some kind of record!"

John grinned, excited at the prospect of owning his old military vessel.

"*Commander* John Blake, proud owner of the Invictus," she stated, making a point of emphasising his rank.

John smiled at the teenager. "Ah, I wondered if you'd picked up on that. It was my old naval rank before I retired."

"Retired?" she asked pointedly, her eyebrow arched.

John was momentarily startled before he replied honestly, "I sometimes forget just how perceptive and intelligent you are."

Alyssa smiled at the compliment.

"Okay, I'm officially retired, but I still hold my rank and I sometimes assist the Terran Federation when I can make a difference." He paused, thinking of the best way to describe his situation. "Think of me as a Special Ops consultant. I help out occasionally, like the rescue the other day. In exchange, I hold a military-grade weapons license and get access to a few handy gadgets."

"Like the chrome device you used to steal that armour, when we saved Calara?" Alyssa volunteered.

John winced. "We requisitioned it, we didn't steal it!"

"Potato, Potahto..."

He laughed along with her. "Okay, okay. But yes, that code breaker works on most T-Fed doors. Anything my rank would grant me access to."

"Sounds awesome, Commander," Alyssa replied, throwing him a mock salute.

John let out a resigned sigh. "You aren't going to let that go, are you?"

Alyssa got up and sat in his lap, kissing him soundly. "No, Sir," she purred in a sultry voice.

She glanced over his shoulder at the console, seeing it would take two hours for the ship to reach the planet. Rising from his lap, Alyssa clasped his hand in hers and led him to their cabin. "It's lunchtime and I'd like my tummy to go down before I try on any clothes..."

Three hours later the happy couple strolled into one of the most exclusive boutiques on the planet. It was a quiet time of the day and the handful of shop assistants were milling around the store attempting to look busy, while not actually doing anything. They all seemed to look up as one and appraise the new customers when they walked in. While the blonde was effortlessly beautiful in a natural kind of way and her companion ruggedly handsome, they both looked to be military from their outfits. Military typically did not mean big spenders in their experience, so most of the girls sighed in disappointment and returned to refolding clothes.

One of the girls though, a very pretty brunette, approached them with a friendly smile on her face. "Can I help you?"

Alyssa read the girl's name tag. "Well Rachel, I need lots of new clothes so I look really hot for my man," she explained helpfully. "The gentleman

requires new outfits as well, so we'll need someone to assist so that he looks his most handsome." She glanced over at John to check if he approved.

He laughed and nodded, enjoying seeing the beautiful teenager enjoying herself.

"He's also very wealthy, so I'd like you to be especially nice to him!" Alyssa added for the benefit of the rest of the assistants.

The other shop girls had been eavesdropping the conversation and their ears pricked up at the revelation that John was loaded. They flocked around him, suddenly very eager to help.

The next couple of hours passed by in a blur. Alyssa liked Rachel, the only genuinely nice shop assistant in the place. She worked with her to select a broad array of outfits that would keep her suitably attired for almost any eventuality. Rachel seemed to be able to instinctively know what clothes would best accentuate Alyssa's stunning figure and the various outfits she selected were exquisite.

Alyssa allocated the rest of the sales assistants to help keep John distracted. At one point she turned to watch as the half dozen pretty shop girls gathered around him, flirting outrageously.

"None of those gold-digging bitches are good enough for him," she thought protectively. Alyssa narrowed her eyes, imagining how they'd all look after an evening with John, bellies huge with his spunk. She was surprised to find the thought extremely arousing and she found herself getting very turned on.

The final hour was hard work for Alyssa. John tried on a charcoal suit that made him look exceedingly handsome and she kept glancing over to watch the girls fawning all over him. If that wasn't turning her on enough, Rachel's soft hands kept gliding over her curves, smoothing the fabric of

each outfit into place. Alyssa found she liked form-fitting garments, so this was happening a lot. At one point, she felt her cheeks flush as the kneeling brunette ran her hands down Alyssa's shapely legs, making sure the fit of the slinky dress was correct. The two made brief eye contact and Alyssa realised that Rachel was enjoying the intimate contact of the fitting session as much as she was. The lovely tawny-haired girl shared a knowing smile with the beautiful blonde, before looking away quickly.

At the end of their visit, John stood by the till as one of his assistants ran up the bill. He would have balked at the cost, but he figured his young lover deserved to be spoilt for once in her life. He turned to look for the gorgeous teenager and noticed Alyssa pulling Rachel aside and whispering in her ear. The attractive brunette blushed prettily and then nodded, before handing something to the gorgeous blonde. Alyssa tucked whatever it was into her impressive cleavage and then turned back smoothly to join him.

Alyssa saw his questioning look, to which she smiled archly. "She was really nice. I thought she might want to join us for dinner one evening."

John was rendered speechless. He followed her out of the shop, their bags overflowing with purchases as they walked to the waiting hover-limo. They made a couple of additional stops for Alyssa, while John stayed in the limo and booked them a room at a plush hotel.

The limo pulled up and the concierge handed John the keys to their best suite. A couple of porters led them to the room, carrying all their retail trophies from earlier. John enjoyed watching Alyssa looking around at their surroundings, her eyes trying to take in all the sights at once, astonished at the opulent luxury of the hotel.

He handed the bellboys a tip before closing the door behind them. He turned to look for Alyssa, but she had disappeared into the bedroom. He heard her gasp of delight before she came running out to find him.

"This place is amazing, John!" she gushed. "I've never seen anything like it!"

"A beautiful room for a beautiful lady" he replied, smiling at her reaction. "Now get dressed, I'm taking you out for dinner!"

Alyssa practically bounced up and down with excitement as she turned into a blur of activity, getting herself ready to go out. John enjoyed a relaxing shower before getting dressed in his new charcoal suit. He waited for Alyssa in the lounge area of the luxurious suite, admiring the view through the glass wall of their apartment.

Gravitus was originally a volcanic planet and the main habitation and retail zones were built in the terraformed areas. This hotel was built on a floating platform that overlooked one of the remaining volcanic areas. The magma flows and spouting lava plumes painted the darkly lit room in flickering red and orange hues. The place felt dangerous and exciting, which he supposed was its main appeal to tourists unlikely to see any real danger.

His attention was pulled away from the dramatic scene in front of him, when he heard the rhythmic clicking of high heels coming from the bedroom. They stopped just as he turned, and his breath caught when he saw the vision of beauty waiting for him. Alyssa was draped in a figure-hugging black dress that seemed to hug her curves sinfully. She posed coyly for him, turning with effortless grace so that he could see that the dress was backless. It offered a breathtaking view, from her finely muscled shoulders all the way down her toned back to the dimples of Venus above her bottom. The contrast behind the midnight black of the velvety material and the glowing perfection of her tanned skin was striking. Whoever designed this garment was a master of showcasing the female form.

She had applied light make up that accentuated her flawless complexion and the overall effect was spectacular. Finally, her luxuriant golden locks

framed her face perfectly, making her seem almost luminous in her beauty. He strode forward to offer his arm so that he could lead her from the room. Alyssa looked at him and blushed, suddenly feeling self-conscious in the revealing dress that only just bordered on the decent side of modesty.

"You look absolutely incredible," he complimented her. "I've never seen anyone quite so beautiful."

Alyssa looked at him, basking in his adoration and soaking in the heartfelt emotions she could sense from him. She sighed happily and floated along at his side, her four inch heels nearly letting her match him in height.

The handsome couple returned to the lobby, heads turning to stare as they walked to the waiting hover-limo. They arrived at the exclusive restaurant and Alyssa started blushing when she realised so many people were stopping what they were doing to watch them. She had never been the focus of so much attention before.

John leaned over to whisper in her ear, "The women all wish they were you, and the men all wish they could be with you." His soothing voice calmed her nerves and she glided along with him, glowing with confidence as they were led to their table.

The rest of the evening seemed to pass by in a blur to Alyssa. She remembered John ordering for both of them and they savoured a lovely wine with a gloriously succulent steak. Conversation flowed naturally between them and she found herself absorbed by his stories of adventure from his youth. Eventually they found themselves back in their hotel, as he led her by the hand to stand by the window to watch the dramatic lavascape below.

"Thank you for tonight John, it's been a magical evening," she said appreciatively.

"It isn't over yet," he said, smiling as he moved closer to kiss her.

With the benefit of her high heels, she nearly matched his height and he enjoyed the slightly different feeling as they kissed each other. John's hands cupped her taut bottom, each cheek round and firm under his grasp. He squeezed them gently as he pulled her forward, so she could feel his throbbing erection against her midriff.

They lost track of time as they kissed one another like this, their passion steadily growing. Eventually they broke for breath and Alyssa turned to lead him to the bedroom, her smoky, lust-filled eyes entrancing him as he followed. She led him up to the bed and then turned, waiting expectantly for him. John brushed his hands up the smooth softness of her arms before hooking his fingers under each shoulder strap of the figure hugging dress. He lifted the straps carefully and gently off her shoulders, before letting the material fall and pool at her feet.

The exquisite teenager stood nude before him, except for her high heels. He rested his hands lightly on her hips, enjoying the feel of her supple young skin, warm and yielding beneath his touch as he moved in for a kiss. Alyssa returned the kiss briefly before stepping gracefully away, around and behind him, peeling the suit jacket from his shoulders. John stood still and let the gorgeous young woman move back in front of him again.

She loosened his tie before dropping it in the pile of clothing on the floor. Next she unbuttoned his shirt, her fingers moving carefully and deliberately, before running her hands over his muscular chest. The shirt joined the discarded garments before she undid the clasp on his belt. She pulled it free in a long elegant motion, the flick of her wrist as it cleared his waist causing the leather belt to crack like a whip behind her. At the loud snapping sound, she looked into his eyes, her eyebrow raised suggestively. She then dropped down smoothly to a squat, so that her head was level with his cock. She undid the button of his trousers, the zip following after sounding loud in the tense silence of the room. Letting his

trousers and briefs drop, Alyssa leaned in to lick at the swollen throbbing head before her. She then undid the laces on his shoes, allowing him to step out of them.

Alyssa rose to stand again, before stepping daintily out of her heels. This dropped her back to her five-foot-eight height, forcing her to look up to him again, which felt natural and right.

He offered her his hand, and the naked couple moved gracefully on to the bed together as though performing a well-practiced dance. Alyssa lay on her back, looking up at him, as John hovered over her, his much larger frame dominating her own.

"Make love to me," Alyssa whispered enchantingly.

She could hear John's thoughts forming into the question about protection, but as he opened his mouth to speak, she silenced him with a gentle finger pressed to his lips. She spread her silky smooth thighs invitingly, her legs moving to either side of him and gently stroking his thighs and flanks.

John's pelvis tilted and he nudged between her labia, the head of his cock pulsing and swollen with lust. Alyssa gasped at the contact, her body arching off the bed. He leaned in to kiss her tenderly, enjoying the soft full lips against his own, before he parted her lips and slipped his tongue into her mouth. She sucked at the tip gently, before licking it with a curled caress of her tongue.

He pushed forward with his hips, spreading her pussy open wide, delighting in the excited gasp this elicited from the pliant teenager. Her pupils were heavily dilated with lust, as she gazed up at him. He pushed further forward and looked down to watch the athletic girl move fluidly under him, her legs tilting back and spreading wider, so that she could cradle him in her hips.

His pulsating cock pushed to the limits of the young girl's pussy, entering unexplored ground as his girth stretched her wide open. Around half of him was buried inside her when he reached her cervix. He held still, not wanting to hurt her, but Alyssa's hips began to move rhythmically underneath him, as though coaxing him to explore further inside. He pushed again and her pliant walls spread to accommodate him, inch after inch disappearing inside the tight sheath of her body. She arched her back and moaned in satisfaction when she felt his heavy, taut balls resting on the upturned cheeks of her ass. His blunt, broad head was deep in her uterus and she revelled in the feeling of being impaled by him.

They began to move together, slowly and in small movements to start, before working up to deep penetrating thrusts. They moaned and gasped as John pounded into the young girl spread out before him, alternating between furious kissing and holding back to look at each other as they fucked.

Alyssa's beautiful young body stretched tightly around him as he drove his cock deep into her. He cradled her head in his hands and looked into her eyes as he stroked in and out of her pussy. He didn't know for sure if she was using protection or not, and that thought added an illicit thrill to the act. She was pinned on her back underneath him and there was no way she could prevent him from filling her receptive womb as he held her tightly in his arms. She was young and her perfect body was vibrant and healthy. She would be a perfect vessel for his cum if he chose to impregnate her.

Thoughts of her looking at him lovingly as she stroked her swollen stomach, the product of their lustful union encased within, was powerfully erotic. Alyssa was looking up at him doe-eyed as though tuned into the very same thoughts. She nodded slowly as her hips rocked beneath him, coaxing him to fill her fertile young belly.

John felt a huge orgasm well up from deep inside of him and he drove his beautiful young partner into the bed one last time before he arched his

back and thrust up to the hilt inside her. He threw his head back and came, his shout of release echoing around the room.

As his balls clenched and began to fire off long blasts of cum into the teenager's womb, he felt her body joining his in climax. Her pussy rippled along his throbbing length, urging him to empty himself inside her. She moaned and gasped beneath him before her voice climbed to a crooning cry, joining him in wordless, animalistic need. He felt the soft skin of her tummy against his own, as the pints of spunk he was driving into her womb rounded out her belly. Alyssa's pussy lips were stretched to the limit around the base of his massive girth, so there was nowhere for the cum to go, forcing her stomach to expand to carry all his cum.

His spasming cock finally jerked one last time as his balls were gloriously emptied into the gorgeous girl underneath him. He felt satisfied in a way he hadn't fully experienced before and he looked down at his young lover as she rested beneath him. Her face was glowing and she looked radiantly happy. He leaned down to kiss her lovingly before rolling to her side, being careful not to squash her under his heavy weight. Alyssa hooked one leg over his hip as she rolled with him, so that he remained buried inside her. They lay like that for a while, relishing the intimacy.

Eventually Alyssa rolled back and his cock slid from her slick pussy. His heavy viscous load seemed to be quite happy where it was for the moment, so she lay back, stroking her semen-packed belly. John raised himself up on one elbow and covered her hand with his, joining in with the gentle circling motions.

"So, am I about to become a daddy?" John asked, smiling down at the young girl he was caressing protectively.

Alyssa smiled back at him. "No, not yet," she replied truthfully. She gazed into his eyes and continued in loving tones, "Tell me whenever you're ready to become a father and I'll have your baby."

He felt momentarily stunned at the extent of his young lover's selfless dedication to him. Unable to express what he felt in words, he kissed her passionately instead, hoping that she would understand. Alyssa seemed to understand his meaning perfectly and she returned his kiss with the same depth of feeling.

They eventually settled down to sleep, marvelling in the sense of completeness they felt with each other.

\*\*\*

John awoke the next morning to feel a soft stroking sensation along his left ear. The delicate touch trailed up one side, reaching the pointed tip, before gently caressing down the other side. He opened his eyes to see Alyssa studying his ears intently as she stroked them with a slender finger.

"John..." she asked hesitantly.

He could guess where this conversation was going already and he smiled wryly. "Yes Alyssa?"

"Would you mind if I asked you a question?"

"No honey, ask me anything you want and I promise I'll answer honestly," he replied, his tone matching his open expression.

Alyssa smiled at his sincerity and her mind suddenly raced at the possibilities in his offer. She decided to stick to the original line of questions.

The lovely teen watched him closely as she said, "You never speak about your childhood or parents. Would you mind telling me about them?"

He studied her anxious expression and was touched that she was that concerned about upsetting him. "No, I don't mind. I don't normally talk to people about it, but you're special" he admitted.

Alyssa sighed happily, her heart bursting with joy.

"I know nothing about my father," John began, launching into his tale. "I must get all my unusual physical attributes from his side of the family though, as my mother was human."

"What was her name?" Alyssa prompted him.

"Jessica..." he replied, a wistful look on his face. "Jessica Blake worked for the Terran Federation as a Xeno-Biologist and was part of a deep space survey team. Basically, her mission was to explore the far reaches of the galaxy and discover new alien races."

Alyssa brushed her fingers through his hair and gently caressed his head. "What happened to her? It sounds like she's been gone a long time."

He nodded and let out a heavy sigh. "I discovered all that from her service record. My mother went missing shortly after I was born."

Alyssa sensed a deep well of sadness in her lover. She was shocked to realise he had grown up an orphan, just like her. "I'm so sorry, John," she murmured, leaning down to give him a tender kiss.

When they parted he smiled at her in gratitude, then continued, "My mother's final mission was shrouded in mystery. I tried to piece together what I could from ship's logs, but by the time I was old enough to handle the investigation myself, a lot of the sources had dried up."

Alyssa was fascinated by his tale, but at the same time sympathised with him over the gaping hole in his early life.

"There was some kind of accident that killed all of my mother's teammates. I was never able to find any kind of accounts from them about what had happened on their last mission together. My mother went missing and was eventually declared legally dead. I grew up with my grandparents, who were nice people." He smiled sadly. "They passed away a few years ago."

Alyssa stroked his arm comfortingly and waited for him to continue.

"I was the sole beneficiary of my mother's pension, so I was able to get a decent education and then followed her footsteps into the military. You already know about my exploits on the Invictus," he said with a faint smile.

"Do you know what species your father was?" Alyssa asked gently.

"No," John replied, shaking his head. "I've searched through descriptions of thousands of different species but I've never read about anything like these..." He glanced down at his cluster of four balls.

Alyssa snuggled in to him, pleased that he would open up to her like that. "Thank you for telling me about your past."

He smiled, feeling relieved to have shared it with her. "No problem, it was actually nice to talk to someone about it."

"I'm very glad you told me," she said, the hint of a smile on her lips. "Do you know what that means?"

John shrugged, having no idea what she was referring to.

"It means that you're truly unique amongst billions of people," she explained, a radiant smile lighting up her face. "Which makes me the luckiest person in the galaxy!"

He laughed and shook his head. "I'm definitely the luckiest one in our relationship; you do realise how wonderful you are, right? I still can't believe we're in bed together! What makes you think you get the title?"

Alyssa's eyes smouldered as she cupped his heavy balls in her hands, massaging them with a gentle touch. "Because I'm the only one who gets to empty these..."

He groaned as she stroked him, spreading his legs to give her easier access. The mischievous girl leaned closer to his quad, moving her hands lower to caress the second cum-filled spheres.

"You boys are packed full again. Would you like me to make you feel all better?" she asked his balls lovingly, caressing the weighty globes. John's rapidly hardening cock flexed in response and Alyssa went to work.

"That's right honey, it's breakfast time," John sighed contentedly, as the beautiful teenager moved to her familiar place, kneeling between his legs. Soon her mouth was encircling the base of his shaft and John relaxed, knowing Alyssa would soon be swallowing down his load like the good girl she was.

The week flew by in a lustful haze. John and Alyssa didn't leave the suite and made extensive use of room service. He revelled in having unlimited access to the beautiful young woman's body and he used her shamelessly to her eager delight.

A few times John awoke from the deep sleep that only blissful sexual exhaustion can bring, to hear the excited chatter of young female voices in the lounge. Alyssa had kept her promise to stay in contact with Calara and the two were becoming best friends. John was worried about the young Latina however. He had seen first-hand the devastating impact PTSD could have on a person and he hoped the medical staff at Port Heracles were taking good care of her.

One morning, John was lying in bed, watching the Holonet for updates on the conflict with the Kintark. He could overhear the two girls having a lengthy animated conversation in the lounge, but he tuned it out to focus on the reports of border clashes and territory disputes.

A short while later, Alyssa strode into their bedroom, alarm written on her face. "Calara is in trouble John, we have to help her!"

# Three Square Meals Ch. 07 – Breaking in the new ride

John wondered what the problem could be. The After Action Report he had submitted to Federation Command last week had made it pretty clear what had happened aboard the Corvette. He was unsure what kind of trouble the young Latina could be in, as there was certainly nothing in the AAR that implicated her being responsible in any way.

"What kind of trouble?" he asked Alyssa.

"Calara said she was being accused of 'dereliction of duty'. She mentioned something about a possible court martial!" she replied, waiting anxiously by the doorway.

John snorted in disbelief. A court martial? That was absurd. "Is she still on the Holo-feed?"

Alyssa nodded, darting a worried glance back into the lounge. "She doesn't know what to do! I said I'd ask you for advice..."

John stood and strode out of the room, grabbing a towel to wrap around his waist on the way out. He could see Calara's face on the holographic screen as he walked across the lounge. The black eyes had mostly healed up, but the bridge of her nose was still swollen from where it had been broken, marring her otherwise pretty face. The heavy bags under her eyes told a tale of troubled sleep.

"Don't worry Calara, we'll get this straightened out," he said reassuringly.

Calara looked back at him with frightened eyes. "I can't be Court Martialed, John! It would destroy my family!"

"It won't come to that. We'll be with you at Heracles as fast as we can. Call us if there's any more developments," he stated firmly.

The Latina looked downcast as she nodded and closed the call, the holographic image of her anxious face fading away.

John turned to look at Alyssa who had watched the brief conversation over his shoulder. "Okay, let's get moving, it looks like we haven't finished rescuing her yet!" he said with a smile.

Alyssa moved in to hug him fiercely. "Thank you John, you're a good man."

John hugged her back before they broke apart to gather their belongings. In a matter of hours, they had checked out of the hotel, taken a hover-taxi to the planet's starport and boarded the Fool's Gold. They set a course for Olympus and two hours later were approaching the bustling shipyard, Terran Federation craft drifting by civilian traffic as they went about their business. The intercom began an insistent buzzing, the flashing light on the console indicating an incoming communication. John pushed a button to answer the call.

"Incoming freighter, please identify yourself and your business at Olympus," a military communications officer requested politely.

"He sounds exactly like the last one!" Alyssa whispered, causing John to chuckle.

"Commander John Blake, requesting clearance to land at the docking bay housing the Invictus," he replied, following formal military comm protocol to speed up the conversation.

"One moment please Commander," the disembodied voice replied.

After a short pause, the voice came back. "Please proceed to Docking Bay Thirteen," the communication officer stated, before closing the channel.

"Unlucky for some," Alyssa said ominously.

John laughed, grinning at his young companion. "You don't believe in those old superstitions do you?"

"You can never be too careful!" she replied archly, tilting up her chin.

Docking Bay Thirteen was part of the dry-dock and used for retrofitting spacecraft with upgraded equipment and weaponry. This meant they had to circle the huge shipyard to approach from the opposite side, the journey painfully slow as Alyssa dutifully stayed under Port-Speed until they reached their destination. This side of the shipyard saw much less traffic and the damaged spacecraft awaiting repairs looked lonely and forlorn.

"What did that?" Alyssa asked in awe, pointing to the devastated foredeck of a Terran Federation destroyer as they slowly passed it by. They could see numerous battle scars measuring dozens of metres in length as the hull loomed overhead.

"That's Plasma damage," John explained sadly, looking at the charred wreckage."That ship's been fighting the Kintark. They're the only race that use Plasma Cannons."

They left the damaged ship behind and moved on to begin landing manoeuvres at Docking Bay Thirteen. Alyssa's breath caught when she saw their new vessel and she glanced at John, finding that he was similarly spellbound.

The assault cruiser was docked in the centre of the gigantic bay. Massive maintenance gantries were slowly backing away from the flanks of the vessel, as though wary of the lethal looking warship. The sleek lines and bristling gun ports clearly identified the ship as a ferocious predator, one not to be trifled with. The craft was painted a dark military grey, with soft

blue lighting illuminating the name "Invictus" in twenty-foot-high lettering along the hull.

The Fool's Gold touched down and the tremors shaking through the ship awakened the pair from their reverie. John flashed a wide grin at Alyssa as he stood quickly and offered his hand to follow. They walked briskly down to the cargo bay of the freighter and John's foot tapped impatiently as he waited for the airlock door to spiral open.

They walked outside before stopping to stand in awe, looking up at the magnificent vessel as it towered above them. At just over five-hundred metres in length it dwarfed the couple and their comparatively tiny freighter.

"Welcome to your new home," a friendly voice said from behind them.

They turned to see Charles Harris had come to greet them at the dock. He walked up and shook John's hand in a firm grip, before turning to smile warmly at Alyssa and shaking her hand too.

With the greetings out the way, Charles got down to business and handed John a Holo-reader. "Here's everything you need to know about the Invictus: schematics, weapons, controls, specifications, everything!"

The maintenance teams had worked furiously to complete the retrofitting to the tight schedule set by Vice Admiral Harris and from the data on the reader, it looked like everything had been finished on time.

"She's a hell of a ship," Charles sighed, looking behind them at the Cruiser he once captained. He smiled wistfully as he turned back to the couple. "You never forget your first command..."

"It's amazing!" Alyssa exclaimed, staring up at the massive assault cruiser with wide eyes. "I can't wait to take it for a spin!"

Charles nodded, clasping his hands behind his back as he joined the young blonde in gazing at the Invictus. "I wish I could come with you on your shakedown voyage, but do tell me how she performs. If you run into any problems, just get in touch," he offered helpfully. Turning to look at John, he added, "What do you want to do with your freighter?"

John smiled as he looked back at the ship that had been his home for the last eleven years. "You know, I haven't really thought about it to be honest. Would it be okay to moor her here for a few weeks until I decide?"

"Having trouble letting her go?" Charles laughed good naturedly. "I know the feeling! I'll have her secured nice and safely for you."

"Thanks Charles, I appreciate everything you've done for me," John said, shaking hands with his old friend.

"It was my pleasure," Charles replied with a broad smile. He waved goodbye and left them to settle in to their new ship.

John and Alyssa worked quickly to transfer their belongings from the Fool's Gold to an anti-grav sled that the maintenance teams had left for their use. John wasn't a hoarder so his belongings mostly consisted of clothing, armour and the contents of his weapon locker. Alyssa, had no personal possessions, except for the bags full of new clothes she'd just bought on Gravitus. From the information on the Holo-reader, the Invictus had been fully stocked with supplies, so there was no need to transfer the foodstuffs from his meagre kitchen and storage room.

John let Alyssa control the grav sled and she had fun steering the humming platform to the new ship. John turned around to look at the freighter one last time and after glancing over his shoulder to make sure Alyssa wasn't watching, he threw the Fool's Gold a nostalgic salute.

"Thanks for looking after me all those years, old girl," he said quietly, before turning to follow his enthusiastic young shipmate.

The door to the Hangar Bay of the Invictus was huge and it yawned open in front of them impressively. It was large enough to comfortably house a decent sized dropship, so the grav sled looked tiny and a bit pathetic parked by itself in the bay. John pushed the button on a wall mounted panel and the external door in the hull began to shut, a force field springing into place to internally seal the huge portal.

The couple walked hand in hand through a sturdy set of doors into an adjacent corridor. They found the waiting elevator, so they entered and John pushed the button to take them up to the Command Deck. The hum of the elevator filled the room as they rose upwards.

"Has it changed much since you were last here?" Alyssa asked quietly.

"There's a lot less people around for one thing," John joked. "This ship used to house three-hundred rowdy marines and a navy crew of forty. Now there's just the two of us!"

Their conversation was interrupted as the elevator door opened with a smooth whir, ending in a soft click. They walked out of the elevator to look over the Command Deck for the first time. John was overcome with memories, staring out across the Bridge as he relived events from his past. Alyssa carefully peeled the Holo-reader from his distracted grasp and then went off to explore.

The bridge was shaped in an oval, with the Commander Chair placed centrally on a podium, surrounded by glowing consoles. To the right of the commander's seat and set slightly lower down, was a similar setup for the Executive Officer. Numerous other stations were placed at regular intervals around the room, but they were all currently dark, automation replacing the crewmen who would have operated them.

Alyssa followed the brightly lit steps that led up to the command podium and settled herself in the XO chair. It felt wonderfully soft and the chair's ergonomics seemed to hug her lovely curves perfectly. She spun the chair happily in a circle, noting that being up here provided an excellent view of the rest of the room. She spotted two doors on opposite ends of the bridge that she hadn't noticed from the elevator and made a mental note to explore them later. Stopping the spin so that she faced the curving consoles in front of her, she placed the Holo-reader on one of the control panels and began to learn how to operate the ship.

John was roused from his memories by an ominous thrum of power as the brand-new engines on the Invictus were fired up for the first time. He looked up to see that Alyssa had settled herself in to the XO's position and had begun charting their course to Port Heracles. She pushed a button and their route was displayed in a large holographic display that spun slowly in the centre of the bridge. He climbed the illuminated steps up to the Command chair for a better view.

"Just under four days to reach Port Heracles, John," Alyssa announced, smiling at him when he stood beside her. "This beast is a whole lot faster than your freighter!"

John slowly sank into the Commander Chair, feeling its luxurious fabric moulding itself around him comfortably. He had served on this vessel for ten years and it was proving surprisingly difficult, adjusting to having the right to sit here now. He spun the chair slowly to look back down the steps. He remembered standing down there over twenty years ago and saluting the Ship's Commander for the first time. He had been green and naive then, but full of the eagerness of youth.

He turned to face Alyssa, watching her as she learned how to operate the ship. She was enthusiastically checking the Holo-reader then pressing buttons on her console, letting out excited squeals when the corresponding systems activated with a hum. Holographic Tactical grids

and Galaxy maps sprung into life around them, bathing the Bridge in a soothing blue glow.

"Course laid in and all systems look good to go. Just say the word, Commander!" Alyssa said, as she saluted him respectfully.

He smiled at her fondly. "Take us out of here, XO."

Alyssa grinned at him and the Invictus lifted smoothly from the floor of the Docking Bay under her expert control. The cruiser pulled away from the shipyard, overshadowing the damaged destroyer as they passed it by. There was a steady flow of traffic heading from Olympus Shipyard towards the system's Nav beacons and Alyssa weaved past a long convoy of huge freighters and a battleship with an escort of six cruisers.

The freighters were heading the same way as the Invictus, but the formation of military vessels changed course, joining a flow of grey armoured warships flying in the opposite direction. Alyssa noticed John's interest in the military ships and read the transponder tag on the battleship, which identified it as the Artemis.

"I wonder where are all those warships are heading?" Alyssa asked, pointing towards the imposing flotilla.

John's expression darkened. "Probably the Dragon March. There's increasing tensions with the Kintark..."

Wanting to avoid upsetting him with talk of war, Alyssa darted a glance around the Bridge, looking for a good distraction. She activated their FTL drive and as soon as the Invictus had jumped into hyper-warp, she asked, "What's behind those doors, John?"

"That one leads to the Briefing Room," he said, pointing to the door on their right. Spinning his chair, he pointed at the door on the left side of the Bridge. "And that one leads to the Commander's Ready Room."

"Mmm, sounds intriguing..." Alyssa replied. "Is the Commander ready?" she asked, rising from her chair and walking towards the door, looking coyly over her shoulder.

John laughed heartily. "Your casual disrespect for naval traditions is going to take a bit of getting used to," he said as he followed after her, watching the alluring sway of the beautiful young woman's hips.

She waited for him at the door, letting him lead the way into his Ready Room for the first time. The room had a big window running the full length of one wall, offering a spectacular view of the shipyard as they departed. At the far end of the room was a big desk and a comfortable looking chair. On their side of the room was a seating area, with several sofas arranged in a square, a coffee table placed centrally between them.

John took in the Commander's Ready Room feeling a little overawed. This all belonged to him now, but he still found it hard to believe. Alyssa gracefully moved to his side, her hand moving up to caress the back of his neck.

"Don't feel intimidated, John," she whispered in his ear. "You just need to stamp your authority on the place. It will feel like home in no time."

He nodded in response, marvelling at how perceptive the lovely young girl was. It sometimes felt like she knew exactly what he was thinking... He felt extraordinarily lucky to have met such a wonderful woman who could read him so well and always seemed to say just the right thing.

"So Command-her," Alyssa purred seductively, deliberately mispronouncing his rank."I think it's time we christened this room." She posed for him, arching her back, thrusting out her chest. "How do you want me?" she asked, giving him a dazzling smile.

John grinned and decided to play along. "As the new Commander, I think the first thing to do is make sure my XO knows her place on board my vessel." He walked over to sit in the chair behind the desk.

Alyssa watched her handsome man take charge... she found it intoxicating!

"You're my second-in-command, but it's important for you to remember that as the person in charge, anything I need comes first," he went on, suppressing a grin.

"Oh definitely, Sir, you always cum first, whenever you need," Alyssa breathed excitedly as she walked slowly towards him.

"That's very good XO. I think we'll have a great working relationship," John said, nodded his approval.

Alyssa unzipped her figure hugging jumpsuit and left it crumpled on the floor next to her calf-length boots. She sank to her knees in front of him and licked her lips, her mouth watering.

"If it's okay with the Command-her, I'd like to lighten his load. Help relieve any kind of pressures that might have built up. It must be hard to concentrate on running the ship if you are all backed up," Alyssa purred, her cerulean eyes smouldering with excitement.

"I'm impressed with your initiative XO. I'm going to enjoy spending many hours stretching you to the limit of your abilities. I think there are lots of ways we can make you grow in this role," John said, while unbuckling his belt and removing his trousers and boots.

Alyssa could barely contain herself. She loved this kind of playful banter with him and she could tell John was really getting into it. She could feel his excitement level rising to match her own and she was determined to make this one to remember. She leaned forward opening her mouth to

take in the broad helm of his shaft, delighting in how her lips had to stretch wide to engulf him completely. A natural instinct wanted to take over and have her suck down his entire length immediately, but she resisted. Instead, she took a deep breath, relaxed and then gradually took his length down her throat, using her lips to pull him inside a few millimetres at a time.

John sighed contentedly as the beautiful teenager slowly wrapped her throat around him. He brushed his fingers through her hair, then gently clasped her head, revelling in the feelings of dominance and control.

The talented fellatrix massaged his throbbing shaft with her tongue, the velvety wetness dancing over him and allowing him to penetrate her throat more readily. She began to swallow repeatedly, the muscles in her slim neck gripping him tightly and massaging him. It felt like there were half a dozen eager young women jerking him off, all using their hands on him at the same time.

His thoughts drifted back to that moment back on Gravitus when he had been surrounded by the pretty shop girls. One of them had been "checking his neck size", leaning into his back and brushing against him with her soft breasts as she stroked his neck. Two more were "checking his arm length", which consisted of feeling his biceps and whispering naughty things in each of his ears. The last three had been kneeling on the ground in front of him, "helping him with the fit of his trousers", their soft hands gliding up and down his legs suggestively as three sets of eyes looked up at him invitingly.

"Those naughty bitches!" Alyssa thought as she listened to John's inner voice, only now realising just what they'd been up to. Thinking about all those pretty women all lusting after her man got her extremely turned on and she squeaked in surprise as her thighs clenched together and she came hard.

John looked down at the young girl deep throating him, as her eyes screwed up tight and she moaned around his shaft, the vibrations feeling incredible along his length. "God, she's just so sexy," he thought, as he remembered seeing Alyssa sharing a lustful look with Rachel, the lovely brunette in the store. The tawny-haired girl had been on her knees, stroking Alyssa's legs, and the sight of those two looking so intimate together had nearly made him cum right there in the boutique!

"Oh fuck! He'd seen that?" Alyssa thought. She could feel his arousal at the thought of her with another woman and she could only suck on him mindlessly as her body reacted with another earth-shattering orgasm.

The beautiful blonde teen let him pull her head down until he was fully embedded inside her throat, his gentle but insistent grip moving her mouth up and down his cock. "I'm his little fuck toy," she thought to herself proudly, revelling in the overwhelming feeling of submission as she knelt there, being used for his pleasure. She opened her eyes to look up at him, loving seeing the determined look on his face as he stroked his shaft in and out of the clutching grasp of her throat, bringing himself closer and closer to orgasm.

She could feel him enjoying every moment of being so dominant with her, as he moaned loudly with each thrust. Suddenly he pulled back, sliding his engorged, throbbing tool from the tight confines of her body. His plan flashed into her mind and she rolled backwards, supporting her weight with her hands and arching her back for him, her big breasts presenting a perfect target.

John stood, looming over her as he panted heavily and fisted his massive shaft in his right hand.

"Do it!" she hissed at him, her eyes ablaze with lust. "Cover me in your cum!"

"Aaahhhhhhh!!!" John bellowed as his quad lurched and a fountain of cum blasted out over her heaving breasts. He stroked out long heavy spurts, covering her quivering chest in his spunk, before moving on to unload all over her gorgeous young face. Alyssa opened her mouth wide to present him with another place to aim and she swallowed down big gulps of his delicious seed as he filled her mouth. Her body writhed with ecstasy and she joined him in orgasm.

Finally spent, John collapsed back in his chair and struggled to regain his breath after his exertions. He looked at the teenager through lidded eyes, admiring his handiwork. The girl was lying on her back, liberally glazed in a thick layer of cum. She used one of hands to massage it into her breasts, while she greedily sucked the spunk off the fingers of her other hand.

The two shared a lustful look, grinning slyly at each other.

John recovered and got to his feet. He offered Alyssa his hand, and she rose gracefully to stand in front of him.

"Maybe time for a shower?" she suggested, smiling up at him as rivulets of cum dripped off her beautiful face and onto her pert breasts.

"Good idea..." John laughed and led her to a bathroom in the corner of the room.

There was a decent sized shower in there and they had fun making sure Alyssa was nice and clean. They dried themselves off and then cleaned up the mess by his desk, until finally, both they and the room were spotless once again. Alyssa walked over to the window and stood completely nude, watching the view of the stars gliding past the window as they raced along in hyper-warp. John walked up behind and wrapped his arms around her in a warm hug. He rested his chin on her head and she felt loved and protected as they enjoyed the intimacy of their embrace.

"Feel like you've marked your territory now?" Alyssa asked him playfully.

John let out a belly laugh. "You're incredible, do you know that?" he asked, as he turned her around to face him.

The lovely teen raised herself up on tiptoe and clasped her hands behind his neck before kissing him soundly. "Yes, and I'm all yours!"

They separated to get dressed and then walked out onto the Bridge hand in hand.

"What now, handsome?" Alyssa asked.

"How about we check out our bedroom?" John replied. "It's just on the deck below".

The young beauty nodded eagerly and they took the elevator down one level. The elevator door opened out into a corridor on Deck Two that led to the officers' quarters.

"The Commander's quarters are the biggest, they're down at the end," said John, pointing down the corridor. "The XO's quarters are at the end on the right."

They walked down the corridor, passing a dozen doorways. They checked a few and found them all to be identically furnished and comfortable officer suites. When they got to the end of the corridor, they were in for a surprise.

"That's odd," John said, as they reached the blank wall where the door to the XO's quarters should have been. Shrugging, he turned towards the Commander's room and touched the wall-mounted panel beside it, causing the door to swish open quietly. They walked inside and flicked on the lights.

"Wow! this place is amazing!" Alyssa gasped, shocked by the grand bedroom.

The rest of the officers' rooms had been large and comfortably furnished, but built to a minimalistic military design. It was as though they were built to some faceless bureaucrats' specification and duplicated thousands of times throughout the fleet.

This bedroom however had obviously been refurbished very recently. It was opulently luxurious in its design, with a magnificent four-poster bed dominating the huge room. There were two doors in the right hand wall and the couple took one each. John took the furthest one and found a large and roomy bathroom featuring a big shower and enormous bath, all beautifully finished.

John heard an excited gasp from his young lover and she poked her head around the door. "John, you've got to see this!" she pleaded. He smiled, nodding and walked back to join her. Alyssa suddenly took notice of the bathroom. "Ohh, that bath looks amazing!" she said with a happy sigh, before reluctantly tearing herself away.

The excited teenager led him through the adjacent doorway into a massive walk-in wardrobe. There were clothes rails along each side with well placed mirrors in the middle that allowed someone to see themselves at all angles. At the end of the room were extensive, wall-mounted weapon racks.

John narrowed his eyes, a growing suspicion forming in his mind. Whoever designed all this seemed to know them both very well indeed. After looking around for a while, and playing with the fixtures and fittings, they walked back into the master bedroom. They were momentarily surprised when the room lights dimmed and a holographic recording sprung into life in front of them. It was Vice Admiral Charles Harris.

"I hope you like the ship, John," the distinguished figure smiled amiably. "I'm sure you don't mind, but I took a few liberties with the redesign of your room. I hope I didn't misjudge your relationship with your Executive Officer, but I suspect I haven't." He gave them a mischievous grin, his moustache twitching.

"She's lovely John, you deserve someone who makes you happy. Consider this a tiny payback for the big debt I owe you." The older man saluted respectfully. "Thanks John, and all the best for the future."

The room lights returned to the previous levels and the hologram disappeared.

"Wow! What was that about?" Alyssa asked, her curiosity piqued.

"I saved his life in a bad situation a long time ago. I told him he should forget it," John said, as his hand waved it away.

"Well I'm glad he didn't, he has amazing taste!" Alyssa replied as she ran her hand over the wonderfully soft bed covers. She darted John a coy smile. "I can't wait to be ravished on here later..."

John darted forward scooping her up in his arms, before throwing her onto the middle of the bed. Her musical laughter echoed around the room as he leapt on the bed to join her. She looked up at him, giggling happily as he laughed along with her. They kissed and then hugged each other tightly.

Abruptly Alyssa's laughter died and he looked down to see what was wrong.

"I'm worried John," she said quietly, answering his unspoken question. "I didn't think it was possible to be this happy and now I have so much, I'm worried it might all go away."

The young girl suddenly looked small, scared and vulnerable and John had a flashback to the frightened waif that had stowed away on his ship all those weeks ago. He held her close to him, wrapping her tightly in his arms.

"Don't worry honey, this is your life now. It will take a little while to get used to all these changes, but you will. You're allowed to be happy," he said to her reassuringly.

Alyssa looked up at him, her eyes welling with tears. "I love you, John."

"I love you too Alyssa" John replied, gazing into her beautiful cerulean eyes.

They kissed sensuously and lost track of time. Eventually the kissing escalated and they made tender love, gently caressing each other with soft touches, as though exploring each other's bodies for the first time. It was a very different coupling to their normal frenzied encounters, but one that bonded them even closer together. They slept for a long time afterwards, their sleep blissfully peaceful and uninterrupted.

The next morning they awoke in each other's arms, John's stomach grumbling angrily. Alyssa looked at him in mock alarm. "You poor man, we need to get some breakfast inside you! You need to keep your strength up!"

John nodded, agreeing with her sentiments and the two had a quick shower together before getting dressed.

"So where do we eat around here?" she asked.

"Wherever I decide to feed you," John laughed, stroking her toned stomach suggestively.

Alyssa laughed with him. "No silly, where do we feed you?"

"If I'm not mistaken there should be an officers' mess at the other end of that corridor," he said, pointing towards the hall outside their room.

"Lead on then, Commander!" Alyssa joked, holding out her hand for him to take.

They walked down the corridor, hands clasped together until they reached a larger set of doors at the other end. John pushed a button beside the doors and they swished open quietly, revealing a large room, filled at their end with comfy sofas and chairs. Long windows flanked the room on each side, with a bar placed strategically on the right hand side of the lounge. Towards the back on the left was a long dining table and the entrance to a kitchen was carefully concealed on the far wall.

The couple worked together to cook up a tasty looking breakfast and John tucked in with gusto, ravenous after his exertions the previous day. Alyssa on the other hand only picked daintily at her plate, trying a bit of each thing they had cooked but only eating a small portion. She watched him eating heartily with a happy smile on her face.

"Not hungry honey?" he asked, his voice filled with concern, as he finished wolfing down his own breakfast.

"I was leaving room for desert" Alyssa explained, before she pushed her chair back and slid under the table out of view. He felt her skilful hands unbuckling his belt and he smiled at her cheeky face as she looked up at him from under the table, grinning mischievously. He helped her shimmy his trousers down then spread his legs wide to make room for her as he slumped back in his chair.

"What a way to start the day," John sighed happily to himself, feeding the beautiful girl her own hearty breakfast a few minutes later. He helped her up again afterwards and she stretched contentedly, her swollen belly packed full of his sperm.

"Ahh, that meal was wonderful," she said with a happy sigh, stroking her full tummy. "My compliments to the chef!"

Now that they were both satiated, they cleared away their dishes, then set about their chores for their first full day aboard their new home. They hauled up all the gear from the grav sled they had left in the Hangar Bay, storing most of it in their walk-in wardrobe. John let Alyssa have one entire side of the room for her many different outfits, while his much more limited selection of clothing took up the first half on the other side. The last section they used to store their combat armour. After that was stowed securely, John began stocking the weapon racks with his small arsenal of equipment.

He stood looking at his collection of armour and weapons, stroking his chin thoughtfully.

"What are you thinking?" Alyssa asked when she saw him looking over the gear. His thoughts were buzzing with military jargon which she found more than a little confusing.

"Now that I have money to spend, it might be worth getting some upgrades. Rarer, custom gear, that kind of thing," he explained, his mind whirring with all the possibilities.

Alyssa nodded, happy to go along with whatever he decided was necessary for their personal security.

"That reminds me," John continued. "There should be an armoury and shooting range near where the barracks used to be. I think they only removed the barracks to make room for the cargo bay, but the rest should all still be there. We should go have a look and see what we can find."

"Sounds like a good plan," Alyssa agreed. "I definitely need some more weapons practice!"

"You were great your first time in combat. With a bit more training, you'll be an expert marksman in no time!" John said encouragingly.

Alyssa mulled it over and realised this was actually a great opportunity. She could learn to better protect herself and her man, and was suddenly eager to get started.

"I'm done here if you'd like to go have a look now?" Alyssa asked, excited by their planned excursion.

"Sure, let's go!" John replied, eager to look around himself.

They left their room and strolled to the elevator. John hit the button for the level above the cargo bay, which should house the armoury and firing range if his memory served him right. The elevator hummed happily to itself as it dropped to the desired level. The door opened into a branching network of corridors. They had a look at the other rooms on this level, using John's memory as a guide. The first room they went into was a large, high-tech medical bay, with dozens of empty beds.

"An assault cruiser is basically a well armed and armoured troop carrier. You need a large medical bay just in case a mission goes badly," John said soberly.

Alyssa nodded, realising he spoke from experience. They left the sterile medical bay behind, neither of them wanting to linger there any longer than they had to. John took a cursory glance into the ship's Pharmacy, only checking to see that it was fully stocked.

Next, John led her to the armoury. This room had the capacity to store gear for three-hundred marines, but it was no longer sensible to carry that much equipment with the barracks gone. When John had last been in here, the walls had been stacked floor to ceiling with a huge assortment of body armour and weaponry. Now the weapon and armour racks were

standing forlorn and empty. The marine munitions team had not bothered to remove the ammunition however, so they found thousands of boxes full of most varieties of caseless ammo.

Finally, they entered the Firing Range. There were half a dozen lanes, with plenty of room to test fire weapons from standing, kneeling or prone positions. John led Alyssa to the back wall of the range and pressed his thumb against the lock on the weapons locker there. The door rolled back to reveal a dozen standard issue assault rifles, several SMGs and around 20 pistols of a variety of calibres. There was also enough ammo stored here for months of sustained practice.

"Excellent," John said, rubbing his hands together happily. "Ready to get started?"

"Definitely!" Alyssa agreed, her eyes gleaming at the prospect.

John went through safety drills again, recapping the lessons he had given her two weeks before. Alyssa began to quote the lessons back at him half way through, repeating his training verbatim with a grin on her face. John listened to her amazed.

"Your memory is incredible! Okay then, Miss smarty pants, time for the advanced lessons!" he said, throwing down the gauntlet.

Alyssa was an attentive student, hanging on his every word. They sat together and he went through everything he could think of, from standard and then advanced infantry tactics, to the use of hand signals to allow for silent communication. Several hours flew by as the young woman absorbed as much as she could from his many years of combat experience.

John eventually grew hungry again, so they took a break for lunch, heading back to the officer's mess. John enjoyed a tasty sandwich which he held with one hand, while the other stroked the beautiful blonde's

head as she bobbed away eagerly between his spread legs. They both felt pleasantly full as they headed back to the firing range.

He decided that Alyssa had studied enough theory for one day and he wanted to build up her practical shooting experience. He handed her one of the standard assault rifles, explaining the normal operation of the weapon. He began with her firing off single rounds at first, getting her used to the kick of the weapon and allowing him to adjust the weapon's scope accordingly. She proved to be a decent shot, holding her breath and steadying herself before firing, and grouping her hits together nicely.

They fired off a few three-round bursts so that Alyssa could get familiar with the extra recoil and improve her accuracy. Finally, he had her unload a full clip at a target, letting her experience the barrel climb as she blew through the magazine.

"You did brilliantly today, honey," John said to her as he showed her how to clean the rifle before putting it away. "Feel free to come down here and practice whenever you want; you don't need me to supervise you any more."

"Thanks for spending today training me," Alyssa said with an appreciative smile. "You're a good teacher."

"You're welcome," he replied, as he tipped an imaginary hat. He offered his hand and they walked back to the officers' quarters for the night.

The couple awoke early the next morning and were raring to go. After having breakfast together they discussed their plans.

"I think I'll explore the rest of the ship," John said, eager to see what secrets the other decks held.

"If it's ok with you, I'll continue practicing at the Firing Range," Alyssa proposed, impatient to continue her weapons training.

"That's fine by me, honey," John readily agreed. He leaned over to stroke her already full belly. "Meet back here for lunch?"

"Mmmm," Alyssa replied, licking her lips. "I'll look forward to it!"

John spent the next couple of days wandering the ship, visiting every location onboard. There were dozens of rooms dedicated to housing machinery and computers that ran vital ship functions: Life support, environmental systems, sensors, fuel control, the list seemed endless. The engine room, the drive room and the ship's magazine were slightly more interesting, but as everything had been automated, there wasn't that much to interact with.

He went to visit the gym and found it had been modified significantly since the days he had served on the ship. No longer having to cater for three-hundred fitness obsessed marines, the huge weights area had been greatly reduced. Dozens of treadmills and other fitness machines had also been stripped out, which meant that the gym was now about a tenth of its original size. In exchange, the freed up space now held a large pool and a Jacuzzi. John enjoyed swimming and was looking forward to showing the new pool area to Alyssa. "Let's just hope the artificial gravity never fails!" he laughed to himself.

Finally, he had a good look over the new Cargo Bay. It replaced a large section of the lower two decks that had previously held the barracks for the marines. The Cargo Bay was situated to the aft of the main hull, accessed by double doors near the ship's airlock. It ran the full width of the Invictus and there were huge hull doors on both sides of the ship that would allow easy loading or unloading of bulky cargo. The Cargo Bay was heavily automated, with massive loading arms looming overhead, ready to assist in the movement of cargo.

Alyssa meanwhile spent the time practicing solidly in the firing range. The first day was spent firing thousands of rounds with the Assault rifle,

before her eyes eventually got tired of staring through the scope. She concentrated mainly on firing while standing or kneeling, figuring it unlikely that she would be firing from a prone position in most random shootouts they were likely to encounter. Besides, it was a bit uncomfortable lying on her stomach while she was carrying one of John's heavy loads.

By the second day, her accuracy had improved dramatically. She was able to consistently land all the bullets from a three-round burst on target, even when firing at the maximum distance capable in the range. She met up for lunch with John and enjoyed hearing about all of his exciting discoveries. He promised to show her a nice surprise in the gym that evening, and she felt herself wondering what it could be while she sucked him off. He suddenly climaxed and she enthusiastically gulped down his tasty cum.

Immediately after lunch, they called Calara on the Holo-feed to let her know that they'd be with her tomorrow. The young Latina looked relieved that they were nearly there and she waved them goodbye with more hope on her face than they had seen in some time.

Alyssa spent the afternoon researching everything she could find on the field of ballistics, before finally heading over to the gym to meet up with John. Anticipation for the evening's big reveal had been building all afternoon and she wondered what he had in store for her. John was already there waiting for her when she arrived and she could see he was excited to show her something. She deliberately blocked out any of his thoughts, not wanting to ruin the surprise.

"Good evening, Alyssa!" he greeted her eagerly.

She grinned at him, enjoying seeing his uncharacteristic enthusiasm. "Hey John."

"Close your eyes," he told her playfully, before leading her into the room.

When he'd carefully positioned her, he said, "Now open them!"

Alyssa opened her eyes, quickly adjusting to the bright lights inside the gym. John had led her to the edge of a large, deep pool. Her face twisted in fear at the sight of all that water and she backed away carefully.

"What...I don't understand?" John asked, clearly disappointed and concerned by her reaction.

"I... I can't swim," Alyssa stammered, upset at ruining his surprise.

"Oh honey, I'm so sorry I scared you! I didn't know," John said as he moved over to wrap the frightened teenager in a comforting hug.

Alyssa peeked over his shoulder to watch the pool warily. "I've never seen this much water before!"

"Well I'm a good swimmer, so you're perfectly safe," he reassured her. "Would you like me to teach you how to swim?"

Alyssa nodded, looking up at him trustingly.

"Ok, let's take things slowly," he said, giving her a reassuring smile.

He offered her his hand which she took gladly, but she was startled when he led her out of the gym. They headed back up to their room and he urged her to lie down on the four-poster bed and wait for him a moment. John disappeared into the bathroom, before coming back to join her. He moved over her on the bed, and cradled her head gently in his strong hands as he kissed her full lips tenderly.

"Ohhh" Alyssa sighed, as her mouth responded to the brushes of his lips against hers. They made out for a while, losing themselves in the sensations.

They were roused from their passions by the soft sound of music coming from nearby. John climbed off the bed and held out his hand for Alyssa to follow him, then led her into the bathroom, opening the door to the soft glow of candlelight. Their large bath was filled with water, the surface now covered in soapy bubbles which sparked in the light of the candles surrounding the tub. John smiled warmly at the astonished young woman.

"Sorry I frightened you earlier," he apologised again. Gesturing to the enticing bath, he continued,"I did say we would start slow..."

"Oh John, this is wonderful, thank you!" Alyssa gasped in delight as she threw herself into his waiting arms.

John swirled her around effortlessly before dropping her back lightly on to her feet. They grinned at each other as they stripped off quickly, clothes discarded in random piles on the bathroom floor. Alyssa managed to get undressed first and she eased herself into the blissfully hot water.

"Oh my God! This feels amazing..." she groaned, slowly sinking up to her shoulders in the water and closing her eyes in bliss.

He climbed into the other end of the enormous bath, finding plenty of room to sit comfortably, his feet just brushing against hers. They relaxed in the hot soothing water for a while, feeling their troubles float away. Alyssa eventually opened her eyes, to find John watching her enjoying the comforting embrace of the water. She glided through the water towards him, ripples fanning out in her wake.

She slipped her toned legs to either side of his muscular thighs, and slid effortlessly into his arms, plenty of room for them both at this end of the large bath. She sat astride him, her pussy pressed up against his groin and she enjoyed the feeling of his rock hard cock as it throbbed beneath her. She raised herself up higher, looking down at his face as she positioned his pulsing head at the entrance to her pussy. Her labia were forced wide

apart as she moved slowly downwards, the pressure increasing until her slippery lubrications allowed him to slide into her. John circled her narrow waist with his hands, enjoying the feel of her flared hips under his eager fingers.

"Oooh, you're so big" she moaned, as her tight channel was slowly forced wide open. The sensitive ridges inside her pussy were smoothed out as her supple young body was forced to accommodate the massive girth of his pulsating shaft.

They stopped for a moment when she reached the depths of her pussy, the broad-headed intruder nudging at her cervix.

"I want all of you," she urged, needing to feel him deep inside her.

John helped her tilt her hips and open her pelvis as she rocked back and forth, letting him inch his way deeper. She held on to his shoulders with her hands, her toned back arched away from him and her held tilted backwards as he pulled her down the full length of his cock. Her lips were parted and she let out a satisfied groan when the tightly stretched entrance to her pussy reached the base of his prick.

"You feel so hot and huge inside me," she murmured, moving one hand to feel the flexing invader that was pushed deep into her belly. With a sigh of contentment she rested against him. "I feel so full..."

John enjoyed feeling the perfect spheres of her ass settling gently on his fully loaded quad. He was buried up to the balls inside her and the beautiful young woman was writhing on top of him, revelling in the deep penetration. He moved his hands up to stroke and squeeze her firm breasts, loving the way her slippery, pliant flesh yielded to his touch. His exploring hands brushed the film of bubbles from her tits, enjoying seeing her responsive body react to his touch. Her lovely pink nipples hardened from the contact, pointing upwards on her gravity defying rack.

They began to rock together, gently at first, before getting more vigorous in their sensuous movements. Alyssa enjoyed being on top of him, feeling more in control as she worked her hips back and forth. His strong hold on her body and the support of the water made it easy for her to ride him, impaling herself over and over again.

John lay back, revelling in the sight of the gorgeous teenager gliding up and down his painfully hard cock. Her breasts felt incredible in his eager hands and he massaged her sensitive flesh as she moaned and gasped above him. Water sloshed violently in the tub as they fucked with increasing passion, the bubbly water cascading out of the bath. He was too pre-occupied to care and his hips worked to thrust himself deeper inside her clutching pussy, her fantastically hot body constricting around him rhythmically.

Eventually the sensations became too much to resist and he shoved himself upwards as far as he could, as she ground herself down on the base of his cock. Her taut buttocks trembled against the swollen orbs of his balls and it was the final trigger for him to explode with a rumbling groan. Alyssa joined him in her own climax as she felt powerful spurts of cum shooting into her womb, his engorged shaft jerking inside her.

The well-defined muscles of her toned stomach bowed outwards, as her bloated womb was packed full of cum in a relentless surge. She moved one hand from his shoulders to her tummy and savoured the exquisite feeling of being stuffed full of his spunk. She rocked back and forth gently, her pussy coaxing out every last pulse of his seed. John's spasming balls eventually finished emptying their load and the tension in his body flowed out of him.

"That was awesome," Alyssa sighed contentedly, as she lay there resting lightly on top of him.

John loved seeing the look of sexual satisfaction on his young lover's face and knew he wore a similar look himself. He helped her slide free from her impalement and the two gingerly stepped out of the bath.

They expected the bathroom to be totally flooded after their sexual debauchery in the bathtub, but the cleverly designed floor had directed the water away to a carefully concealed drain. Relieved at not having to clean up any mess, they went into the bedroom and collapsed on the luxurious bed. They lay together facing each other and before they knew it, the luxurious bed had lulled them into a deep and restful slumber.

John awoke the next day to the delightful sounds and sensations of a warm, wet teenage mouth bobbing energetically on his morning wood. He looked down the bed to see Alyssa's smiling lips stretched wide over his cock. She reluctantly backed up and let him slide from her loving lips.

"Good morning handsome!" she greeted him cheerily.

"Good morning to you too beautiful!" John replied, as his cock throbbed angrily in the tight grip of her hand.

"You looked lovely and hard this morning, so I just had to have a taste," she explained with a broad grin.

"It was a wonderful way to wake up," John agreed, affectionately brushing his fingers against her cheek.

Alyssa rolled over on to her tummy, her rosebud glistened with lube invitingly.

"If it's okay with you, I'd like to have a slim tummy when we meet with Calara later this morning," she said, looking at him over her shoulder. "Besides, we haven't done it this way for a while and I like how doing it like this makes you very naughty!"

John laughed as he moved to cover her smaller body with his own. "Are you saying that the thought of fucking your tight little ass gets me extra excited?"

Alyssa sighed happily, nodding, "Yes, that's it exactly."

John slotted himself into position and began to push gently. "How's that baby?" he crooned softly in her ear. "Not too painful?"

"No, not painful," she gasped, matching his mounting excitement. "My muscles aren't designed to work this way, so you forcing your way in feels strange but good."

"Well, you feel lovely and tight to me," he groaned, pushing in further.

"I love pleasing you with my body," she murmured, crumpling the bed sheet with her clenched fists.

Alyssa let out a low groan as John slid smoothly up to the hilt in her ass, her firm round cheeks pressed into his groin. He held still a moment to let her adjust to the long, thick shaft penetrating her, his huge girth forcing her anus wide open.

"Ohh," she moaned, getting used to the huge intruder in her belly. When she'd finally adjusted to that lovely feeling of fullness, she turned to give him a lustful glance over her shoulder. "So how does it feel to have a tight little teen to use, however and whenever you want?"

"It feels pretty fucking good," John said roughly, as he pulled back and thrust into her again, right up to the quad.

"Unh," she grunted, taking the thrust well. "But you're old enough to be my father" she teased him, her eyes shining with arousal.

John thrust into her more forcefully.

"Unh," she grunted again. "Does that turn you on? Would you like me to call you daddy?" she hissed at him, gripping the bed sheet tighter in her small hands.

"No," he said sternly, as he thrust powerfully into her ass.

"Unh," she grunted again, as his balls slapped against her pussy, his broad head driving in deep. "Why not?" she demanded.

"Because one day I want to knock you up and a daddy isn't supposed to want to do that to his little girl," he punctuated his explanation with another powerful drive into her pliant young body.

"Unh!" Alyssa moaned loudly as his groin slapped into her taut ass with a smack. "Ah, so that's what you like? You want to impregnate hot young women?"

John covered her small hands with his own, holding her in place as he began to bugger her with long rhythmic strokes.

"Unh, unh, unh!" Alyssa grunted in time with the powerful fucking. "That's your secret huh? You want a stable of hot teens, their bellies all stuffed full of spunk!"

John was breathing deeply, getting more and more turned on. Alyssa's tightly clutching ass felt impossibly good and the things she was saying...

"Unh, unh, unh," Alyssa panted, her body writhing with lust. "Yeah! A big group of us, all beautiful and all knocked up!" she screamed, as she began to climax.

"Fuck yeah!" John bellowed, as he ground his hips forward, driving the yielding teen into the mattress. He hunched back and forth, trying to fuck his way deeper into her as a mighty orgasm overwhelmed him.

"Aaahh!" He groaned, as his cum blasted out of his balls to fill up the prostrate teen's belly. With his weight firmly pinning her in place, she could only lie there and take it, her gorgeous young tummy rounding out with the heavy spunk he was pumping into her. Alyssa's tight little ass gripped him like a fist, as she convulsed in her own orgasm. Each clutching squeeze seemed designed to coax out as much of his cum as possible.

Finally drained completely dry, he collapsed, trying to keep his weight from squashing the young girl beneath him. He rolled over and slipped out of her, as the exhausted pair panted for breath.

"Yeah, very naughty..." she said with a giggle and grinned at him. John could only moan in response.

Alyssa leaned over and kissed him on the forehead as he laboured for breath, before she got up and headed to the bathroom. "I'll see what I can do," she whispered quietly as she left, a broad grin on her face.

They relaxed in bed for a while, before getting dressed for the day. John wore his charcoal suit, looking the part of successful businessman. Alyssa wore a delightfully tailored jacket and pencil skirt in an identical colour to his suit, that accentuated her shapely curves perfectly. Breakfast was over and done with quickly, with Alyssa eating conventional food for a change.

Holding hands contentedly, they headed back up to the Bridge before separating to sit in their corresponding chairs. Timed to perfection, the Invictus dropped out of hyper-warp into the Nerus system, home of Port Heracles.

"Let's go say hello," John said to his beautiful companion.

Alyssa nodded eagerly and laid in the course that would take them to the space station and their awaiting friend.

## Three Square Meals Ch. 08 - A rescue left unfinished

The Invictus followed the course laid in by Alyssa, making quick and determined progress towards Port Heracles. Not quite at the same scale as Olympus Shipyard, this space station was still an impressively large base, with twenty separate docking bays to cater for all the shipping. As the last major space station in this sector of Terran territory, the facility was buzzing with merchant and military traffic. The communications officer who contacted them sounded surprised that the assault cruiser was a civilian vessel, but such things were not totally unheard of. He granted them docking clearance for Docking Bay Four.

The Invictus stalked closer, before gliding into the brightly-lit docking bay under Alyssa's careful hand. It was a tight fit, but with her skilful guidance they avoided any mishaps. Lateral thrusters fired as their ship eased up to the docking gantry, and once they had finally made gentle contact, docking clamps locked them securely into place.

"Nice job," John said, admiring her handiwork.

"Thanks," she said, smiling up at him. "Flying something this huge is so much fun!"

They headed out of the ship across the docking gantry, and then up an elevator into the Spaceport proper. Although not on anywhere near the same physical scale as Olympus Shipyard, this spaceport had a large retail and trading emporium because it saw a lot of traffic from independent traders. Those traders included a broad selection of space-faring aliens, which had Alyssa whirling around wide eyed to take them all in. She gawped at the exotic creatures, marvelling at their bizarre shapes and colouring.

John leaned over to the gawking teen. "Try not to be too obvious," he whispered into her ear quietly. "Some of these species don't like to be stared at."

He smiled as he watched the curious young woman darting furtive glances at the various different aliens, whilst trying to be discreet. He looked around himself, and noted that the Kintark were conspicuously absent.

*Excuse me, young one,* a melodic voice sounded in Alyssa's head. She whirled to see a dark green, solid looking, gelatinous blob stopped at her side, waiting to pass by.

"Oh, pardon me!" she exclaimed, before stepping out of the way. The creature squelched past, followed by a pair of robotic humanoid porters that were loaded down with boxes.

*It is of no consequence. Be well, young one,* the kind melodic voice chimed again.

"What was that?" she asked John quietly, as soon as the creature was out of earshot. It had no ears, so she hoped it couldn't overhear.

"That was a Bolon," John explained. "They're a friendly species, but communicating with them is very difficult as they can't speak. They use the robots as interpreters when trading."

"Ah okay, thanks," Alyssa mumbled distractedly. "How very interesting..." she thought to herself.

John led Alyssa to the Terran Federation medical facility where Calara was recuperating. John nodded courteously to a couple of soldiers standing guard outside, and they were ushered into the reception area of the facility. The walls and floor in the sterile facility were blindingly white, which took a little getting used to.

The receptionist was a middle-aged woman, who looked up from her work at her console and smiled at them in welcome. "Hello, can I help you?" she asked the smartly dressed visitors courteously.

"We're here to see Calara Fernandez," John replied, bracing himself for questions if it turned out that she had been hauled off to the brig.

"Certainly sir, one moment," the receptionist replied, before scanning through a list of names on the console.

"Ah yes," she said, finding Calara amongst the list. "May I see your identification please?" she requested politely. John and Alyssa handed over their IDs, which were scanned by a nearby reader, logging them as visitors.

"Take the elevator up to floor three, Lieutenant Fernandez is in room 347," the receptionist said, passing back their IDs, and pointing to the elevators in the corner of the room. "I'll let her know you're on your way," she added kindly.

John and Alyssa thanked the receptionist and then walked over to take the elevator up to the third floor. The hospital was well sign-posted, and they found room 347 easily. John knocked politely on the door.

"Come in!" Calara's excited voice drifted out from the room.

He opened the door and saw Calara standing by a desk, turning to face them as she closed the call with the receptionist. Alyssa glided past him and the two young women came together in a warm embrace.

"It's so good to see you!" Calara gasped, overwhelmed with relief to see her visitors.

"You too!" Alyssa exclaimed, a beaming smile on her face. "You look so much better!"

Calara reached up to touch her nose self-consciously, still swollen from the break that had been straightened. Her black eyes had mostly disappeared now, and John could see that the young Latina was actually very pretty. Unfortunately, the stress and her lack of sleep made her look very tired, with big bags under her eyes.

John moved forward to greet her with a hug and she moved into his arms, holding him tightly. "Thank you for saving me, both of you," Calara mumbled into his chest. "You don't know how wonderful it is to see you again."

"It's great to see you too," John replied, holding her gently and trying not to aggravate any of her injuries.

Alyssa stepped up behind Calara and they both hugged the distraught young woman, wrapping her in a comforting embrace. After some of the tension had relaxed from her shoulders, they stepped away, with John taking the nearby reclining chair, and the girls sitting on the bed.

"So, Calara, tell me more about the trouble you're in?" he gently prompted her.

A dark wave of depression seemed to crash over the poor girl, and her shoulders slumped in defeat.

"I'm being charged with 'dereliction of duty' and there's going to be a court martial!" she exclaimed, her voice panicked. Alyssa moved closer and put an arm around her shoulder, supporting her comfortingly.

John frowned, his face showing his disbelief. "That's completely crazy! How could you be responsible for what happened?!" He took out a small handheld device and connected to the station's security network.

"He said I'd have to answer for my shocking lack of judgement. That I was to blame for the Corvette being boarded and all those people being killed!" Calara blurted out, on the verge of tears. "I was asleep at the time though! As the junior tactical officer, I had handed over the next shift to Lieutenant Crowe."

John searched through the Port Heracles' judicial log for formal proceedings, but he could find nothing logged in relation to Calara Fernandez. He put down the device then leaned forward, reaching out to hold one of her trembling hands. "Who is 'He'?"

Calara shuddered with revulsion. "Commander Rupert Grant. He's in charge of Port Heracles, and has jurisdiction of this sector. He was my commanding officer for a while, before I requested a transfer."

Alyssa guessed there was probably more to this story, as she watched the Latina visibly withdraw into herself. "Why did you ask for a transfer?" she asked quietly, while stroking Calara's arm.

Calara's eyes were downcast and she looked ashamed. "He... He kept coming on to me. I kept telling him no, so he threatened to end my career if I wouldn't go out with him. Commander Bryant arrived at the station on the Corvette Griffon, so I applied for an immediate transfer. He accepted, and I joined his crew the next day."

"This Grant guy didn't take that well then, I guess?" Alyssa asked darting a pointed look at John.

"No. When I told him about the transfer, he was furious. He swore at me a lot, and called me all sorts of horrible things," Calara said, blushing with embarrassment.

John's eyes narrowed dangerously. "I think it's time I met Commander Grant."

They calmed Calara down, reassuring her that everything would be fine, and promising they would be back shortly. She watched them leave, nervously biting a nail.

Alyssa followed after John as he strode towards the elevator. He was absolutely fuming with rage, and she had never seen him like this before.

*Fucking with someone who has PTSD!* he snarled to himself. *What the fuck does he think he's playing at?!*

Alyssa decided to let John focus on the situation at hand and stayed quiet. She matched his pace as they stormed out of the medical facility, then walked briskly to the Station Commander's office in the main Terran Federation military compound. Alyssa tuned in to John's inner voice and was pleased when he calmed down, finally deciding against shooting the Station Commander. John swiped his ID at the entrance to the compound and the guards waved him inside.

They travelled through a number of corridors in the base until they finally reached the Commander's office. John opened the door without knocking and strode purposefully into the reception area.

A pinch faced man in a naval uniform looked up and saw that two civilians had entered his office. "Yes, what do you want?" he snapped, making no attempt to hide his irritation.

"My name's John Blake. I'm here to see Commander Grant... about Calara Fernandez," John informed the adjutant through clenched teeth.

The man tutted in annoyance, deliberately taking his time before pressing a button on a console. "There's a John Blake here to see you about Lieutenant Fernandez, Sir," he said obsequiously.

There was a long pause before a voice on the intercom said, "Send him in."

John and Alyssa walked towards the door, only for Alyssa to be stopped by the adjutant's raised hand. "Not you miss, you can wait there," he sneered, pointing at a nearby chair. She was relieved John didn't carry through with his fleeting desire to break the man's arm. Well a bit, anyway.

"I won't be long," John said to Alyssa, before he opened the door on the other side of the office and strode in.

Alyssa watched John enter the room and saw a portly man in his fifties slouched behind a desk.

"Ahh, the irrepressible Mr Blake! I read about your exploits in Lieutenant Fernandez's report... I must admit I'm surprised to find you aren't eight-feet-tall and breathing fire. What can I do for you?" Commander Grant sneered, his contempt quite obvious.

"Shut the fuck up and scan this," John demanded in a tone that brooked no argument, slamming his military ID down on the Station Commander's desk. He closed the door behind him, cutting off Alyssa's view.

They were in there for what seemed like forever to the impatient teenager, who desperately wanted to know what was happening. Alyssa discovered that she was too far away to listen in to John's thoughts, so the silence was maddening. The adjutant kept throwing salacious glances her way and she suddenly realised the reason why he had insisted she had to wait behind. She deliberately ignored him and tried her best to wait for John's return.

Eventually the Station Commander's door was thrown open and John strolled out. Alyssa glanced inside the room as she got up to join him and saw the corpulent Rupert Grant slumped in his chair, his face a mask of fear and dread. The couple walked away quickly, eager to leave the loathsome presence of both contemptible men.

"I've sorted it out," John said to a relieved Alyssa. "We just need to speak to Calara and find out what she wants to do."

They walked back to the medical facility, eager to bring the good news to the troubled young woman.

\*\*\*

Meanwhile back at the medical facility, Calara thrashed around violently on her bed, gripped in a terrifying nightmare.

It had been such a relief to see her two saviours again, and she had felt safe and protected when in their presence. When they had gone, she found herself fighting off waves of exhaustion and had curled up on the bed to try to get some sleep. The nightmare had started as it normally did...

The horrific screams gurgled to a halt as the second crewmate died horribly at the hands of the Largath.

"It's all my fault!", Calara berated herself. "Those women and all the other crew died because of me!"

The twisted faces of the surrounding pirates loomed large before her dazed eyes, leering at her and baying for blood. A crude spear was thrust into her hand and she was dropped awkwardly into the pit to face the hideous creature. Her back was a sheet of agony from where she had been flogged by that demented cyborg, the pain enough to nearly make her pass out. She struggled to find her footing again as the monstrous Largath approached with a sickening leer on its ugly face.

She waved the metal pole in front of her, desperate to keep the rampant beast at bay. It was deceptively fast for something so huge, and she had to work hard to keep out of its grasp as it lunged at her time and again.

Calara knew her situation was hopeless, that she could only fend the Largath off for just a few minutes and then she'd be torn to pieces, violated to death in the most horrific way imaginable. Her heart pounded with terror and she knew that she was doomed.

Calara misjudged one strike, underestimating the Largath's reach and it whipped its arm to the side, catching her in the chest. The force behind that blow was terrifying and she screamed at the explosion of pain. There was a sickening crunch as her ribs broke and she sailed through the air before landing on her back, the wind knocked out of her. Frantically trying to regain her breath, she struggled to her feet as the creature came forward, a sickening hunger burning in its four eyes. It roared in victory to the cheering pirates, showboating for the depraved spectators...

"Bzzzzt!"

The insistent buzzing of the intercom broke through her terrifying nightmare and Calara lurched upright on the bed, her chest heaving for breath. It took her a moment to realise where she was, but when she saw the gleaming sterile environment of the medical facility, she let out a shuddering sigh. She was desperately relieved to have escaped from the Largath's clutches and her racing heart began to calm. Taking a deep breath, she steadied herself before answering the call. It was the receptionist again, politely informing her that John and Alyssa had returned. Calara's heart lifted with joy at the thought of seeing them again and she darted over to the door to watch out for their arrival.

\*\*\*

John and Alyssa left the elevator and turned to walk towards room 347. They saw Calara's hopeful face looking around the door to her room and she gave them an anxious, tentative smile when she saw them. The Latina stepped out into the corridor and ushered them into her room. They walked into Calara's room and John turned her to face him.

"It's over," he stated simply, looking into her big brown eyes as she stared up at him hopefully. "You won't have to face any charges and there's not going to be a Court Martial. None of what happened was your fault."

Calara's face crumpled with relief as she fell sobbing into his arms. He held her in a warm embrace, being careful not to aggravate the young woman's healing wounds. Alyssa stood at his side and stroked the brunette's long dark hair, her face filled with compassion. They stood like that for some time, until Calara was able to regain her composure. She looked up at them both with sincere gratitude on her face.

"Thank you," Calara said fervently.

"You're welcome," John replied, giving her a reassuring smile.

He felt a lump in his throat. This poor girl had been through so much, and then that asshole Grant had made things so much worse. This was serious, he realised suddenly. He needed to report what had happened but he couldn't do it from here using the Port Heracles comm network, as Grant might be monitoring outbound traffic.

"I need to talk to someone about this," John said apologetically, as the blonde and brunette looked up at him. "Grant isn't going to get away with the way he's treated you."

"It's okay, I'll look after her," Alyssa said kindly, as she smiled at the other young woman.

They agreed that he would come back to meet them after he had visited the ship and he left Alyssa hugging Calara, the two of them talking softly. He made his way back to the Invictus, so that he could use its powerful communication relay to contact Terran Federation Command.

\*\*\*

A short while later, John stood deep in thought, as he took the elevator back up to the concourse. He had made his report and recorded his detailed allegations against Commander Rupert Grant. He had lost some friends to PTSD in the past; good men, their lives taken by their own hand. He would be damned before he let anything like that happen to this young woman. The elevator door opened and he was surprised to see Calara and Alyssa walking towards him.

"Second Lieutenant Calara Fernandez reporting for duty, Sir!" The pretty Latina said formally, before snapping a sharp salute and standing rigidly at attention.

"What...?" John blurted out, surprised by her actions.

"I told Calara we had a vacancy in our ship's roster, after my recent promotion," Alyssa told him, her beautiful blue eyes flashing mischievously. "She just agreed to join us!"

"Now wait just a minute!" John blurted out, remembering Alyssa's old job title.

"Uh-uh, Commander!" Alyssa admonished him playfully, waving a finger from side to side. "As your Executive Officer, I'm in charge of all recruitment."

John was about to speak again but she cut off his forthcoming objection with a piercing gaze that startled him into silence.

"Second Lieutenant Fernandez graduated near the top of her Academy class, specialising in naval tactics," Alyssa said, before she turned to face Calara. "Lieutenant, summarise your career for the Commander, please."

"I joined the Terran Federation Navy at sixteen and spent two years at the Academy. My first posting was at Port Heracles, before I transferred to the Corvette Griffon," Calara informed him, standing at attention as she

began listing off the impressive achievements and citations of her fledgling career.

"Besides," Alyssa continued, once Calara had finished. "The Invictus has a lot of big guns. I don't know anything about ship-to-ship combat, do you?"

John paused, mulling this surprising turn of events over in his mind. He was a Marine at heart, specialised in ship boarding and infantry tactics. He realised he had subconsciously shied away from anything to do with the Invictus' gun batteries, feeling a little wary of their massive firepower. A Tactical Officer could actually prove to be very useful and with that realisation, he quickly came to his decision.

"Welcome aboard Lieutenant!" he said to Calara, snapping her a crisp salute, then smiling at her warmly.

The pretty Latina returned his salute, smiling back at him as she relaxed. "Thank you, Sir. You won't regret it."

"Yay!" Alyssa squealed, rushing forward to embrace her friend in a hug. Calara returned the beautiful blonde's enthusiastic embrace, groaning slightly at the sharp pain in her ribs.

"Oh, sorry!" Alyssa apologised, before quickly releasing her.

They walked over to the window overlooking the docking bay, which offered Calara her first view of her new home. The Invictus loomed in front of them, and Calara gazed in awe at the intimidating sight of the huge warship, knowing exactly how much firepower lay hidden within its hull.

"Oh yeah..." she said in a low voice, her head nodding appreciatively, a broad grin lighting up her face.

"Come on, let's get you settled in," Alyssa said eagerly. "You're going to be so happy here, I promise!"

Calara turned back to retrieve her duffle bag, but John waved her away. "You haven't fully recovered yet. Let me carry that for you."

She nodded to him in gratitude, then smiled at Alyssa as the blonde clasped her hand and led her towards the elevator. John watched the departing teenagers for a moment, wondering just what he was getting himself into, before he scooped up Calara's duffle bag. He carried it easily over one shoulder, and followed behind them to the lift that would take them down to the docking gantry.

The elevator took a few moments to drop down to the docking level, then the trio walked briskly towards the towering hull of the Invictus. Alyssa pressed her hand against the DNA reader and the airlock spiralled open for them. They walked inside and headed up to the officers' quarters, while Calara recounted what had happened while John had gone back to the ship.

"So, after Alyssa offered me the job as Tactical Officer on board the Invictus, I called Commander Grant to request the transfer. He offered me an indefinite leave of absence!" she exclaimed, still shocked by how eager he had been to help. "That means I can stay on the ship for as long as you guys want me here," she added with a happy sigh.

Alyssa grinned at John over the excited brunette's head as they walked along the corridor on Deck Two. He smiled back at her, both of them pleased to see Calara's dramatically improved mood. They reached the end of the corridor and Alyssa pressed the button on the door to the left of the Commander's room.

"Our room is just over there, so I'd like you to have this one," Alyssa said, as the door to the officer's room swished opened quietly. "Then we'll be close by if you need anything."

Calara nodded and they walked into the room. "Wow, these quarters are huge! This room must be at least three times as big as my berth on the Griffon," she exclaimed, as she looked around the corner. "And my own bathroom too!"

"Decorate it how you like, but please keep it nice and tidy," Alyssa said with a warm smile.

"Yes Ma'am," Calara replied respectfully, as John placed her duffle bag next to the door.

Alyssa's musical laughter filled the room. "There's no need for all that military stuff, except when making fun of John!" she said with a wink.

John grabbed the playful blonde and tickled her relentlessly until she begged for mercy, while Calara watched them with a bemused smile. John eventually let Alyssa go and she panted for breath.

"Come on you two, let's go have some dinner," John suggested jerking his thumb towards the Officers' Lounge.

"Yes, Sir," Calara replied automatically, before catching Alyssa's mock frown of disappointment.

"Yes... John. That would be lovely," she answered again, glancing at Alyssa for approval.

Alyssa smiled at her in delight. "Much better!"

John laughed at the blonde and rolled his eyes. "I thought the Executive Officer was supposed to enforce discipline amongst my crew?"

Alyssa arched an eyebrow at him. "I thought we discussed what my main role was supposed to be?"

John flushed with embarrassment. "Very good, XO."

They walked off to the Officer's lounge, enjoying the playful banter. This was such a change from the rigid discipline enforced on Terran Federation ships, that it came as a bit of a shock to Calara. She soon relaxed though, with both John and Alyssa putting her at ease with their welcoming friendliness. They enjoyed a great dinner, and it turned out John was an excellent cook when he put his mind to it. The trio then relaxed in the comfy chairs of the Officers' Lounge.

"This ship is amazing," Calara said with a contented sigh, before looking over at John. "You really own this yourself?"

He nodded and grinned happily at her. "After my service in the military, I worked as a trader for eleven years and finally made a big score. This..." He spread his arms wide "Was the result."

"Plus, he got me in the bargain," Alyssa said with a playful smile.

"I guess I did," John said with a chuckle, and they looked at each other fondly.

Calara stifled a big yawn and then looked at them apologetically.

"Sorry to bore you," Alyssa said with a smile.

"No, no! I'm just really tired!" Calara answered hurriedly, worried that she had offended them.

"Relax, I'm only joking," Alyssa said gently.

"Come on ladies," John smiled at them both. "It's probably time for bed anyway."

He stood and then offered each of them a hand. Both girls accepted and rose to join him, before walking back down the long corridor to the other end of the Officers' Deck. John and Alyssa stopped at Calara's door and the exhausted brunette half stumbled into her room.

"Remember, just come and ask if you need anything," Alyssa said pleasantly. Calara nodded her thanks and the couple left her to get settled in.

Calara went into her bathroom and completed her night-time routine, then collapsed onto the big comfortable bed. She struggled out of her clothes and pulled on a big comfy T-shirt, before crawling under the covers and turning out the light. Even though she was tired out and badly needed to rest, she was scared of the terrifying nightmare that had plagued her every night for the last two weeks. She lay half-dozing in bed, desperately fighting her exhaustion as she knew the terrors sleep would bring.

She was roused from her half-awake state by the sound of an excited gasp. Calara looked at her clock and saw that it was eleven at night, realising she'd been lying there for around an hour. She mulled over the life changing events of the day, which brought a hopeful smile to her face, when she suddenly heard the unmistakeable sound of a lusty moan. Her mind immediately recalled that time back on the Fool's Gold, when she had stumbled across Alyssa pleasuring the handsome Commander.

Feeling a little guilty, but unable to resist the siren call of the enticing feminine sighs coming from the other room, Calara got up and padded to her door. She had been so tired, she had forgotten to close her door earlier, and she saw that the door to Alyssa and John's room had been left open too.

"Alyssa probably did that in case I needed anything," Calara thought to herself, shaking her head in wonder. "How can someone so impossibly beautiful, be so kind and caring as well?"

"You shouldn't peek on them after they've been so welcoming," said the good angel on one shoulder, adopting a pious expression.

"But John's so handsome and Alyssa's so beautiful," countered the naughty devil on the other shoulder with a wicked grin. "What would it hurt to take a quick peek? Besides, Alyssa didn't seem to mind last time!"

The devil convincingly won that argument. Calara crept forward and looked into their room, her breath catching at the sight in front of her.

John was on his back, with his head towards her, as the dim light in the room cast shadows over his muscular chest. Alyssa was riding him like a cowgirl and her slim, tanned body moved with a sensual grace as she slowly rocked back and forth. John's hands cupped the beautiful teenager's big firm breasts, and the pink nipples seemed to point towards Calara enticingly, as though begging to be kissed. Alyssa was leaning forward, her lustrous mane of golden hair flowing around her as she moved. It was clear they were trying to stay quiet, but the couple couldn't help but make little gasps or moans when something felt too good.

Calara's thighs ground together and she felt a surge of arousal wash over her for the first time in weeks. She let out an excited little moan as she watched them with growing excitement.

John was oblivious, totally absorbed with the ravishing young beauty who was riding his painfully hard cock. Alyssa however, heard the quiet moan from the doorway, and looked up under her shroud of blonde hair to see Calara silhouetted in the doorway. She raised herself up slightly, putting on more of a show for the voyeuristic Latina, and writhed smoothly on John's lap. She noticed Calara's hand slipping down between her legs to rub herself in time with Alyssa's rhythmic motion and she watched the gorgeous brunette with growing excitement. The beautiful blonde sat up and tilted her head back, brushing her long, lustrous hair away from her

face with both hands. She then looked forward and glanced over at Calara, making eye contact with the brunette.

The sight of Alyssa riding John so passionately had Calara quivering with excitement and she watched them with feverish eyes as she brought herself closer to climax. Suddenly, she noticed that the gorgeous blonde was looking right at her, watching her rub her pussy. Letting out a frightened squeak and flushing with embarrassment, she made to bolt for her own room, but something in Alyssa's piercing cerulean gaze had her rooted to the spot.

"Come join us, beautiful," Alyssa purred seductively, and beckoned the shy Latina towards her. John tilted his head back to see what was happening, suddenly aware of their late night-visitor. Alyssa pressed a finger gently to John's lips with the other hand, silencing any objections, before leaning in close to whisper in his ear, "She needs this John."

Calara moved forward hesitantly, transfixed by those perfect blue orbs, which invited her in.

"That's right, there's a good girl," Alyssa crooned soothingly as she slid up and off John's massive shaft. Pivoting with a dancer's grace, she landed lightly on her feet by the side of the bed. She walked towards the brunette, her effortless poise reminding Calara of a catwalk model.

The beautiful blonde reached out to take the lovely brunette's hand and she led her back to the bed. They turned to face one another and Calara gasped when Alyssa slid her hands down to take the bottom of the oversized t-shirt, before gently pulling it over her head. The hypnotic effect of those incredible blue eyes was momentarily broken, but Alyssa moved in and kissed Calara gently, reinforcing her bewitching hold over the brunette. Calara moaned into Alyssa's mouth as the two kissed tenderly, both of them exploring lovely soft feminine lips for the first time.

John was stunned by the recent turn of events. He had tried to object when Alyssa had beckoned over Calara, worrying about the Latina's fragile state after all the trauma she had experienced over the last two weeks. He sat up and turned to face them as Calara came over to the side of the bed, hand in hand with the blonde teenager he loved so much.

He had to stifle his own gasp as Alyssa removed the T-shirt from Calara and the two moved together to kiss softly. They held each other in a tender embrace, their youthful breasts pressed together as they relished their first kiss.

This was the first time John really had a chance to study Calara's body in a sexual light, his previous worry for the young woman overriding any such thoughts. She was shorter than Alyssa, probably about five-foot-six compared to the five-foot-nine of the statuesque blonde. Calara was slim and athletic which he liked, but she was looking thinner than when he had first met her, the strain of the last two weeks taking their toll. Finally, her breasts were a lot smaller than the blondes, probably about a 30B if he guessed right.

John's cock throbbed with excitement as he watched the beautiful sight before him. The girls obviously held great affection for each other, and it was wonderful to see them express it physically. Their full, soft lips brushed lightly over each other, their tongues meeting as they explored this exciting new aspect of their relationship.

Alyssa sighed with happiness as Calara moaned into her mouth. She was bigger than the lovely brunette and she felt protective of the smaller woman. "I wonder if this is how John feels with me?" she asked herself, glancing to the side, to see her man drinking in their bodies as they made out in front of him. Alyssa leaned back slightly, breaking the kiss.

"Poor John, we've forgotten about him," she said quietly, as she turned and climbed on to the bed, holding Calara's hand so that she would follow.

"Don't you want to show John how much you care about him too?" she asked the lovely Latina.

Calara nodded in agreement, and climbed on to the bed, moving forward to face her handsome saviour. John brushed her long dark hair away from her face so that she could look him in the eyes.

"Are you sure about this?" he asked her gently, cupping her face with tenderness.

"He's still looking out for me, even now," Calara thought to herself, touched by his concern. She leaned forward and initiated their first kiss, linking her hands behind his neck as her lips met his.

John cradled the lovely brunette in his arms and savoured the exquisite pleasure of kissing this pretty girl. Her brown eyes gazed at him beneath long eyelashes and he could see the passion in those lovely soulful orbs.

Alyssa sat to their side and watched lovingly as her friend and lover explored each other's lips for the first time. This felt so right to the blissfully happy blonde and, with a contented sigh, she knew the brunette would fit in with them both perfectly. She watched them relish their kiss, thrilled by the sexual tension in the air as she waited until they paused to take a breath.

When they finally parted, Alyssa leaned forward to whisper in the Latina's ear. "Would you like to taste me?"

Calara's eyes opened wide at the thought and she blushed before answering with a tentative nod.

Alyssa embraced the Latina and their lips made contact again. "You're such a good girl, and so lovely," the blonde murmured to the brunette.

Calara glowed with the praise and kissed her back fiercely. John watched up close as the two girls made out only inches in front of him, and he could hear every breathy moan, every sigh, every gasp of delight. Calara's darker olive tones provided a thrilling contrast to the fairer-skinned blonde and his eyes roved over them both, watching slender fingers brushing over soft skin. His rock-hard cock throbbed with excitement and he couldn't recall being this turned on before.

Alyssa eased back from Calara and then guided the brunette to her knees in front of John, his massive cock throbbing, as if pleading for attention.

"You're absolutely huge!" Calara gasped, eye-to-eye with his equipment for the first time.

Kneeling beside her, Alyssa nodded, her bright blue eyes gleaming at the sight. "I know! We're so lucky!" She put her arm around the Latina and added, "Definitely plenty for us to share."

"Didn't you want me to taste you?" Calara asked in confusion.

"You saw me with him," Alyssa replied to the brunette with a knowing smile, to which Calara nodded, blushing slightly. "Well he's coated with me," Alyssa added, seeing the light of understanding go on in Calara's soulful brown eyes.

The Latina smiled coyly, and then moved over John's cock, parting her lips into a wide oval. She leaned forward and carefully enveloped his broad head in her mouth, licking him with her tongue. Alyssa watched intently, feeling incredibly turned on as the brunette sucked on John's cock, her tongue lapping away at the throbbing hardness filling her mouth. John's balls were overjoyed when his burgeoning prick started to receive attention once again and they served up some fresh pre-cum for this new teenager to savour.

Alyssa leaned down and kissed the side of John's shaft, just below where Calara worked on the head. She licked and caressed him with her tongue as she watched the brunette's eyes grow dazed and heavy lidded. Soon the Latina's brown eyes were closed and she began to bob in his lap rhythmically, brushing up against the blonde's face on the downstroke.

Alyssa backed away to let the Latina go to work, watching from close by. She saw the girl pause when he reached the back of her mouth, unable to fit his girth into her throat. The lovely brunette seemed determined however and she visibly relaxed, sucking gently all the while on his pulsing length. Eventually she moved forward again, swallowing this time, and coaxed the broad head of his cock into her throat. Alyssa reached out to gently stroke Calara's neck, feeling John's shaft make steady progress. She marvelled at the way the girl's slim neck bulged out, accommodating the thick tool that was now embedded deep inside her. John eased all the way back, and Calara took a deep breath before swallowing him down again.

Alyssa moved to stand by John's side, her firm breasts sandwiching his left arm. "This is so fucking hot," she whispered softly into his ear. "Did I look like that when you broke me in?"

John's brow was furrowed with concentration as the brunette pleasured his shaft, massaging him as she swallowed. "You were smaller... tighter... I had to be very careful," he replied with a groan.

Alyssa slipped a finger between her thighs and stroked her swollen clit. She came instantly. "Oh my God!" she moaned in his ear, clinging to him as her body shook with pleasure.

The wonderful sound of an orgasming young woman nearly made him cum there and then.

"You own me now, John," she gasped devotedly. "I'm yours forever, if you'll have me?"

John grunted his agreement, grabbing the beautiful blonde so that he could give her a fierce kiss. Alyssa moaned into his mouth, until she finally pulled back, looking down to stroke Calara's head as she sucked mindlessly and rhythmically on his cock.

"Do you want to own her too?" Alyssa asked, feeling an overwhelming desire for him to agree.

John moaned and could only nod, his hips gently thrusting him into Calara's sucking mouth.

"Then fill up her belly!" Alyssa urged him passionately. "Show me what we'll look like when you make us both pregnant!"

"Oh, fuck!" John yelled as his balls flexed and he began to shoot long spurts of cum into the compliant Latina's awaiting stomach.

Calara's slim tummy filled out immediately and she sucked harder, as though determined to get every last drop of his seed. Alyssa's eyes widened, her pupils dilating, as she felt the climactic wave overcome John. Her thighs ground together and her hips twitched as she joined him in an explosive orgasm. The trio eventually collapsed in a heap, completely spent, curling up together as they panted for breath.

When John and Alyssa had recovered, they looked down at Calara who was now fast asleep between them. Glancing at each other over the lovely Latina, they shared a loving smile. After carefully manoeuvring the comatose young woman into the middle of the bed, they lay down beside her, cuddling Calara between them. Their hands met as they gently stroked her hugely swollen belly, the olive skin stretched taut to carry several pints of cum.

\*\*\*

John woke up the next morning with a young woman in his arms. He was spooned behind her, and enjoyed the feel of her slim, toned body against him. He moved his hand up to cup Alyssa's firm breast in his exploring hand, but instead found himself cupping a smaller but still delightfully pert breast. He opened his eyes to see dark brown hair instead of blonde in front of his eyes, and it took him a moment to remember what had happened the previous night.

Alyssa's face suddenly appeared above Calara's head and he looked up into her bright blue eyes as she smiled down at him, looking happy and content. They rested together on either side of the young Latina, both feeling protective of the peacefully slumbering brunette.

\*\*\*

Calara had fallen into a deep sleep, and the nightmare started as it normally did, with the second crewmate dying at the hands of the Largath.

"It wasn't my fault," Calara suddenly reminded herself. "Those women and all the other crew died because of the evil pirates... there was nothing I could have done to prevent it."

A crude spear was thrust into her hand by the foul pirates and she was dropped into the pit. The Largath lumbered towards her and she waved the metal pole in front of her to keep it at bay. The crippling sense of terror was gone this time and she looked at the hideous monster in disgust, wondering how any creature could be so cruel and vicious.

Suddenly there was a blinding flash above her and two angels appeared in that blazing radiance. The heartbreakingly beautiful woman was surrounded by a golden halo, the sight of her lifting Calara's heart and filling her with joy. The angel pointed at the Largath as it lurched around the cargo bay and its head exploded, sending it keeling over on its side where it would never bother Calara again.

The gloriously handsome man scooped Calara up in his powerful arms, sending a thrill of elation through her body. She knew his tender embrace would protect her from all harm and she relaxed against him, her worries fading into nothingness. The angelic figure carried her away from danger and he gave her a benevolent smile as she gazed up at him in adoration.

"You're safe now, no-one will hurt you again," he said, his voice strong and vibrant.

Calara felt safe, warm, and loved, as she fell into a deep untroubled sleep.

\*\*\*

John and Alyssa stretched as they woke up, then got out of bed. John kissed the beautiful blonde, smiling happily before heading to the bathroom, while Alyssa stayed behind, as she wanted to see how their new bedmate was doing.

The worry lines had smoothed out on Calara's face and she slept like a baby, tucked up in the comfortable bed. Alyssa checked the girl's back and saw that the horrific welts and lacerations were healing nicely, the angry red marks not nearly so inflamed as they had been last night. Careful not to wake her, she walked around the other side of the bed to check the Latina's face. She noted that the fading black eyes had disappeared completely, and the swelling on her nose had gone down a bit too.

"Perfect," she said to herself quietly, nodding in satisfaction.

This was working out exactly as she had hoped and she turned to follow John into the shower. She found her lover enjoying the feel of the hot water as it flowed down over his face. Sliding in behind him, Alyssa wrapped him in a warm hug, her heart full of love for her man.

The couple left Calara to rest and went to the Officers' Lounge to get some breakfast. John was pleased when Alyssa joined him in eating a hearty breakfast, but was then surprised when she made no move to go down on him like she normally did every morning.

Alyssa laughed at his bemused expression and cupped his face lightly in her hand. "I think I've been spoiling you!"

John looked a bit abashed and started to mumble an apology, but Alyssa cut him off. "If you're really horny, of course you can have me any way you like," she offered sincerely. "But I'd prefer you to save up a big load and give it to Calara when she wakes up."

"Give it to Calara?" John asked, with a confused look on his face. "Why?"

Alyssa stood silently and lifted her figure-hugging top, revealing the lovely bronzed skin of her toned abdomen. She turned slightly to her left, showing him her right flank. "What do you see?" she asked, watching him carefully.

John looked closer, wondering what the beautiful young woman was getting at. He ran his hand over her side, but all he could see and feel was her absolutely perfect, unblemished skin.

"You're flawless honey. Other than your gorgeous body, I can't see anything out of the ordinary," he replied with a shrug of his shoulders, admitting defeat.

"I grew up in abject poverty, surrounded by fighting black market gangers," Alyssa explained as she pulled off her top completely, showing him acres of breathtaking perfection. "There's no way my skin should be like this. Shouldn't there be a few scars here or there?"

John nodded, "Sure, that makes sense, but there aren't any."

"Exactly," Alyssa confirmed, with a satisfied grin.

John laughed and shook his head in bemusement. "Sorry, honey. All the fun last night must have blown my mind and made me a bit dense this morning. Please could you explain it for me, using small words."

Alyssa smiled at him lovingly. She remained standing and showed him her right flank again. "When I was fourteen, I was caught up in a street fight. A fucker with a knife stabbed me here," she said as she pointed to an area of unblemished skin. "I had a scar that went from here... around to here," she added, as she traced a line just above her right hip.

"It wasn't that noticeable unless you looked closely, but now it's completely gone," she said, looking to see if he understood.

"Light gunshot wound - right arm, burn - left wrist, mole - lower back..." Alyssa said as she began to list her scars and imperfections, pointing to the unblemished locations on her body. "All gone," she added, as if that explained everything.

John finally realised what she was saying. "So you had all these scars, but now they've gone, and you think it's linked to the changes in your body?"

Alyssa nodded emphatically. "Yes, exactly," she agreed, reaching between his legs to gently stroke his quad. "I think that when these gave me a full body makeover, they healed all my scars at the same time."

"And now you're hoping the same will happen to Calara?"

"Mmm-hmm," she agreed, gazing into his eyes.

"I'll wait," he said with a broad smile, glad he might be able to really help the young Latina's physical recovery.

The beautiful blonde leaned over to give him a tender kiss. "Thank you. I know this'll help her." She eased back into her seat and looked at him quizzically. "So aside from topping up Calara, what's our plan now?"

"Well I thought we might head back to Karron," John suggested, watching Alyssa carefully for her reaction. "I know you were desperate to leave there before, but when I bought the last load of Tyrenium I could only afford ten tons, and I know the mine still had a bit more. It would be worth our while going back to pick that up, even if it's just a couple of tons."

Alyssa didn't react aversely, she just seemed to be mulling things over in her mind.

"Is that okay with you, honey?" he asked, not sure if she had heard him.

"Oh, sorry," she apologised. "I was just thinking about something I left behind there. Sure, a trip back sounds great!"

They headed up to the Bridge and Alyssa laid in a new course for Karron. She hit the button on her console and the large holographic display showed the winding path through the stars.

"There we go: eleven days, twenty-two hours," she said, satisfied that she couldn't reduce the journey time any further.

"That journey took me over four weeks in the Fool's Gold!" John exclaimed, marvelling at the difference his talented young companion and their powerful new ship had made.

"You're welcome!" Alyssa smiled at him, tipping an imaginary hat, making John laugh at her mimicry of him. "Permission to get under way, Commander?"

"Take us out of here, XO," John said, as he smiled at the beautiful young woman.

After getting permission to depart from Traffic Control, Alyssa grinned and flipped the switch to release the docking clamps. She clicked a couple more buttons and the engines throbbed with power, the massive cruiser slowly gliding out of the docking bay under her smooth and steady hand. The five-hundred-metre long behemoth pivoted elegantly, in a manoeuvre that seemed unnaturally graceful for a ship of that size, and then leapt forward as Alyssa engaged full drive power. They reached the Nav-beacon in what seemed like no time, before the cruiser eagerly clawed its way into hyper-warp.

"We better get back to Calara," John said, looking at the ship's chronometer. "Fourteen hours are nearly up."

"Can't wait to round out that lovely olive-toned tummy again, eh?" Alyssa asked with a teasing smile.

"You're such a vixen!" John exclaimed as he laughed. "You know I just want to make sure she's okay."

"I know, that's why I love you!" the beautiful blonde said, standing eagerly. "Come on, let's go see how sleeping beauty is doing."

They didn't have to wait much longer before Calara started to stir. Her eyes fluttered awake, and it took her a moment to realise where she was. When the events of last night began to flood back to her, she huddled into the covers, blushing with embarrassment.

"Hello there," Alyssa said, smiling at her warmly. "How are you feeling?"

"A bit thirsty," Calara mumbled, self conscious to find herself in Alyssa's bed.

As if on cue, John appeared with a chilled glass of water. "There you go, honey. Drink this, you'll feel a lot better," he said as he carefully handed it to her.

Calara took the glass and gulped down the water gratefully. Her throat was parched and the soothing chilled water felt amazing. As she finished drinking, a small drip of water fell from the condensation on the glass and landed on Calara's right breast, the cold water making her gasp as it slid down her warm skin.

"Let me get that for you," Alyssa offered, and she leaned forward to lick the water droplet off the Latina's breast with a salacious flourish of her tongue.

This caused Calara to gasp again, this time in shock at the brazen blonde's actions. The glass jerked in her hand, causing more water to drip, but this time on to her other olive-toned breast.

"Mmm, there's some for you as well, John," Alyssa pointed out helpfully.

John climbed on to the bed and looked into Calara's eyes as he moved forward to lick the water droplet from her other breast. Gradually, her shocked expression relaxed and she sighed contentedly as he continued to lick her skin with long, drawn out motions of his tongue. Alyssa moved back to join them and gently pulled down the covers, fully exposing the Latina's erect nipples, the hard buds begging to be kissed.

"Oh God!" Calara groaned helplessly, as John and his beautiful blonde assistant suckled on her nipples.

The contrast between their slightly different tongue techniques was driving her mad with lust. She held the backs of each of their heads firmly to her heaving breasts as she writhed under their ministrations. Her eyes squeezed tightly shut as she gasped and moaned in pleasure.

Alyssa began to kiss lower, moving steadily down the young brunette's body. She held John's gaze as she trailed kisses over the Latina's olive-toned stomach, her blue eyes lusty and suggestive. The gorgeous blonde moved nimbly between Calara's twisting legs and smoothly spread them open, exposing the girl's sex. Calara gasped in shock, but that quickly turned into helpless moans, as Alyssa ran her delicate tongue over the woman's labia.

The blonde began to lap at her clit with gentle strokes, and the brunette kissed John fervently as her senses were overloaded. Soon Alyssa's skilfully probing tongue had the lovely Latina arching her back as she came hard, clinging tightly to John. The couple let her ride out her orgasm, before they settled down on either side of her, holding her protectively between them. The lovely Latina could only shudder with the aftershocks, her chest rising and falling rapidly as she struggled to regain her breath.

"You look like you enjoyed that," John said to Calara, impressed by Alyssa's performance. His cock throbbed painfully, and he was very turned on from watching the stunning blonde teenager between her equally young friend's legs.

"That was so good; I've never come that hard before!" Calara gasped, staring at the two of them in amazement.

Alyssa gave the bewildered girl a gentle kiss. "You looked amazing when you came," she said softly.

Calara relaxed between the two and stifled a yawn. "I'm so sorry!" she apologised profusely.

"No need to apologise, honey, you've had a tough couple of weeks and your body needs rest to recover," John told her reassuringly.

"Would you like a nightcap before getting some more sleep?" Alyssa asked the brunette, who nodded tentatively in response, not exactly sure what the mischievous blonde meant.

"Great! This will make you feel so much better," Alyssa replied enthusiastically, and offered Calara her hand.

John watched the Latina follow the beautiful blonde trustingly, getting out of bed and standing at its edge facing her. Alyssa leaned forward and kissed her gently, her left hand reaching down to stroke the olive-skinned girl's firm bottom. The contrast of her lighter coloured hand on the darker skinned girl's buttock made John's cock throb urgently. Alyssa held her other hand out to him and then beckoned him forward.

Wondering what his adventurous young lover had in mind, John inched forward until he sat on the edge of the bed, his thighs spread wide to give the teenagers plenty of room to make out in front of him. He reached out with both hands, to cup a delightfully firm cheek with each. He loved the tautness of their teenage flesh, the way both of the bottoms yielded to the careful touch of his strong fingers.

Alyssa was momentarily distracted by the searching lips of the eager brunette standing in front of her. Kissing a woman was lovely, so gentle, so soft. She felt John's hand cupping her ass cheek and massaging her with a skilled touch. It got her even more aroused and she nearly turned around to mount him.

She remembered that they had to take care of the lovely Latina, so she broke away from Calara's gentle kisses and carefully guided the brunette to her knees in front of John. Dropping to her knees close behind the smaller girl, Calara's firm bottom felt warm and pliant against her as Alyssa snuggled in closely.

"No wonder John likes to fuck me in the ass so much, this feels amazing," Alyssa thought to herself lustily. She began to wonder what it must be

like, having a big hard cock that she could plunge into a receptive young woman this way.

She looked over Calara's shoulder to see that the eager brunette had wasted no time. Her hands rested lightly on John's thighs, the darker skin contrasting with his fairer colouring in a most exciting way. Calara's dark hair bobbed smoothly back and forth as she enveloped his cock in her mouth, and from the rhythmic way she was letting him glide into her throat, Alyssa realised that the Latina had succumbed to the effects of John's pre-cum.

John delighted in the feel of his broad head disappearing into Calara's grasping throat. She was a natural at this, and her full lips were soft and inviting as they eased their way down his shaft. His balls were sensitive and fully loaded, annoyed at missing their regular morning emptying. The orbs felt taut and packed to the brim, four orange-sized spheres swollen with spunk. He saw Alyssa leaning around to look at Calara's face, taking in her glazed eyes and then looking up to him, nodding eagerly.

The gorgeous golden-haired blonde moved her hands around Calara to stroke her tummy. The Latina's stomach muscles were well defined and toned, evidence of the athletic girl's dedication to physical fitness. Alyssa looked up at John and saw that his eyes were hooded with lust.

"She's ready for you," she said to him, hugging the brunette gently from behind. "Her toned little tummy feels so flat and empty. Are you going to be a good host and give her a big meal?"

He nodded, feeling tremendously excited and relishing the different feel of another lovely young girl servicing his length.

"That's good," Alyssa crooned softly. "I want to feel you fill up her belly," she added as she looked up at him with her piercing blue eyes. "Show me what I look like when I empty your balls."

John's breathing was getting laboured now. He could tell Alyssa was turning herself on with her lewd commentary as she was panting excitedly too. He closed his eyes for a moment and just focused on the rhythmic motion of Calara's lips, tongue, and throat as she slid up and down his length, massaging every inch of him.

It was like her body was eager for his cum, desperate to feel him filling her up. He looked down at the lovely brunette as she took him deep down her throat and started sucking insistently at his root. Seeing the girl's full lips suckling at him was the final trigger, and he cradled her head gently in his hands as his orgasm overtook him.

"Ahh!" he groaned with satisfaction as his balls began to unload their contents. This orgasm wasn't like the frenzied ones with Alyssa, he felt more in control; it was a long and drawn release, rather than an explosion of pleasure.

He watched Alyssa gently cupping Calara's slender neck with her right hand, her delicate fingers feeling his cock jerk in the tight confines of the brunette's throat. The other hand was rested on that slim olilve hued stomach, as it began to rapidly inflate with his spunk.

Alyssa could feel John's cock throbbing under her fingertips and she imagined the thick ropes of jism being blasted into the Latina's slim tummy. Her other hand rubbed Calara's stomach gently, as though encouraging it to expand and make room for all that delicious cum. She moaned with excitement as her slim little waistline was blown outwards, and eventually she had to cradle the semen-swollen tummy with both hands to feel it's engorged majesty. She experienced John's lengthy, controlled climax and joined him with her own orgasm as she embraced the quivering brunette.

Eventually John was drained dry, and he collapsed back on the bed with a satisfied sigh, his spent cock sliding easily out of Calara's throat and mouth. The brunette sat in a serene daze, her thighs spread wide to make

room for her bloated belly, while her hands stroked the sperm-packed sphere protectively. Alyssa followed Calara's hands with her own, marvelling at the way the brunette's stretched stomach could handle such an enormous load. She felt a slight protrusion in the middle of her swollen abdomen, and realised the girl's belly button had popped out to make extra room for all John's spunk.

The statuesque blonde rose to her feet and helped the comatose brunette to rise too. John reached over to help and they positioned the Latina so she was lying comfortably on the bed. They sighed contentedly and it didn't take long before they joined Calara in her nap.

\*\*\*

Four hours later, Calara awoke from another deep and restful slumber. For the first time since her capture, she had been untroubled by the recurring nightmare and she felt well rested and alert. She was momentarily surprised to see she was flanked by John and Alyssa, who were still fast asleep, until she began to remember some of what had happened earlier.

She tried to sit up, but found it significantly more difficult than normal. When she looked down at the curious weight she felt at her waist, she was astonished to see that her tummy was rounded, looking like she was a few months pregnant. She gaped at her gently swollen belly with wide eyes, rubbing a hand over it experimentally. Her skin felt firm and taut under the probing touch of her fingers, but stroking it like this felt wonderful. She toyed with waking her bedmates to ask them what had happened to her, but they looked so peaceful, she let them sleep.

Calara carefully climbed out of the bed, managing to avoid waking either of them. She walked into their bathroom feeling full of energy and with a spring in her step, despite the extra weight she was carrying in her belly. She looked longingly at the gorgeous bathtub, wishing she could use it

herself and then giggled to herself quietly, knowing that Alyssa would insist on it.

She paced over to the big mirror as she steeled herself to look at her reflection, worrying how her swollen nose would look today. Her anxious face peered back at her in the mirror and Calara was astonished to see that her nose was fully healed, looking just as it always had before it'd been broken. She twisted her head from side to side to look at it from different angles, but it was back to its cute former self, with no swelling in sight.

The Latina sighed happily and stretched her arms above her head without thinking. She suddenly flinched, anticipating the sharp pain such movement would normally trigger. Calara felt nothing though and she tentatively tilted and rotated her upper body from side to side, astonished to find there was no pain from her ribs at all. Her toned tummy was looking significantly more rounded than normal however and she sighed, thinking that perhaps all the bed rest must have wreaked havoc with her waistline. There were definite patchy spots in her memories from last night, so she guessed they must have just had a really heavy meal late at night, and she had overdone it.

Finally, she twisted her shoulders to try and look at her back. She wasn't sure, as she couldn't see clearly, but the welts and lacerations looked much less red and angry. She walked back to the bedroom, surprising herself at her confidence and feeling no sense of embarrassment at her nudity.

Alyssa had awoken and she watched Calara as she walked confidently from the bathroom and climbed back on the bed. The brunette smiled at Alyssa and she moved in for a cuddle when the blonde teen opened her arms in invitation.

Alyssa rolled with Calara so that the brunette was lying on her back and then she leaned over her, checking her nose closely. "You look so much

better!" she exclaimed with some satisfaction. "Please turn over so I can see your back."

Calara rolled over obediently to lie on her tummy, and she could feel her friend's fingers tracing lightly over her back. "Another day or two and these will be gone!" Alyssa declared, sounding overjoyed.

Calara rolled over onto her back again. "How?" she asked simply. She glanced to the side and saw that John had awoken too and was watching them both intently.

"It's probably simpler to show you something first before we explain," John said, his voice quiet and soothing. "It'll make it easier to understand."

He leaned over to the bedside table and picked up a remote. When he moved to lie down again, Calara urged him to sit in the middle of the bed, so that she could cuddle him on one side, with Alyssa snuggled in on the other. It felt right somehow and the brunette shared a contented smile with the blonde across his chest.

John couldn't help smiling too as he wrapped an arm around each lovely teenager. He passed the remote over to Alyssa as his hands were now full of nubile young women. Alyssa looked up at him knowingly and searched through the data dump from the Fool's Gold for the right files. She never ceased to amaze him with her uncanny ability to know his every desire and he marvelled at how incredibly perceptive she was.

After a few moment's spent searching through files, a holographic image appeared at the foot of the bed. It showed a delightfully nude Alyssa, standing confidently with a beaming smile on her face, in all her busty athletic glory.

"You recognise that gorgeous girl, I'm sure," John said, glancing down at Calara.

She nodded and grinned at the blonde across his chest.

A second image flashed up beside the first and John asked gently, "But have you seen her before?"

This new image had been taken over a month ago, the day that John had first met Alyssa. It showed a ghostly pale, petite waif, looking malnourished and nervous.

"Who is that?" Calara asked, her heart full of compassion for the poor girl in the image.

"That was me," Alyssa said in a hushed voice, suddenly sounding vulnerable.

Calara snorted in disbelief, her mind refusing to accept what was obviously some odd joke. However, she went quiet when she noticed something... the eyes. Those same piercing blue eyes stared out from each image. Calara moved out of John's embrace and crawled to the foot of the bed to take a closer look at the images. Now she had a familiar point of reference, she could see it was true, as she looked back and forth between the two images. Similar nose, mouth, jawline, ears, all just made more lovely and perfect.

"How?" she asked, feeling bewildered, before turning and sitting down to face John and Alyssa.

"His cum," Alyssa explained. "I made a deal with John where I offered to service him whenever he wanted. After a few weeks of swallowing his loads, I went from that, to that," she said, pointing at the two images.

"But that's impossible!" Calara gasped, her mind balking at the idea.

"Is it?" Alyssa insisted. "Your nose is fully healed after only two days. I bet the medical staff told you it would take a few weeks for the swelling to fully subside."

Calara reached up to her previously broken nose self-consciously, before stopping and nodding her head in confirmation. She sat and pondered this startling revelation.

"So if I keep swallowing his cum, I'll end up changing to look like you?" she asked, sounding fascinated.

"No, you'll probably look like you. Just a slightly taller, bigger busted, more perfect version of your current athletic self I suspect," Alyssa theorised, studying the lovely brunette.

"Probably? That's not very reassuring," Calara said, smiling warmly at her friend.

"You're happy with the results so far though, right?" Alyssa asked.

Calara nodded enthusiastically, before pausing to look down at her rounded belly. "Is that what this is?" she asked in wonder, as she ran her hands over the gentle curve of her abdomen.

"Yes, you have a stomach full of John's cum right now. That's what triggers this healing," Alyssa explained, reaching out to gently caress Calara's tummy.

"Are you mad at us?" John asked with concern, worried how the lovely young Latina might react.

"I could never be mad at either of you," the pretty brunette said emphatically, making eye contact with each of them in turn, so they could see her sincerity.

John spread his arms wide, welcoming her to join them again, and Calara grinned at him as she bounced over the covers to snuggle into the crook of his arm. They settled back on the bed as Alyssa turned off the Holo-images, and then curled up cosily beside him. John realised that his happy couple with Alyssa had now become a happy trio with Calara. He looked down at the blonde, wondering if she was going to be ok with the dramatic change in their living arrangements. The last thing he wanted to do was upset the beautiful young woman, who he considered to be his soulmate.

Alyssa stared up at him with her bright blue eyes, as though looking into his soul. Her loving smile spoke of happiness and contentment and she linked hands with Calara before resting them lightly on his chest over his heart.

"Luckiest son of a bitch in the galaxy," John thought with delight, as he hugged them both.

# Three Square Meals Ch. 09 – Living the dream

The trio lay cuddled together comfortably in bed. John and Alyssa were both greatly relieved that Calara had taken their surprising revelation so well.

"There is one thing though..." Calara said tentatively after a few moments.

"What is it Calara?" John asked, his voice tinged with concern.

"I still haven't seen the Bridge yet! I'm not going to be much good as a Tactical Officer if you don't let me out of the bedroom" she said, grinning impishly.

Alyssa's musical laughter was joined by John's baritone chuckles. "Okay honey, we can go now if you want?"

Calara could barely contain her excitement as they got dressed. John smiled at her eagerness and stood politely by the door, gesturing for them to proceed before following after them. The lovely teenagers headed down the corridor to the elevator, chatting animatedly, and he admired the enticing sway of their hips as they walked. They stood together in the lift, their chatter falling quiet as Calara's anticipation grew palpable.

The door to the elevator whirred quietly open and they walked out on to the bridge together for the first time.

"Wow!" Calara gasped, her big brown eyes like saucers as she took in the large oval shaped bridge.

Alyssa darted nimbly up the illuminated steps to the command podium and sat in the Executive Officers chair. She pressed a couple of buttons on her console and looked down and to her right, watching the Tactical

Station as it burst into life. Two long curving consoles began to fill with a welcoming glow, as one control panel after another lit up.

John walked up to the awestruck Latina's side and rested his hand reassuringly on her shoulder. "Take your post, Lieutenant," he said to her quietly.

Calara turned to face him as she came out of her reverie. Her sharp salute and the intense look in her eyes silently conveying her deep respect for him. "At once, Commander!"

Alyssa watched the two and rolled her eyes. She smiled, but stayed quiet, letting them have their moment.

John climbed the steps of the podium and sat in his Command Chair, breaking into a smile as he watched Calara eagerly stride towards her new station. She sat in the elaborate Tactical chair and pressed a sequence of buttons on the armrest, powering up her seat. Holographic targeting arrays sprang to life in front of her, as two illuminated controls slowly rose from the armrests.

Alyssa had brought the Holo-reader with her and she walked down to the Tactical Station to offer it to Calara, just in case she needed it to learn how to use the controls. The brunette politely declined and so Alyssa just stood and watched intrigued as the brunette gripped the arm rest controls confidently with each hand.

"This is just like the simulator back at the Academy!" the brunette exclaimed, her eyes bright and alert.

She pressed a couple of buttons and large holographic images appeared in the middle of the bridge, displaying tactical information for all to see. An image of the Invictus rotated slowly before them, looking sleek and menacing. Calara flipped a safety switch and then pushed a foreboding looking red button on the top of her right controller. Armoured panels on

the hull of the Invictus began to slide away, revealing the hidden arsenal beneath.

"Weapons armed, Commander," Calara stated, following standard Terran Federation protocol.

John leaned forward, studying the holographic representation of the Invictus. "I'd like a weapons check please, Lieutenant."

Calara pressed a button on her console and dozens of stubby Gatling lasers spun up, the image of the Invictus showing their many overlapping fields of fire. "This is the laser defence grid, to take out missiles and fighters," she explained for Alyssa's benefit, John already familiar with the assault cruiser's capabilities.

"Laser Cannons," Calara continued, as the overhead image displayed the broad fire arcs of the turreted laser weapons. "They're medium range weapons, designed to take out lightly armoured targets."

She pressed another button and the rotating image in the centre of the bridge showed the six forward-facing Beam Lasers, each barrel over thirty metres in length. "Those are our Beam Laser arrays," Calara stated, as she cycled through the massive firepower at her fingertips. "They've got long range and are powerful enough to punch through heavy shielding!"

"Finally..." she said, with a gleam in her eye. "We've got the Invictus' biggest guns."

She cycled through to the last setting and two pairs of two-hundred-metre-long magnetic rails were highlighted on the glowing holographic image. It was obvious that the ship had been built around these enormous weapons, with power converters and ordnance feeding rooms built adjacent to them.

"These are the Mass Drivers, for when you really want to fuck something up!" Calara exclaimed, her youthful exuberance momentarily getting the better of her military professionalism.

"Want to perform a fire test, Lieutenant?" John asked, the young brunette's enthusiasm proving contagious.

Calara nodded eagerly. "Absolutely!"

John turned to look at the beautiful blonde. "XO, any asteroid belts nearby?"

Alyssa strode purposefully back up to her console and began searching through the systems closest to their current location. Getting caught up in their excitement, she replied, "There's an uninhabited asteroid field in this system, Commander!"

John nodded his approval. "That sounds perfect. Lay in a course please."

A short while later, the Invictus dropped out of hyper warp, the exposed gun barrels looking like teeth bared in a snarl as it prowled closer to its unwitting victims. The unsuspecting asteroids drifted and rotated slowly, as though performing an intricate dance with one another.

Calara focused intently on the targeting grids in front of her. "Firing Beam Lasers!" she said excitedly as her finger caressed the trigger on the right control. Six lances of coruscating energy blasted outwards and sliced an enormous tumbling asteroid in half. The chunks separated cleanly, each chunk glowing from the heat of the incision.

"Main guns!" she cried out, as she cycled through the weapons and unloaded the Mass Drivers.

The Invictus trembled with the recoil, as the huge magnetic coils accelerated the shells to hyper-warp velocity. Two sets of massive impacts

punched into each of the split asteroid chunks causing spectacular craters, before the shells detonated a second later. The two halves of the asteroid detonated into a thousand pieces, devastated by the colossal explosions.

"Laser Cannons!" Calara gasped, as the turreted laser weapons began to track and vaporise the larger asteroid fragments in a cascade of bright energy blasts.

"Point defence!" she concluded, as ribbons of laser fire erupted around the Invictus, the Gatling lasers opening up on the pitiful remnants of the once massive asteroid.

Alyssa watched in awe as the destructive power of the Cruiser was fully unleashed. Having never before witnessed firepower of this magnitude she found it scared her more than a little. She was lost in her thoughts as she looked out over the hazy field of gravel, all that remained of the once huge tumbling asteroid.

Calara's eyes shone with excitement as she grinned up at John, looking for his approval. He loved how vibrant and full of life she looked, as she thrilled at the chance to be in control of such a powerful ship. "Lieutenant, to my Ready Room," he ordered brusquely.

"Yes Commander!" she gasped excitedly, as she practically ran to join him as he jogged down the steps from the Command Podium. They entered the adjoining room together, sharing lustful looks.

Alyssa's quiet contemplation was broken by the sound of excited feminine gasps and the rhythmic slap of flesh upon flesh. Coming back to full awareness, she laughed to herself as she placed the Holo-reader on her console and followed its instructions, powering down the weapons and resealing the armoured hull of the Invictus. Bringing up the Navigation display next, she activated their FTL drive, launching them into hyper-warp and back on their previous course. Once she was satisfied that everything was in order, she got up and followed the lusty noises coming

from the Commander's Ready Room, unzipping the top of her form fitting jumpsuit as she went.

She found Calara kneeling on one of the sofas, grasping the back tightly in her hands. Her mouth hung open as she panted lustily, her head pulled back by John's strong grip on her long dark hair. The beautiful Latina was nude and her skin glistened with sweat as John pounded in and out of her yielding body.

John's other hand was resting on the taut, olive-hued skin of Calara's right ass cheek. He had thrust his entire length into her, right up to the Quad and pulled back before driving forward again powerfully. The panting brunette moaned as the broad crown of his weighty cock pushed deep into her body once again, stretching her pussy wide open to accommodate him. She let out a grunt as the invading monster forced its way deep into her belly, until its throbbing head was cradled snugly in her womb.

Alyssa stepped over the hastily discarded piles of clothes and walked up to their sides, running her hand under the panting brunette's body. Her delicate touch felt the warm bulge in the Latina's otherwise toned, flat stomach.

"I can feel you deep in her womb, John" she purred, gently massaging his throbbing head as he held himself still, deep in Calara's body. "Does it feel good breaking in another tight teenager?"

"Uh-huh, she's gripping me like a fist!" he grunted, as he pulled back and drove forward again.

Calara cried out with pleasure, the innermost places of her body yielding to her man.

"How about you honey?" Alyssa asked the lovely brunette. "Does it feel good?"

Calara tried to nod, but was unable to, what with her head pulled back and her body held so tightly in place. "His cock is so big... never had anything so deep in me before..." she groaned helplessly.

Alyssa got down on her knees and then ducked under John's swaying balls between his parted legs. He had the brunette's thighs spread wide open as he thrust away, so it meant that Alyssa had plenty of room to manoeuvre. She slid under Calara's body facing upwards, and arched her back so she could support John's throbbing balls on her big firm tits. Now she was at the perfect angle to see where his mighty girthed shaft had spread the Latina much wider than she ever had been before. The beautiful blonde lapped away at the tightly stretched skin, making it easier for her friend to take the solid pounding she was receiving.

Calara moaned when feeling the soft, wet delicate touch on her overheated pussy. "That feels so good! Please don't stop!"

Her snug grip on John's cock had been heating her up with the friction of his steady thrusts, so the blonde's tongue felt cool and soothing on her taut skin. She could only screw her eyes tightly shut and wail out her orgasm as Alyssa lapped gently at her clit, the sensitive little organ throbbing uncontrollably.

John pushed inside the lovely brunette, enjoying the feel of her rippling pussy as it flexed along his length. He held still as far inside her as he could go and stopped to relish the rhythmic grip of her tight young body. "That's it, come hard for me, gorgeous!"

Alyssa backed off for a moment and as soon as Calara came down from one orgasm, the blonde's rapidly moving tongue was back and licking her clit again. The Latina could only scream with pleasure as her sensitive body reacted to Alyssa's unrelenting mouth and she writhed helplessly as she came hard a second time.

John held the spasming brunette tightly in place and enjoyed the sucking motions of her tight little pussy, as Alyssa made her come over and over again. As Calara sobbed through her fourth continuous climax, he felt Alyssa's tongue lick and caress his balls, as though encouraging them in their efforts. The stimulation from both the provocative teenagers was too much for him to resist and he felt his quad tense up as they prepared to unload.

"Oh fuck!" he groaned, pumping the athletic teenager full of his cum.

Calara yelped as she felt his release, screwing her eyes closed as she felt every jet of sperm fired directly into her womb. Alyssa had the perfect view to watch John's massive cock throbbing purposefully as it delivered its precious cargo. She cradled the brunette's rapidly expanding abdomen, as it provided a warm home for his hefty load of spunk.

"That's it, beautiful girl," she murmured in encouragement. "Help him empty those big balls!"

Eventually John's quad stopped twitching where they lay cradled on Alyssa's chest and she gently moved out from under them. John helped Calara flop down on the sofa, her breath ragged as she recovered from the relentless chain of orgasms. He collapsed on to the sofa beside her, resting his hand possessively on the taut skin of her olive-toned stomach.

Alyssa slid between the brunette's limp legs and gently hooked them over her shoulders. She darted him a wicked smile and said, "Massage her tummy for me please, John?"

She tentatively licked the exhausted teenager's swollen labia, while John's hand moved in firm but gentle circles over the girl's rounded belly. Calara's body relaxed enough to gradually release his load and Alyssa sucked away at the brunette's pussy, enjoying the heady taste of his sweet spunk as she filled her stomach with his delicious cum.

Eventually Calara's laden tummy had slimmed-down to its usual svelte shape and Alyssa rose from between the Latina's thighs, her cheeks bulging. She moved forward on to the sofa so she was kneeling astride the blissed out brunette and cupped her face in her hands as she leaned in for a kiss. John could see Calara's throat bob as she greedily swallowed the mouthful of cum Alyssa passed to her.

"Was the Commander ready for that?" Alyssa asked him with a lazy, well satisfied smile on her face.

John laughed good naturedly. "No honey, you're full of surprises!"

They eventually regrouped in the shower, with Alyssa and John helping the exhausted Latina get squeaky clean. They took her back to their bedroom and the trio settled in for the night.

The next few days established a pleasant routine for the crew of the Invictus. Alyssa wanted to work on her marksmanship, so she spent most of her time training at the firing range. Calara was keen to spend more time getting familiar with her tactical station, so she spent a lot of her day on the Bridge.

John used to spend most of his time aboard the Fool's Gold cleaning and performing maintenance, but the Invictus had a suite of cleaning robots who scrubbed the floors meticulously clean. Even for someone with his exceptionally low tolerance for dirt, he had to admit that they did a phenomenal job of keeping the ship spotless. That meant John had a lot of free time to spend at the pool, which he thoroughly enjoyed. He had kept himself in pretty good shape by being so active on his freighter, but muscles he hadn't really used in years soon reminded him that he could do a better job with his fitness.

The highlight of his day was meeting up with the girls for meal times. They would chat and get to know each other better as they relaxed in the Officers' Lounge. John enjoyed having long, interesting conversations with

Alyssa, as she didn't have her mouth full for a change. That honour belonged to Calara. Alyssa would stroke the girl's thick dark brown hair lovingly, as the beautiful Latina knelt between John's legs and bobbed her head in his lap. Calara was getting three massive meals a day and she loved running her hands over her cum packed belly after he topped her up. She marvelled at how her malleable body was able to expand to hold such a gut-busting feast and how her stomach reverted to its prior toned self a few hours later.

A week raced by and one morning Alyssa and John had a surprise for Calara. As soon as she was awake, they called her in to their walk-in-wardrobe and ushered her over to stand nude in the middle of the room. From here, the cunningly designed mirrors allowed the person in their focus to view themselves from all angles.

"Your scars... they're all gone!" Alyssa exclaimed in delight.

Calara twisted around to look at her body in the reflections, staring at her body in amazement. The swelling on her nose had cleared up completely a week before, as had the bruising around her ribs, but the brutal wounds from the cyborg's whip were the biggest shock. While those lacerations had taken much longer to heal, the doctors at Port Heracles had predicted that her back would bear permanent scarring. She gaped at her reflection, astonished to see only beautiful, unblemished skin.

"Thank you so much!" she gushed, her eyes welling up with tears. "The scars... now they're gone, it's like you've wiped away all those horrible events from my past too!"

Alyssa glided over to the Latina and enfolded Calara in a tight hug, her own eyes filling with tears at the heart-warming moment. John was only a step behind in moving to embrace his grateful young lover, when he suddenly stopped. He stepped back instead so that he could view both the nude teenagers clearly.

"Take another look at your body, Calara," he prompted gently. "Compare yourself with Alyssa..."

The brunette wiped away the tears from her eyes and looked a bit embarrassed, knowing she was nowhere near as beautiful as the ravishing blonde. She reluctantly took another look in the mirrors as she stood beside Alyssa's, readying herself for the hopelessly unfair comparison.

"Oh, my goodness!" she blurted out, eyes widening in shock.

Alyssa was very slightly taller at five-foot-nine compared to the Latina's new five-foot-eight. Other than their distinctive, beautiful faces and their strikingly different skin tone, their youthful bodies were almost identical. They each had a set of large, firm 32D breasts, a slim waist and flared hips that resulted in a breathtaking hourglass figure. Their bottoms were round and pert, perfect globes that sat at the top of long, finely muscled, elegant legs. Their skin was perfectly smooth and free of all blemishes of any kind.

John walked around them both, whistling appreciatively as Calara modelled her gorgeous dusky hued figure in the mirrors.

"You're both stunningly beautiful," he said to the two teens, delivering his final verdict.

Alyssa smiled at him lovingly and glided over to stand on his right side, matched in her movements by Calara who moved to his left. They stood on tiptoe and each planted a tender kiss on one of his cheeks. He looked at his reflection, at the man smiling in wonder at the ravishing young women leaning in to softly kiss his face. He managed to tear his eyes away to watch the girls, as they walked back to the bedroom hand in hand, looking over their shoulders at him coyly.

John recognised that look and so did his cock. It rose to full hardness, eager to be pushed into the warm and welcoming embrace of the female

flesh presented before him. He lost sight of them for a moment as they glided into the bedroom, so he strode after them to follow. He found the luscious girls standing by the side of the bed, waiting for him. He walked up to them, his heart beginning to beat faster as his body prepared for the activity to come. The beautiful teenagers were taller now than when he first met either of them, but at six-foot-two, he still towered over them both.

He leaned down and gently kissed the exquisitely beautiful blonde, before switching to the gorgeously exotic brunette. His eager hands moved to caress each of their pert buttocks, their taut, wonderfully firm young flesh yielding to the strong and insistent grip of his massaging fingers. Both their hips began to writhe as they responded to his touch, their youthful bodies instinctively knowing that they were about to be used.

John broke away from Calara's lovely soft lips and both girls looked up at him in adoration as they waited to see what he wanted to do next. He used his firm hold on their bottoms to gently push the two teenagers together, until their toned tummies were touching each other. From his vantage point above them, he could see four big tits below him. When they were pushed together, their nipples disappeared from view as the proud breasts swelled against each other. It was a breathtaking sight that made his cock throb excitedly.

Alyssa looked over at Calara and parted her lips, running her tongue over them to make them nice and moist. The brunette sighed happily and leaned forward to brush her own soft lips against the blonde's. The beautiful young women kissed passionately, communicating the love they felt for one another with each darting tongue and every breathy moan into each other's mouths.

John could only stare in wonder at the two gorgeous girls he cared more about than anyone in the galaxy. After all those long lonely years spent on his freighter, to have found not just one, but two incredible women who wanted to share their lives with him felt like an incredible stroke of luck.

Alyssa turned to glance at him out of the corner of her eye, her mouth lifting into a smile as she continued to kiss Calara.

John returned her smile and slid his hands lower beneath their cheeks, gently caressed a finger across each girl's clit and drawing excited gasps from the both. He stroked them at a steady, insistent pace and could see the girls panting into each other's mouths as they responded to his skilful touch. Their buttocks trembled against his wrists and they moaned helplessly as he brought them both nearer to orgasm.

Calara and Alyssa stopped kissing for a moment and stared into each other's eyes as their man brought them closer to a shared climax. Their pupils were dilated with arousal and they panted lustily as John got them even more turned on. Their breathing grew more laboured as their heaving chests rubbed together, teasing erect nipples in a way that had them both moaning with excitement.

Combined with the intimate massage from John's fingers, the beautiful teenagers were powerless to resist the crashing orgasms that overwhelmed them. They hugged each other tight as they came long and hard, trembling together and crying out in ecstasy. John eased his finger back and gently slid them up inside each girl's tightly grasping pussy, enjoying the feel of their clutching grip as they rode out their climaxes.

Once their trembling had subsided, the two girls eased back and sighed contentedly as they looked into each other's lusty, heavy lidded gaze. They pulled John's head lower so that they faced each of his pointed ears. They began to whisper quietly in each ear, seductive, arousing things.

"We're going to make you feel so good… " Alyssa purred, planting soft kisses on his earlobes.

"I want to please you, fulfil your every desire..." Calara murmured, her breath tickling him and sending a shiver up his spine.

"Two beautiful, lusty teenagers eager to obey you... are you going to take charge?" Alyssa crooned, her hand drifting down to grasp his throbbing shaft.

"We'll do anything you want!" Calara moaned, pressing herself against him and squashing her breasts against his chest.

John could barely contain his excitement, as he gently eased his buried fingers from each girl and then traced his hands up their slender, toned backs. He placed each hand on top of their heads and applied gentle downwards pressure, letting them know what he expected next.

The gorgeous teenagers looked up at him as they sank to their knees on either side of his engorged member. They pushed their proud breasts closely together and leaned forward to lap obediently at either side of his throbbing shaft. John's eyes nearly rolled into the back of his head at the feeling of their velvety soft tongues, as they stroked up and down his length.

"You're such good girls!" he groaned, gently but firmly holding them in place.

The girls tried to kiss each other around him, but his wide girth meant that their efforts were futile and their questing tongues just massaged him delightfully. He cupped both of their heads in his hands, feeling their wonderfully soft hair beneath his fingers.

The girls glided up and down his length in perfect sync with each other. their eyes meeting over the male tumescence between their lips, as they relished pleasuring their man at the same time. They eventually separated so that one was kneeling in front of him with her mouth over his engorged head, while the other lapped and caressed his quad, reassuring his aching balls that relief was soon on its way. They switched positions a few times and John's cock twitched and throbbed at their enthusiastic attentions. It

was becoming too much for him to take however, so he held both of their heads in place and got them to look up at him.

"On the bed, now!" he commanded.

The teenagers thrilled at his authoritative tone and moved quickly and gracefully to obey. Calara lay on her back, her head towards him, her mouth open invitingly. Alyssa swung lithely over the supine Latina and rested her big breasts on her friend's yielding bosom.

"She's ready for you John, come and use her mouth!" Alyssa invited him lustily.

John shuffled forward, his painfully hard cock leading the way as he pushed his broad head between Calara's welcoming lips. She had become an expert at deep-throating him now and was able to take his throat-stuffing thrust with ease. The Latina felt him push deep inside her body, until her lips were wrapped around the base of his shaft. She looked up to see his heavy quad swinging overhead and moaned hungrily, as John began to fuck her face.

"Does that feel good baby?" Alyssa purred, kissing Calara's stuffed throat. The Latina managed an imperceptible nod, unable to reply with John's cock impaling her.

As John rocked back and forth, Alyssa glanced up at him and smiled. "Don't worry, we'll empty those big balls for you..."

He placed his hands on her head, stroking her silky blonde locks as he gazed into her enchanting blue eyes.

"Would you like to use me too?" Alyssa murmured, biting her lower lip coyly.

John could only reply with a terse nod. He groaned and pulled his weighty cock from Calara's clutching throat, before placing the angrily throbbing head between Alyssa's flushed lips. He held her head in place with both hands as he pushed into her mouth and right down her clutching throat in one glorious thrust.

"Mmm," Alyssa moaned appreciatively as her nose brushed against John's stomach and her chin grazed the top of his balls. She could see Calara's lovely dark-haired head bobbing beneath her as the helpful Latina lapped at his quad.

John was seeing stars as the girls worked their magic on him. He couldn't hold out any longer.

"Aaaahh!" he bellowed as he thrust himself deeply into the accommodating blonde and began to fire long strings of semen straight down her throat and into her waiting stomach. After a half dozen belly expanding blasts, he pulled out of her throat, leaving a final spurt in her eagerly sucking mouth, before moving his jerking cock down to push into the waiting brunette. He slid up to the balls inside her yielding body and rode out the last of his orgasm filling her stomach with his cream.

John shuddered, before he withdrew his wilting prick and collapsed on the bed on his back. "Oh fuck, that was amazing!" he panted as he gasped for breath.

The girls smiled at each other in contentment, feeling their sperm-packed bellies pressing together.

Alyssa leaned down to give Calara a tender kiss. "We make such a great team," she said lovingly to the brunette, enjoying the satisfyingly full feeling in her stomach.

Calara nodded her heartfelt agreement and sighed happily as she looked up at the beautiful blonde. The girls separated and moved to flank John,

snuggling into him as he put his arms around them both and hugged them close.

\*\*\*

The next couple of days proved uneventful until one afternoon, John persuaded Alyssa to come with him down to the pool and begin to learn how to swim. Alyssa trusted John unreservedly but she was still scared of the water, so it was with some trepidation that she followed him into the gym. They had only just started to get undressed when a warning alarm began to flash on John's watch.

"Saved by the bell!" Alyssa grinned at John, zipping up her top again.

He smiled back and pressed a button on his watch, a hologram of Calara's lovely face appearing before him.

"What is it, Calara?" he asked, frowning at her anxious expression.

"Long range sensors are picking up a distress beacon, Commander!"

John and Alyssa's eyes met and a look flashed between them. "Was this real or another trap?" they both wondered at the same time. They darted out of the gym and jogged to the elevator, dodging around a pair of cleaning robots as the automatons performed their duties in the hall. A few moments later they stepped out of the lift onto the bridge and mounted the command podium, taking two illuminated steps at a time.

"What do we know so far, Lieutenant?" John asked as he sat in his Command Chair.

"I'm picking up what looks like four ships, but three of them aren't broadcasting any transponder codes. The last one is a heavy freighter," the brunette reported, her tone professional.

"See if you can contact the freighter, Calara" John replied. "Alyssa, plot an intercept course."

The girl's leapt into action, swiftly following his commands. The beautiful blonde was the first to respond. "Course laid in, John, three minutes until we're in range."

John nodded his understanding as the Invictus surged forwards, as though eager at the opportunity for action.

"Commander, the freighter is hailing us," Calara warned. "The distress beacon is coming from them."

John pushed a button on his console to answer the hail from the freighter. "This is John Blake, Commander of the Cruiser Invictus. What's the situation?" he asked tersely.

"Oh, thank God!" exclaimed a relieved voice, as the panicked face of a middle-aged man appeared on the overhead view screen. "We're being attacked by pirates... slavers I think!"

"We'll be with you in two minutes; hold tight until then," John reassured the freighter captain, ending the conversation.

"Weapons hot, Lieutenant!" John ordered, his strong unwavering voice filling both girls with confidence.

Calara activated the ship's weaponry and the armoured panels on the Invictus slid open, baring its fangs. The ship was thirsty for blood. They surged forward, the cruiser's massive engines throbbing with power and Calara was able to pick up more information on the pirates as they closed in.

"A Lexon class destroyer and two bulk corvettes, Sir!" she exclaimed, hitting a button to bring up the holographic Tactical Map in the centre of the Bridge.

The three marauding pirate ships were clearly displayed on the map as they pursued the limping heavy freighter. Although the smaller vessels were older ship models, they were still in surprisingly good condition for pirate craft. They'd all been painted black, with red stripes down the side. The freighter was a larger Atlas-class merchant ship and John could see its rear was pockmarked with numerous craters, where the pirates had tried to disable the engines with weapons fire.

"XO raise shields," John commanded, before hitting a button that would hail the pirate ships. "Pirate vessels, cease all hostile actions and power down. Follow these orders and you will be spared."

"Go fuck yourself, jerkwad!" came the thoughtful reply from the pirate captain in the destroyer.

John shrugged to himself. If they wanted to sign their own death warrant, so be it. "Fire at will Lieutenant!" he ordered.

Calara was focusing intently on the holographic targeting matrix in front of her and her finger carefully depressed the trigger on the right control. Six scintillating beams of energy punched into the destroyer, overloading it's shields in a single devastating strike and following through to shear off the rear quarter of the ship. Without its engines to hold it steady, the destroyer began to slowly tumble forward in a roll, still maintaining its previous momentum. The Invictus bore down inexorably on the bulk corvettes as they began evasive manoeuvres, desperate to escape from the lethal warship.

"Remaining ships attempting to withdraw, Commander. What are your orders?" Calara asked, turning in her seat to look up at the Command Podium.

"You know the penalty for piracy, Lieutenant," John replied firmly. His sombre voice sounded their death knell. "Finish them..."

Calara nodded grimly and the corvettes came under attack from a withering hail of Laser Cannon blasts. Their weak shields managed to deflect the first couple of impacts, but they were totally outclassed by the military grade laser weapons and soon collapsed. The fleeing pirate hulls lit up from the concentrated firepower and both ships exploded practically simultaneously.

Alyssa brought the Invictus around so that it was directly astern of the crippled destroyer. She could see escape pods blasting clear of the ship, as the pirates frantically deserted the doomed craft. Calara caressed the trigger and the beam lasers cored through the length of the destroyer, causing the front of the ship to explode outwards, scattering glowing debris in a wide arc.

"Excellent work, ladies," John said, nodding in satisfaction. He hit a button on his console to hail the freighter.

"Thank you, Commander!" the merchant captain said as his grateful face filled the viewscreen. "You saved us all!"

"My crew did the hard work, but we appreciate your thanks," John replied affably. "Can you make it to your destination from here?"

"We took a little damage, but nothing too serious. We should be fine from here. Thanks once again!" the merchant said, giving them a friendly wave.

Calara deactivated the ship's weapons and the Invictus' armoured hull resealed itself, the cruiser satiated for the moment. Alyssa adjusted their course for the minor detour and the ship leapt into hyper-warp once again.

"Girls, to my Ready Room please," John requested quietly.

The two teenagers got up and walked to the Commander's private room, both somewhat lost in their thoughts. John entered the room first and waved them over to one of the comfortable sofas and he moved to join them, sitting opposite.

"You handled yourselves like seasoned veterans. I'm very proud of you both," he commended the young women. Concerned how they would react after their first combat, he leaned forward and continued gently, "More importantly though, how are you both feeling?"

"The corvettes could each crew twenty people and the destroyer over fifty," Calara said in a grim voice. Her voice sounded leaden as the enormity of her actions began to sink in and she started to tremble. "I'm probably responsible for the deaths of nearly a hundred people..."

"You've seen first-hand what pirates are like," John countered. He moved to sit beside the brunette and wrapped his arm around her shoulder to comfort her."You should have no regrets about bringing scum like that to justice. Think of it more like wiping out vermin."

"More importantly..." Alyssa interjected, hugging the Latina too. "There were thirty-four crewmen on board that heavy freighter; good people who had never harmed anyone. You helped save them all from a horrible fate."

Calara took a deep breath and let it out slowly, nodding her head as she contemplated the logic behind their words. She straightened and smiled at them both, feeling a newfound sense of pride in her actions.

"How about we go have a drink?" John suggested. "To celebrate our first good deed in the Invictus."

Calara and Alyssa smiled at him and nodded eagerly.

"Okay then ladies, let's go get drunk!" he exclaimed, grinning at them in return.

As they were heading out of the room, he touched Alyssa's arm, holding her back. He glanced at the Latina and requested politely, "Calara, could you go rack up the drinks please? We'll be along in a moment."

"Sure, I'll see you both in a minute," she replied and headed towards the elevator.

Alyssa turned to him with a raised eyebrow. "What's up, handsome?"

"You're taking our first ship-to-ship combat remarkably well," John said, his voice tinged with concern. "I just want to make sure you're really okay?"

Alyssa blinked in surprise that he would even consider her doubting him. She shrugged and replied, "I trust you with my life. You gave orders and I followed them."

John looked equally surprised by her declaration of unquestioning obedience.

Seeing his startled expression, she stepped closer and caressed his cheek as she said, "Putting it simply; we killed some bad guys and we saved some good guys. It's pretty black and white in this case." Alyssa had been reading his thoughts, so she knew that he felt the exact same way about the encounter as she did.

He nodded, looking pleased. "I agree completely. I'm glad you see it the same way."

"You're a good man, John," she said softly, standing on tiptoe to give him a tender kiss. "I trust you; I know you'll always make the right decisions."

Placing his hands on her hips, he gazed into her bright blue eyes and saw only open sincerity in her loving gaze. "Thank you. I promise I'll always do everything I can to keep you girls safe."

She gave him an affectionate smile. "Now we've cleared that up, let's go get drunk! Who knows how you might take advantage of us young women?"

John laughed at her unassailable positivity. "Okay honey, let's go."

The trio reconvened in the Officers' Lounge, with Calara playing bartender. She grabbed bottles of vodka, soda water, and lime then began mixing up some refreshing cocktails for herself and Alyssa. She chucked an expensive bottle of whiskey John's way and he grinned at her as he caught it. His glass clinked merrily when he dropped in a couple of ice cubes and he poured himself a drink.

They brought the bottles with them to the coffee table and curled up on a comfy sofa. The girls got John to tell them his old war stories, and he regaled them with tales of boarding actions and intense fire-fights. He didn't bother to sugar coat his stories as he would for civilians, figuring that they deserved to know the realities that war could sometimes bring. The girls sat enraptured by his stories, amazed at how much he had been through in ten years of military service.

They got progressively drunker as the evening went on, eventually dissolving into fits of laughter as the topic of conversation changed to lighter subjects. It turned out Calara knew a lot of dirty jokes and she had the other two in stitches with her ribald humour. John's face muscles began to ache from laughing so hard for so long.

Close to midnight after several hours of boozing, John sat between the two girls as they looked out the window at the twinkling stars in the

endless sea of blackness. Calara and Alyssa were curled up under his arms, enjoying the view and the quiet peace of the moment.

"I never realised I could be this happy," John said suddenly, his voice catching.

The young women looked up at him adoringly. "I love you John," they both said at the same time, triggering smiles on their beautiful faces as they glanced across his chest at each other.

"I love you too" he said, smiling down at them both.

The merry trio walked back to the Commander's quarters on wobbly legs and collapsed together on the bed in a drunken tangle of limbs. They were all asleep practically as soon as their heads hit the pillow. John had had such a great night, he didn't even regret not taking advantage of his lovely young bedmates.

They awoke the next morning as one normally does after going on a big bender - quietly, so as not to aggravate a throbbing headache. John and the girls gulped down some painkillers and had a light breakfast before returning to bed for a late morning nap to sleep it off. They re-emerged around noon and John persuaded the girls to join him down in the gym.

Somewhat nervous, Alyssa followed behind Calara and entered the leisure area of the ship. Calara was a confident swimmer, so she had no qualms about being around a pool. John had come down to the gym earlier to set up "a surprise", which he convinced Alyssa was not going to be a bad one this time. When he saw the teenagers enter the gym, he strode over to them and led them to the area behind the pool. He had activated the hot tub and the bubbly water gurgled enticingly.

They stripped off their clothes and John climbed in first before helping a nervous Alyssa step after him in to the large tub. Calara slid gracefully into the frothing water moments later and the three of them relaxed on the

submerged benches, feeling the gentle streams of bubbles massaging their skin.

"This feels amazing!" Alyssa said with a happy sigh.

"See, not so scary after all." John smiled at her, pleased that she was enjoying herself.

He had an amazing view as he looked to his side. The girls were sitting next to each other and as they relaxed in the hot tub, their firm youthful breasts rose proudly out of the water, two sets of nipples looking soft and kissable. He tried not to focus on them too much and just enjoy the relaxing warm water, but his cock ached at the thought of being adjacent to so much ripe female flesh.

Alyssa knew exactly what he was thinking of course. She enjoyed his attention and posed for him subtly, without letting him know that she was on to him. The beautiful young blonde found that she was tuning in to John's thoughts every chance she could. It felt like she had a little part of her mind set aside just for him and she revelled in his constant, reassuring presence.

She had found it difficult separating from him to go and train in the firing range, the absence of his thoughts feeling like a dark hole in the mind-space that she had reserved for him. It had felt almost painful to travel more than ten metres from his side, as his wonderful presence suddenly winked out and went silent. Every morning she sat quietly in the firing range and focused inwards, the same way she had seen John do from time to time. Once she had cleared her thoughts and centred herself, she tried to reach out to find him once again, her mind yearning for the contact.

The first couple of days had been frustrating and had not borne fruit, but by the third day she was able to reconnect with him when he was in the gym. It was on the same deck, but still a good fifty metres away which was

a huge improvement, and she was overjoyed as his inner voice resonated in her mind once again. She kept at the routine every morning, trying to connect with him across decks and on the other side of the ship and by the fifth day she had managed to extend her connection to him to such a degree that she could hear him wherever he was on the ship.

As Alyssa relaxed in the soothing water, revelling in the close proximity to her man and her loving friend, she was startled when she felt another budding presence suddenly appear in her mind. This new presence was tiny and embryonic and consisted purely of heartfelt emotions: Love, happiness, contentment, acceptance. Alyssa examined it closely and recognising it for what it was, decided to reserve it a tiny little spot of its own, for her to nurture and watch it grow.

Eventually John's lusty thoughts grew loud and insistent, so Alyssa decided to put her poor man out of his misery. She rose from the hot tub like Venus from the sea, John's eyes snapping to her beautiful form as the water dripped from her glistening body. She held out her hand for Calara to take.

"Come on Calara, I think we should set up our own surprise for John to reward him for this one."

The stunning brunette rose obediently and joined Alyssa in climbing out of the hot tub. They sashayed out of the gym together, hand in hand, with Alyssa turning to smile at John just before they left.

"Meet us in the officer's quarters in fifteen minutes!" the ravishing blonde temptress called to him.

It was the longest fifteen minutes of John's life. Alyssa was correct the other day when she joked that she had been spoiling him. He was used to her or her equally beautiful young compatriot tending to his needs morning, noon and night. They had got very drunk yesterday evening, were hung over this morning and it was now well past noon. Not only

that, he had been only inches away from glorious nude temptation all morning. He felt so full, he was sure his quad was about to explode under the pressure.

He adopted a meditative pose, trying not to bump his painful taut balls in the process and concentrated on clearing his mind and relaxing. At first he wasn't sure whether he would be able to do it, he was wound up so tight, but the warm bubbly water helped him relax and centre himself. He glanced up at the wall mounted clock and saw that it was time, so he climbed out of the hot tub before heading out of the gym, not bothering to pick up his clothes.

The elevator hummed quietly as it rose up to Deck Two and when the door opened to the corridor, John saw that the lights were out. He stepped out of the lift and as the brightly illuminated elevator closed behind him, he was plunged into blackness. It took his eyes a few seconds to adjust and then he realised it wasn't pitch black, there was actually a dim flickering light coming from one of the nearby officer's rooms. He walked towards the light, his curiosity piqued.

John arrived at the door and looked in. It was a large room like all the others on this deck, but this one was had some significant differences. The entire room was lit by candlelight, the warm flickering glow from the circle of candles sending red and gold sprites dancing across the ceiling. All the furniture had been removed apart from what looked like a big mattress in the middle of the floor, covered by some kind of smooth surface instead of the normal bedding.

The centrepiece of the display was the two oil slicked teenagers standing coyly in the middle of the mattress. Their lubricated skin glistened alluringly in the flickering light and they looked slippery, pliant and oh so very willing. Lusty desire smouldered in their eyes, along with the promise of all sorts of sensual delights. His carefully gained focus nearly shattered in an instant, before he managed to just about regain control of himself.

"Come in, John," Alyssa purred seductively, welcoming him into their abode. "We set up a playroom for this special occasion, I hope you approve."

He could only nod mutely.

"Calara has a wonderful gift that she would like to give to you and I thought we should celebrate with our own little ceremony," Alyssa explained enticingly.

"I'm still a virgin in one place," Calara murmured shyly, "I'd like you to be the first and only man to take me there."

John's erection returned with a vengeance, his length hot, hard, and throbbing with need at the enchanting invitation laid out for him. He was drawn into the room by the captivating sirens standing before him. He couldn't remember crossing the room, but soon he was looming over them as they looked up at him trustingly. He reached out to place a hand on each of their curved hips, the oil slicked skin feeling slippery and delicious under his fingertips. He applied gentle pressure and the teenagers moved obediently, standing to face one another. They smiled warmly as John pushed softly at the small of their backs, encouraging them to move forward to embrace each other.

The girls stepped forward until their toned tummies were touching, feeling warm and soft where they rubbed against each other. Their wonderfully round and firm breasts pressed together, causing each girl to shiver at the slippery sensation and then gasp, as their nipples grew hard when they slid across silky smooth young flesh. John moved his hand down under their bottoms and began to stroke each of their excited young clits. Alyssa and Calara leaned together to kiss passionately and moaned into each other's soft searching mouths as he rubbed them closer to orgasm. They clung to each other and shivered with pleasure as John brought them to an amazing climax. Eventually they recovered and turned to lean against him, whispering their thanks.

John revelled in the feel of their slippery and pliant teenage bodies as two sets of large firm young breasts slid enticingly across his chest. His cock pulsed in time to his racing heart as his prick yearned to be encased in a receptive young woman. John let his hands move back from their pussies, so that his fingers were circling each of the girl's rosebuds. Calara breathed heavily, her eyes closed with anticipation, while Alyssa looked up, watching his reactions carefully through lusty eyes. Both teens gasped as he gently pushed a slippery finger into their tight, lubricated channels.

"Does that feel good, John?" Alyssa murmured, clenching his finger with her anus.

He nodded his agreement.

"Widen her out a little first, let her get used to being stretched."

John eased another finger into each slick teenager.

"Mmm, that's good," Alyssa moaned. She smiled at Calara and whispered, "Relax for him, baby. Show him how much you trust him."

At the blondes encouraging words, the brunette visibly relaxed, letting John push two fingers deep inside her incredibly tight passage.

"Now stroke those fingers in and out, let her body get used to being taken that way," she encouraged him.

John carefully pushed his fingers in and out of both girls. "Is that painful?" he asked Calara with concern.

"It feels amazing," Calara murmured and moaned into his shoulder, enjoying the new sensations as he massaged her incredibly tight hole and got her used to his intrusion.

"Gently, that's good," Alyssa said in encouragement enjoying the insistent stroking of his fingers in her body too. She kissed Calara, seeing the passion burning in her deep brown eyes. "She's ready now John."

John gently removed his fingers and the girls stepped back from him and then knelt gracefully on the large mattress. Alyssa lay down on her back, her oil-slicked body sliding on the slippery sheet. She opened her arms invitingly and the Latina knelt in between her splayed thighs, before dropping down to press her big firm breasts to sit on top of the blonde's pert proud chest. Alyssa's hands moved down to Calara's round firm buttocks and gently pulled them apart, allowing John to see his glistening prize for the first time.

The candlelight flickered around the room, highlighting the wonderfully firm muscles of the Latina's olive hued back. Her back arched as her breasts slid across the supine young woman beneath her and Calara gasped when Alyssa's strong hands parted her cheeks.

John knelt behind the beautifully presented young woman, unable to resist his desire to penetrate her. He carefully nuzzled the blunt head of his cock at the Latina's slippery rear hole, the target highlighted by Alyssa's white hands spreading those round tanned cheeks. He applied gentle but insistent pressure, to let Calara know she was about to be stretched more than ever before.

"That's a good girl," Alyssa crooned to the Latina. "Just relax and welcome him inside you."

The brunette nodded gently, her mouth slightly parted as she panted with lust. John pushed forward and Alyssa helped him by holding Calara's firm cheeks wide open to allow him full access to his target.

"Unnhh!" Calara grunted as John's lubricated cock pushed its way inside her body, stretching the tight band of her anus wide open around his

broad head. He held still with just his first few inches encased in the glorious tightness of the Latina's snugly gripping hole.

Alyssa relaxed her grip on Calara's buttocks, letting the oil slicked cheeks snap back to their normal pert position. The firm cheeks of that toned bottom trembled as they bounced back together, looking and feeling wonderful to John who wanted nothing more than to drive hard into that cushiony pillow. Alyssa's helpful hands began to slide over Calara's delightfully soft skin as she glistened in the candlelight. She brought her hands forward to take each of the brunette's juicy breasts in her hands and squeezed them energetically, pinching both nipples.

"Ohh!" Calara gasped, distracted by the rough mauling her breasts were receiving. Her nipples being tweaked distracted her from her focus on her tightly stretched ass and she relaxed back there for a moment.

John felt her body yield to him and so he pushed another few inches into the lovely brunette, making her groan as her rectum adjusted to the huge invader pushing its way into the unexplored parts of her body.

She tensed up for a moment, unused to the strange feelings of something being pushed in to her body in that tight tunnel. There wasn't any pain, she just felt full, stretched and exposed.

Alyssa saw the gorgeous brunette tense as her body was taken in this strange and novel new way. She decided to help her friend again and her slippery fingers moved down from Calara's heaving breast and slid effortlessly over the Latina's ribcage, to then skate down under her belly. With Calara's back arched, her toned little tummy was resting on Alyssa's own firm stomach and the blonde briefly wondered just how many gallons of John's delicious cum they had eagerly swallowed down between them. Her searching hand slid lower until she found Calara's swollen little nubbin and her slicked finger glided over it smoothly.

Calara moaned as her beautiful blonde lover gently caressed her clit. She arched her back even further and squeezed her eyes tightly closed as intense pleasure washed over her. The world closed off around her until all she could concentrate was the insistent stroking of delicate female fingers over her clit and the throbbing shaft currently stretching out her body in ways it had never experienced before. She relaxed as she felt the rising wave of her climax fast approaching.

With a shared groan, John steadily pushed every last inch of his massive cock into Calara's pliant body, taking advantage of her relaxed state. The relentless invader forced her to uncoil and stretch around him as he drove his length deep into her belly. Calara's mouth opened in a silent scream as a moment later, Alyssa rapidly stroked her fingers over her throbbing clit. The Latina's body writhed as she was overcome with the intensity of her orgasm.

John held on to Calara's delightfully flared hips and he looked down to see where his thick cock was pushed into her as far as it would go. Her tightly stretched ring gripped him snugly at the base of his cock and her body massaged him wonderfully as her tight passage rippled with her climax. He took in the lovely arch of her back, the indentation of her spine running in a perfect straight line from her tousled brown mane right down to her flared hips. The muscles of Calara's spectacularly toned, athletic body flexed and moved smoothly under her alluring olive skin and he loved the way she glistened in the candlelight.

Alyssa had outdone herself this time, he thought to himself. She had prepared the exquisite Latina like some kind of primitive sacrifice to an ancient deity and he relished being the one to accept such a wonderful offering from the beautiful young supplicant.

Calara sat up on her haunches, her taut, round little buttocks fitting snugly into John's lap. She kept herself arched as she sat up, so that her back was resting against his chest and she turned her head to one side, so that he could lean forward and kiss her yearning lips. She panted into his mouth

as he gradually eased back an inch, before pushing into her again as far as she could go. He could see the concentration on her face as she forced her body to relax and yield to his desires, making herself as welcoming and available to him as she could.

Alyssa moved smoothly with Calara as the brunette reared up to kiss their man and the blonde admired the way the two of them looked together. She marvelled at the powerful muscles in John's biceps and his impressive masculine physique contrasted with the gentle way he stroked and caressed the dusky hued girl he was taking. Calara was a strong, athletic girl, but John's muscular arms were at least three times as big as the lithe and toned Latina's. It was like he was a hulking dangerous beast that the girls had somehow managed to tame with their perfect young bodies.

Snapping out of her lustful dazed thoughts, Alyssa ran her hands over Calara's heaving, lubricated breasts. The brunette moaned helplessly as John held her in place and began to take longer and longer strokes into her body.

"Unh," she gasped as he pushed himself smoothly up to the hilt inside her again.

"Unhh," she grunted when he pulled back and then drove himself forward again.

"Unnnnhhh!" she groaned as he began to pummel her yielding body in a relentless, steady rhythm.

John was really working the Latina's tight ass now. Her buttocks quivered in his lap every time he thrust forward and slapped into them. They were delightfully firm and felt wonderful as he pushed into her yielding teenage flesh. He held Calara close to him, enjoying hearing her gasps and cries of pleasure as he established his dominance over her eagerly offered young body. Using his firm grip on her waist, he rocked her up and down, letting

her glorious body bounce in his lap as he used her snug little ass to stroke himself closer to orgasm.

Alyssa's hips writhed as she watched John buggering her friend with smooth driving strokes. Calara was taking everything he could give her, the Latina's elastic young body stretching around him like a snug-fitting glove. The blonde could tell they were both working towards an explosive climax, so she moved her hand down Calara's heaving chest and over the perfect oval of her toned tummy. Alyssa gently spread the brunette's velvety smooth labia and began to rub the Latina's clitoris in time with the lunging drives of John's hips.

Calara screamed as she came, her body reacting to Alyssa's skilful touch. Her tight passage undulated along John's length and constricted as tightly as it could around the pulsating invader that was thrusting deep into her belly.

"Fuck yeah!" John bellowed as the rippling sensations of Calara's ass overcame his ability to hold out any longer.

He held her hips perfectly still, pinning her in place as his own hips thrust back and forth mechanically. His taut quad was quivering with need and it felt almost painful when the first powerful shot of cum blasted into the beautiful girl kneeling before him.

"Oh, I can feel him shooting in me!" Calara gasped, as she knelt submissively in front of him, John's convulsing shaft throbbing deep inside her.

"That's good," Alyssa whispered in her ear as she stroked Calara's toned stomach "Relax and let him fill you."

Calara nodded faintly, her hypersensitive body still tingling from her climax. Her belly began to round out as John's jets of cum pumped into her ass, packing her beautiful body with copious amounts of spunk. Alyssa

felt the Latina's stomach round out as she provided a new home for his hot, heavy load. Calara looked relaxed and blissful as John used the tight grip of her anus to milk every last drop of cum from his balls.

Finally spent, John eased gently out of Calara, watching her passage seal up firmly as his exhausted cock left her hot embrace. He collapsed onto the bed and the girls joined him, with Alyssa helping Calara lie back with the awkward, beach ball sized sphere her slender young belly had become. The beautiful blonde had been riding her own powerful wave of pleasure as she felt John climax across their empathic bond. They all relaxed together and just concentrated on regaining their breath as they basked in the afterglow of such an intense orgasm.

Eventually Calara excused herself as her gravid belly rumbled ominously and she disappeared into the bathroom, leaving Alyssa and John resting comfortably together. When she returned, restored to her svelte form, they doused all the candles and cleaned up the room before retiring to the huge shower in the Commander's quarters.

John stood under the soothing jets of hot water, holding Calara in his arms. He felt Alyssa's soft body pressing up against his forearms as she snuggled in behind the Latina, so he encircled the blonde as well. Both girls looked up at him happily as he held them in his protective embrace.

Tired out from all the frenzied activity, they had a relaxing meal together in the Officers' Lounge before cuddling up in bed for the night. Calara snuggled in on John's left side and ran her hand lovingly over Alyssa's long soft hair, while the beautiful blonde eagerly took John's firm cock into her throat. Alyssa worked smoothly and efficiently to empty his balls for the night, but she saved some to give to Calara when they shared a goodnight kiss. John's eyes closed in bliss as they ended yet another incredible day.

Alyssa awoke the next morning, feeling happy and alert. The fresh-faced teenager waited patiently for her lovers to rouse from their own slumbers and when they did, she kissed each of them tenderly in turn, her soft lips

communicating the depth of the love she felt for them. Sighing with contentment, John and Calara looked up at Alyssa as she knelt beside them captivating them with her radiant beauty.

"Now I have your attention..." she said, smiling down at them both. "I want to talk about my past and why I want to travel back to Karron."

# Three Square Meals Ch. 10 – Completing the circle

Alyssa smiled shyly at her lovers and saw that she had their undivided attention. They were waiting patiently for her to begin, intrigued to learn more about this wonderful girl they loved so much.

"As you know, I grew up on Karron," Alyssa began, gazing into the distance. "It's a bleak inhospitable place, a massive asteroid that's been gradually hollowed out as the mines have dug deeper. Slums have built up in the old abandoned tunnels and there's many thousands of people living there now."

Calara didn't know much about Alyssa's history at all, so she lay there enraptured by the tale. John nodded encouragingly for the beautiful blonde to continue.

"My mother died shortly after childbirth," she said, with a mournful sign. "My father was a miner and died in a mining accident when I was only six years old."

"He was a good man, but we lived on the breadline even when he was working. After he was gone, I had nothing and no-one to turn too, so I was put in an orphanage," she said, continuing with her tragic tale.

Her exquisite mouth twisted with distaste at the memory. "In a terrible, dangerous place like Karron, there's no end of orphans, so the orphanage was cramped and overcrowded. I stuck it out there for a couple of years, but the vicious bullying made it as bad a place to be as the streets, so I left. I tried begging and scavenging for a while, just barely managing to get enough food to stay alive. By the time I hit eleven and had started to physically mature, I learned I had to watch out for other kinds of predators," she continued a grim expression on her face.

"When times got really bad, I..." she paused, struggling to go on for a moment.

Calara got up and knelt at Alyssa's side, offering her a comforting arm around her shoulders. John laid his hand reassuringly on her leg, his heavy grip feeling warm, reassuring and supportive.

Alyssa continued haltingly, "...Sometimes I did what I had to, just to survive. Some men were nice, some weren't..." She shuddered involuntarily.

Calara and John were shocked. They had no idea their warm and bubbly young companion had experienced such a horrific start in life. John hadn't known his parents, but at least he had grandparents who had loved him dearly and had looked after him in his formative years. Calara's family were career military and she had had a strict but enjoyable upbringing, living with her loving parents and three older brothers.

"Anyway, I'm sure I would have ended up getting killed by some deranged miner, but that's when I met Sparks." For the first time in her tale, Alyssa's lovely face brightened.

"I was fourteen years old when I first met her. Sparks was the same age as me and we ran into each other scavenging in a junk pile. Sparks is extraordinarily gifted at fixing machines and she was looking for parts. I offered to help, even though I had no idea what I was looking for, and we soon became great friends." Alyssa smiled wistfully at the fond memories.

"Sparks was an orphan too, but her skills at fixing things made her useful to one of the gangs. She was kind of adopted by the Diablos and she kept their gear in good shape in exchange for food. She used to share it with me and in exchange, I'd scrounge parts for her."

"I kept my head down and managed to survive, largely thanks to Sparks. I never had to... get extra money, ever again," she said, darting a look of

embarrassment at her lovers. "Unfortunately, one of the gangers took a shine to me... there was an incident and I had to escape." Alyssa gave John an affectionate smile and concluded, "That's when I snuck on board your freighter and now here I am."

John opened his arms for Alyssa, wanting to hold her close and reassure her that nothing bad was ever going to happen to her again. She smiled warmly as she lay down beside him, cuddling up at his side as Calara embraced her from behind. Alyssa could feel the brunette shuddering as she tried to suppress her tears at hearing her lover's terrible tale. Over their empathic connection, Alyssa could sense overwhelming sadness tinged with heartfelt love and compassion coming from the young woman. She reached back to stroke the Latina's leg comfortingly.

"Thank you for telling me your story, Alyssa," John said gently. "I'm sorry you had such an appalling start in life."

The lovely blonde gave him a tender kiss. "It wasn't your fault; you have nothing to apologise for. I appreciate your kind thoughts though," she said, smiling up at him lovingly.

"So what prompted you to tell us about it now?" he asked, gazing into her bright blue eyes.

"Well we're only a day from Karron now. I know we're going there for more Tyrenium, but I wanted to ask you two if you'd mind us bringing along another passenger?" she asked tentatively.

"Another passenger, what do you mean?" John asked, brushing her blonde locks away from her face.

Alyssa took a deep breath and replied, "Sparks..."

John could see how much this meant to her, so he stayed quiet and let her continue uninterrupted.

"I owe that girl my life and I think she'd make a great crewmember. She's amazing with machines and I think she'd be really useful." Alyssa's voice trembled as she added, "Besides... I'd like to save her from Karron... she's too special to waste another day in that shithole."

John looked over Alyssa's shoulder and made eye contact with Calara, who eagerly nodded her agreement, a warm smile on her face.

"Who am I to argue with my XO?" he said, smiling at Alyssa who was waiting anxiously for his answer. "She is in charge of recruitment after all!"

Alyssa felt relief washing over her as her musical laughter filled the room. "Thank you, John. You don't know how much this means to me," she replied, her voice full of emotion.

"No problem," he said, leaning in for a kiss. "Besides, look how well your last hire turned out!"

Calara grinned at them and they cuddled up together.

"Hey Calara," Alyssa asked. "Do you think we should be worried?"

Calara frowned, suddenly looking concerned. "Worried, why?"

"Well John just agreed to expand our crew. Maybe the two of us aren't enough to satisfy him any more?" said the mischievous blonde.

"Hey, wait a minute!" John cut in. "I didn't mean it like that!"

Calara sat up and played along. "Maybe we should show him we're good girls and can take care of him properly," she said to Alyssa. The Latina looked at John, gently stroking his quad."We're so sorry you had to miss an emptying the other day."

The girls moved smoothly as one so that Calara was lying on her back with Alyssa astride her, their lovely firm breasts pressed together. They closed their eyes and presented him with two soft pouting mouths shaped into ovals.

John's denials died abruptly when he saw the gorgeous teenagers offering themselves up for him like that. His rapidly growing erection led the way as he shuffled over and sank into Alyssa's welcoming mouth, bottoming out deep in her accommodating throat. He held her head as he began to stroke in and out, delighting at the soft wet touch of Calara's tongue as she licked each of his balls in turn.

"You're very good girls," John said earnestly as he enjoyed the exquisite tightness of her throat.

John pulled back out of the young blonde's mouth and then aimed lower and pushed forward between Calara's soft lips. He thrust forward until her lovely mouth encircled the base of his shaft, his balls brushing over her forehead. Alyssa kissed his stomach tenderly and then sat up to kiss him on the mouth as he fucked the pretty brunette's face.

"Doesn't that feel better John?" Alyssa asked him, before giving him a heated kiss.

"It feels so good," he agreed, trembling as Calara sucked harder.

Alyssa heard his breathing get more uneven as he started losing control and she broke away from the kiss and looked him in the eyes. "Now remember to share, we both want a nice breakfast." She lowered herself down again so her nipples were brushing Calara's and lovingly kissed his stomach, waiting patiently for his creamy load.

John panted as he became increasingly turned on. He had not one, but two lovely teenagers eager to service him and now Alyssa wanted to add

a third? That thought drove him over the edge and his balls tensed up, ready to deliver their hefty contents. He hunched forward as he came, holding on to Alyssa's shoulders to keep his balance.

The lovely blonde teen was looking down directly over Calara. She watched the bulge in her olive toned neck in fascination, kissing her throat while it throbbed in time with the jerking of John's cock, as he pumped his load directly into the gorgeous Latina's empty stomach. Alyssa could feel the brunette's toned abdomen start to rise underneath her own slim tummy, as spurt after heavy spurt rounded out the young girl's belly. She saw the bulge in Calara's neck begin to move back up and Alyssa knew that it would be her turn soon.

She moved down so her mouth was practically on top of Calara's, so John could switch girls without spilling a drop. His broad head was suddenly pushing at her lips and a blast of sweet tasting cum filled her mouth. She swallowed it down as his massive cock glided over her tongue and then began sliding effortlessly down her throat, his way lubricated by the slick layer of cum. Alyssa made sure he was deep inside her with her lips wrapped around his root and she suckled at him, coaxing him to empty every last drop out of his balls straight into her stomach. She made sure to swallow continuously so that her throat would massage his length and heighten his orgasm.

John groaned as his taut balls finally stopped flexing, having released all their cum into the girls beneath him. He gently slid out of Alyssa's mouth and flopped backwards on to the bed, making sure he was in the middle so the girls could lie on either side of him. Alyssa moved to his right and Calara to his left as had become their custom and they snuggled up to him feeling warm and soft against his body. He noticed both girls were absent-mindedly stroking their gently rounded tummies, his enormous load big enough to comfortably fill both their stomachs.

Alyssa noticed him watching her and she looked up at him. "Just let me know John, whenever you're ready..."

"Whenever he's ready for what?" Calara asked curiously.

"Alyssa..." John cautioned her, but of course the beautiful blonde ignored him completely.

"I told John that he can be a daddy whenever he wants," Alyssa announced, gazing at Calara while her fingers traced lazy circles over his chest.

"Wow, you're pregnant?!" Calara gasped, her eyes widening.

"No, not yet," Alyssa clarified. "When John decides he's ready, he just has to let me know and he can get me pregnant."

Calara's thighs began to rub together as she grew excited. "That's actually really hot!"

"Have you ever thought about having children?" Alyssa asked, her face an artful mask of innocent curiosity.

"Alyssa..." John growled in warning.

The mischievous blonde just smiled at him and gave him an impish wink.

Calara looked contemplative as she thought it over. "I hadn't planned on having children until I was a bit older, after having a successful career in the military. I hoped to eventually become Tactical Officer on a big ship and really be able to make a difference, before finding the right man and falling in love. Then when we were ready, I'd have children then."

"Sounds like a sensible plan," John said encouragingly, seeing a chance to deflect where this was heading.

"Then again, I'm already making a difference on the Invictus and I've fallen in love with the perfect man!" Calara gasped, turning to look into his eyes. Her gaze softened and she continued in a hushed voice, "John, let me know when you'd like me to have your baby and you can get me pregnant too."

John groaned helplessly. "I'm honoured Calara, truly, and I love you so much, but..."

Alyssa grinned at the brunette in delight. "We could get pregnant at the same time! We'd both have matching baby bumps and be mummies together!"

Calara squealed excitedly, climbing lithely over John to wrap Alyssa in a loving hug.

John thought to himself for a moment. "What's the matter with you? Just look at them for God's sake!" His heart skipped a beat when he sat up and looked at the gorgeous women he loved so much.

"Ladies..." he said and both girls looked up at him expectantly.

"You're both stunningly beautiful women and I love you more than anything in the galaxy. You're intelligent, kind, and caring, and would make perfect mothers for my children." John said honestly.

Two sets of doe eyes looked up at him in adoration and they sighed happily together.

"But I still think we should wait a little while as you're both only eighteen. I promise you though, I want to start a family with both of you when the time is right," he said, gently stroking their rounded tummies.

Calara and Alyssa moved swiftly to embrace him, their eyes filling with blissfully happy tears. They cuddled together feeling happier than any of them had thought possible before.

\*\*\*

The rest of the day proved uneventful after all the startling revelations and declarations of love in the morning. The girls were good to their word and at lunchtime Calara knelt between John's legs eagerly sucking his cock, impatient for him to fill her stomach again. In the evening, it was Alyssa's turn to be the vessel for his cum and she smiled contentedly after he gave her a huge load to keep her tummy warm that night.

They awoke the next day and dressed quickly before heading up to the bridge. The Invictus was about to arrive at Karron and they were all keen to see their destination after almost two weeks of travel. The cruiser left hyper-warp and Alyssa plotted a course that would dock them directly with the mining colony. Karron look bleak and uninviting, the red from the star casting a crimson pall over one side of the massive asteroid's dark-grey surface.

There were only three available docking bays available at Karron and the Invictus was too large to fit into two of them. They had to wait twenty painfully slow minutes until a huge heavy freighter pulled clear of the last bay and headed off into the blackness of space. Alyssa docked the huge cruiser, carefully guiding the ship into the tight fit of the bored-out tunnel that opened into the docking bay. As the Invictus glided to a halt with the aid of retro-thrusters, massive airlock doors creaked closed behind them and a force-field sprung into place over the tunnel as an extra precaution against depressurisation.

"Okay, let's get moving," John said to Alyssa.

They had decided earlier that Calara would stay back on the ship, to keep watch over their home. An assault cruiser was a whole lot more tempting

that a small, worn old freighter like the Fool's Gold, so John was far more wary of leaving it undefended. Calara was disappointed not to be able to come along too, but she understood his reasoning and didn't make a fuss. She kissed her lovers goodbye, with warnings to stay safe and be careful.

"So where to first?" Alyssa asked John, as they exited the airlock in the side of the Invictus.

They had landed in a huge rough-hewn docking bay, designed to load the hulking freighters that came to take away the thousands of tons of valuable ore that were mined from the asteroid. Loading equipment and storage crates lined the darkened edges of the bay and loomed in the shadows, making the dock seem sinister and foreboding.

"I thought we could go and meet your friend first," he suggested. "We've waited two weeks for the Tyrenium, a few more hours won't hurt."

Alyssa nodded eagerly and led him out of the docking bay through a towering set of doors and into the dusty and grimy spaceport that guarded the way into Karron. The couple were dressed in street clothes, as wearing combat armour and carrying assault rifles would have attracted too much unwanted attention. Going completely unarmed would have been foolish though, so they each carried a heavy pistol on their hips.

The spaceport was busy with dockhands, who had all just finished their shift after loading up the departing freighter. As the crowd of dockers left the port, chatting raucously amongst themselves, John cast a disapproving eye at a motley group of spaceport guards who leaned against a wall drinking bottles of beer. They were too far out on the rim for there to be a Terran Federation garrison here, and security at the spaceport was handled by private contractors.

John followed Alyssa through the initial huge open cave areas, which housed the spaceport and the mercantile district. There were no aliens to

be seen here, the crowds bartering noisily around the bustling market consisted entirely of pale skinned humans, or "worms" as they were known to the less than polite visitor. John wove through the throng of people, following behind his beautiful companion as she skilfully navigated the crowds. She led him away from the central hub of the colony and soon the tunnels got smaller and more claustrophobic, as they wound their way deeper into the bowels of the asteroid.

John would have been completely lost without his infallible teenage guide, who knew these tunnels like the back of her hand. His mind flitted back to Alyssa's tragic tale of her life on Karron and his heart felt heavy at the thought of his wonderful girl having to go through so much at such an early age. They eventually reached Diablo territory, which was made obvious by the red jacketed, pasty white gangers slouching insolently at every intersection.

"Aren't you worried that someone might recognise you?" he whispered to Alyssa.

She turned slightly to face him, a gleaming white smile on her tanned face, her golden hair tumbling past her shoulders and down her back. She was a picture of vibrant health and beauty.

"Okay, silly question," he said, with a wry grin.

Alyssa finally led him up to a closed steel door, flanked by two heavily-scarred men in gang jackets.

One of the ghostly pale gang members glanced up from the heavy pistol in his hands and watched John warily, while the second asked, "Hey chief, what do you want eh?"

Before he could speak, Alyssa cut in, "We're here to buy some custom gear from Sparks. We don't want any trouble." She handed each man a

credit stick for one hundred credits, while enchanting them with a disarming smile. "For your assistance..."

Powerless to resist such a beautiful woman bearing gifts, one of the gangers let them through with a casual wave of his hand. His dour faced companion punched a button on a wall-mounted panel and the locks clanked, letting the reinforced door swing open for them with an ominous creak.

John followed along behind the blonde, the darkly lit tunnels reverberating with wolf whistles as she strolled elegantly past gangers. The flirtatious comments and whistling grew quiet in her wake as the gangers spotted John and eyed him suspiciously. They eventually reached a workshop cut into a side tunnel, the bright light from a welding torch casting dancing shadows through the entrance and on to the wall of the tunnel opposite.

"Hey Sparks! You got a moment?" Alyssa called out in a friendly, familiar manner to a small, wiry figure bent over a workbench.

The welding torch cut out a moment later and the figure stood bolt upright, lifting the heavy welding mask from her face as she half-turned towards them. John could see a pasty white face looking hopefully in their direction, before the hopes were dashed and replaced by a dark scowl.

"Custom gear's over there, Blondie," she said dismissively as she waved a hand at weapon racks on the wall, before turning back to continue with her welding.

John followed the direction of the girl's pointing finger to see a surprisingly clean and well cared for set of weapon racks, filled with elaborate custom pistols and sub-machine guns. The weapons gleamed in the dull light of the workshop, looking vicious and deadly. He walked over to look at them more closely and saw that the sinister-looking black and chrome weapons were actually the work of a highly skilled gunsmith. He

picked up a heavy bore pistol and was impressed by its excellent craftsmanship and balance as he turned it carefully in his hand. Even the scope was surprising, with its powerful zoom and infrared capabilities, far beyond anything he expected to see in a colony like this. He carefully replaced it on the weapon rack, feeling a newfound respect for its creator as he turned to focus on the reunion in the workshop.

Alyssa moved closer to the tetchy figure and tried again. "Don't you recognise me, Sparks?" she asked tentatively.

The wiry girl seemed to tense with irritation before deactivating the plasma torch. Pulling off her cumbersome welding mask, she turned right around to look at them squarely. Now that John could see her clearly, he noticed a livid looking red scar all over the left side of her face and running down her neck. The girl could have once been considered pretty, if not for the disfiguring burn that looked to be many years old. She was ghostly white like all the locals at Karron and her small figure was topped by a shock of short, spiky red hair.

"Oh yeah, I remember you from our old modelling days!" Sparks scoffed. "Now why the fuck are you bothering me?!" she blurted out, annoyed at the interruption to her work.

"It's me..." the stunningly beautiful blonde continued. "Alyssa..."

Sparks snorted with laughter. "Haha! Good one, who put you up to it? Fat Tony? Choppy Bob?"

"It's not a joke, it's really me," the blonde said calmly, smiling at her friend's reaction.

Sparks rolled her eyes and laughed derisively.

"Four years ago, we got caught in a street-fight and one of the Fletcher brothers stuck me with a knife, right here," Alyssa said pointing to just above her right hip.

Sparks laughter died as she looked at Alyssa more closely for a moment. She then shook her head and grinned. "Nice try Blondie, but plenty of people were there at that fight."

"Yes, but it was only us there when you helped stitch me up. You told me that holding on to your lucky penny would make it hurt less," Alyssa said, her melodic voice catching.

"How in the hell did you know that?" Sparks blurted out, before throwing the welding gear aside and striding right up to Alyssa.

Now that she was this close, the ghostly pale teenager did a double take as she stared at the beautiful blonde's lovely features. She recognised the piercing blue eyes, her mouth, her ears; she could see parts of her old friend's face, but this stunningly attractive woman was over six inches taller than her friend, just to start with!

"What are you?" Sparks said, her eyes narrowing with suspicion. "Some kind of a robot?" she poked Alyssa's arm. "What the fuck did you do to my friend?!" she demanded, growing angry.

"It's me Sparks!" Alyssa said, growing exasperated. "We met four years ago. I used to gopher for you in exchange for food. I used to sleep over there," she said, pointing to a tucked away corner of the workshop. "I left here six weeks ago, because Georgio tried to rape me and I stuck him with a knife!"

The ghostly pale teenager stood there opened mouthed at Alyssa's outburst. "Fuck me... It really is you..." she whispered in a stunned voice, her eyes wide. "But you're tall and so beautiful now! What happened? Was it some kind of luxury bodysculpt job or something?" she asked,

while walking around Alyssa, her face showing her shock as she studied the blonde's incredible body.

"My body changed, but it's still me," Alyssa said, a warm smile on her lovely face.

"You don't even sound the same any more!" Sparks blurted out. "Your voice used to be more scratchy. Now you sound like... liquid honey," the confused girl said, struggling to find an appropriate description.

Alyssa's musical laughter filled the workshop.

"See! That's what I mean! No-one should sound that happy, it makes me want to smile just hearing your laugh!" Sparks said, desperately trying to reconcile the new Alyssa with the old.

"I know it's a lot to take in Sparks," Alyssa said, reaching out to stroke her friend's arm. "I stowed away on that freighter, like you suggested I should and it turned out it was owned by this guy." She turned and darted a smile at John.

"Nice to meet you," John said, offering his hand.

"John, this is Sparks," Alyssa said, smiling at them both. "Sparks, this is John."

Sparks shook his hand warily. "Yeah, hi."

Alyssa met the redhead's curious gaze and continued in an excited rush, "So I joined John on his ship, then my body went through a bunch of changes and I've been on a load of adventures. We decided to come back here to Karron and I wanted to come and see you, and get you to come with us and leave this place!"

"Leave?" Sparks murmured, sitting down on a nearby stool in a daze.

Alyssa nodded excitedly. "Yeah! All those times we talked about leaving this fucking dump! Now's our chance, Sparks!"

The spiky haired red-head sat quietly for a moment, thinking things through. "If what you're saying is true, then I'd love to come with you. But what about the Diablos? They aren't going to just let me walk, they make too much money from my custom work," she said, darting a cautious glance at the tunnel behind them.

"Just say you're going scavenging and then meet up with us on the ship! By the time they realise you're not coming back, we'll be out of here!" Alyssa said enthusiastically.

"But what about all my gear?" Sparks said, turning to look around her workshop in consternation. "I can't just leave all my shit behind, it's taken me years to collect all these tools and equipment!"

"Don't worry about that, I'll replace anything you leave behind," John interjected.

"Gee thanks, Daddy Warbucks!" Sparks blurted out sarcastically. Waving her arms around to encompass the workshop, she sneered, "Do you have any fucking idea how much it would cost to replace all this stuff?"

John shrugged nonchalantly. "Alyssa wants you to join us, the cost isn't a problem."

"Come see the ship," Alyssa urged the sceptical girl. "You'll see we're absolutely genuine once you're on board."

"Okay," she exhaled as she reached her decision. "I'll come see, just for old time's sake," Sparks said, not daring to build up her hopes.

Alyssa grinned happily and wrapped the smaller girl in a tight hug. "Thanks Sparks! This is going to be amazing!"

"I haven't agreed to anything yet," the redhead grumbled.

They broke apart and Alyssa saw Sparks eyeing her chest suspiciously. "Go ahead," she said, her tone matching her warm and encouraging smile. "They're real!"

Sparks reached out tentatively and gently cupped Alyssa's firm breasts in her small pale hands. "Wow, they're fucking awesome!" she gasped in wonder.

"I know, right?" Alyssa beamed happily at her friend. "Don't worry, I'll explain everything properly back at the ship. We're in Docking Bay Three."

John and Alyssa exited the workshop, leaving a very confused and bewildered girl behind them. They left the Diablos base without any trouble and wound their way back through the claustrophobic tunnels to return to Karron's central cave network.

Alyssa had been bouncing along happily beside John and she threw him a curious glance. "Do you want to go to the mine now?"

"No, I don't think so, not yet. Let's go back to the ship and gear up. If there's any chance of getting into a gunfight with a street gang, I want you in body armour," he replied, his voice tinged with worry.

She smiled and nodded, touched by his overprotective nature.

John pressed a button on his watch and contacted the Invictus. Less than a second later, Calara's anxious face appeared as a holographic projection above the watch.

"Is everything alright?" she asked with a worried frown.

He gave her a reassuring smile. "We're fine, but I just wanted to let you know we're heading back to the ship. We'll be back in a couple of minutes, alright?"

She nodded and visibly relaxed. "I'll see you soon," she replied, blowing him a kiss.

John and Alyssa strolled back through the spaceport which seemed almost deserted now. This far away from civilisation, there weren't many visitors to Karron, so the docks didn't see a great deal of activity. They followed their own footprints back through the dusty, grimy docking areas until they reached Bay Three and saw the welcoming sight of the Invictus. Calara was waiting for them at the airlock and she greeted them both with a hug as they came back onboard.

"It's just a fleeting visit, honey, we wanted to get our combat gear," John explained. "We might run into some trouble with a street gang and I don't want to take any chances."

Calara nodded her understanding and came up with them to their quarters to help them get suited up in their body armour.

John picked up his deadly looking assault rifle and loaded the bullpup magazine with a satisfying click. He followed his normal weapons check and held the high-tech rifle to his shoulder to look through the integrated scope and made sure everything was fully operational. He turned to look at Alyssa and was surprised to see her holding his backup rifle, the sister to the one he carried. She slapped in a magazine and performed an identical check with the scope. Alyssa saw him watching her and she winked at him impishly.

They said farewell to Calara a second time and asked her to watch out for their recently invited guest. Leaving the docking bay again, they strode through the spaceport terminal at a determined pace, with their rifles

slung over their armoured shoulders. The slouching guards looked alarmed when they saw them brazenly carrying assault rifles into the colony, but a stern glance from John had them backing down before they'd even taken a step in their direction. John hailed a rugged-taxi and asked the driver to take them to the Mortimer Mine.

The journey to the mine seemed to flash by, and in no time John and Alyssa were in the mine owner's office. Seb Mortimer seemed delighted to see John again and clasped his hand in a warm handshake. Alyssa watched the interaction half-heartedly. Once the initial exhilaration of seeing Sparks again had worn off, being back on Karron had proven tough going for the young woman. During the taxi ride, everywhere she looked seemed to dredge up bad memories from her past.

"Hey Seb, it's great to see you again. How's the mine been running?" John asked the mine owner politely.

"Great thanks! It's really good to see you again too, John," Seb replied cheerfully.

*You fucker, you have the balls to come back here after ripping me off?!* someone snarled furiously.

The incandescent rage in that livid voice had Alyssa whirling around, her eyes darting about trying to find whoever it was that had just spoken.

"Are you okay there, Alyssa?" John asked, wondering what his young lover was doing.

She nodded distractedly."Yeah, I'm fine, don't worry about me."

"Sorry Seb, I'm being rude. This is Alyssa, my Executive Officer," John said, introducing them courteously.

Seb glanced at her with a smile on his face. "Nice to meet you, miss."

*So you spent my money on whores, and you flaunt this slut in front of my face?!* the enraged voice barked.

Alyssa looked around bug eyed. Where was this other person? Why was no-one else reacting to the crazy stuff he was saying?!

She realised John and Seb were both looking at her in confusion and she stammered, "Err, nice to meet you."

John wondered what had gotten into Alyssa, he had never seen her behave like this before. He turned back to look at Seb and asked, "I was wondering if you'd mined any more Tyrenium? I was looking to purchase some more if you have any for sale?"

"Well we tapped out that vein in the end, but we managed to get another twenty tons out of it before it ran dry," Seb replied, an ambivalent expression on his face. "Interested in buying the rest?"

*Come around for a second bite? You little fuck, payback's going to be a bitch!* the savage voice ranted.

"That's great news!" John grinned. "I'd be interested in buying all of it. Same price per ton as last time?" he asked hopefully.

"Sounds like you have a deal mister!" Seb exclaimed, grinning back.

*Yeah, and I'm gonna take your ship and your whore too...* the voice growled dangerously.

"Let me go tell the foreman to get the Tyrenium ready for transport. You own that big fancy cruiser down at the dock right?" Seb asked pleasantly. When he saw John's startled expression, he added, "Word gets around pretty fast when something like that appears in Karron!"

"Yeah, that's my ship, the Invictus," John confirmed for him. "We're in Docking bay Three."

Seb beamed a big smile and stood up to leave the office. "I'll be back in a few minutes. It shouldn't take long to get the ore ready to go."

*My own warship... I'm going to fucking end you, then I think I'll make myself Lord of Karron...* the voice gloated.

Alyssa watched Seb leave, her eyes wide with panic. As soon as they were alone in the office, she grabbed John's arms with both hands, surprising him with the strength of her grip as she gasped, "He's going to betray you!"

John stared at Alyssa, mouth agape. "What's gotten into you?"

"He's pissed about the last deal! He thinks you ripped him off! He's going to kill you and take me and the ship!" she blurted out, desperate for him to understand the danger they were in.

"Why would you think that?!" John gasped, shocked at her sudden outburst.

He watched Alyssa's eyes dart from side to side as though she was rapidly turning things over in her head. She suddenly locked eyes with him, having come to her decision.

"I can read minds. I heard his thoughts!" she exclaimed, gazing into his eyes so he could see she wasn't playing some silly prank.

"You can what?!...." John stammered, stunned by her shocking declaration.

"It's only been you up until now..." Alyssa tried to explain.

"You've been reading my mind?" John exclaimed in astonishment, as he tried to desperately wrap his head around this latest revelation.

Alyssa broke eye contact with him and lowered her gaze, looking guilty. "I'm sorry, I should have told you earlier..."

Their conversation came to an abrupt end as they heard Seb's heavy boots outside the office door.

"Hey, welcome back," John said to Seb, managing to hide his earlier shock. "Everything good to go?"

"Sure John, let me just sort out the paperwork," the faux-friendly mine owner replied as he sat behind his desk and began to prepare the auth device, which would transfer ownership of the Tyrenium to John.

John threw a glance Alyssa's way. *Are you reading my mind now?* he asked experimentally, forming the question in his mind without actually saying anything.

Alyssa met his gaze and gave a slight nod of her head, looking a bit contrite.

*Well I'll be damned!* John thought, his eyes widening in wonder.

Unfortunately, further experimentation was cut short, as Seb held the prepped Auth device at the ready. John handed him the logging manifest for the Invictus and Seb plugged in the device and pressed a couple of buttons to authorise the transaction.

"There we go," he said, smiling. "It'll take a few minutes for the Merchant's Guild to log the trade. Are you sure you want to bother with all that?"

John gave him a helpless shrug. "Sorry, my backers are real sticklers. Any trades I do need to be registered or I get no end of grief."

Seb stifled a frown, then seemed to notice their ceramic plated body armour for the first time. "You two in some kind of trouble?"

"Oh, you know how it is with all the local gangs," John replied with an amiable smile. "Better safe than sorry."

*I'll give you sorry alright you fucker... I'm going to make you sorry you were born!* Seb thought to himself smugly.

They sat in rather uncomfortable silence for a few minutes, Seb's slight shift in demeanour more than enough for John to believe Alyssa's suspicions.

"Okay, we're all set," Seb finally said, when there was a beep confirming the deal had been logged. He smiled at them and continued in a helpful manner, "You two head back to your ship with the cargo and I'll come and meet you there with some extra boys to help speed up the loading."

*Just wait until you load that ship, then it's time to pay the piper,* Seb thought to himself, crowing over his impending victory. *This fucking idiot won't even see it coming!*

John and Alyssa stood and shook Seb's hand, before leaving his office to meet with the truck driver who would be taking them back to the Loading dock. The whole experience was becoming increasingly surreal for Alyssa, especially when she had to smile and shake hands with Seb who was planning to kill John and abuse her horribly.

They climbed up into the cab of the massive truck and John greeted the pale skinned driver with a friendly nod. He moved to sit in the middle with Alyssa by the door. The engine rumbled loudly and the cab began to

vibrate as the chunky six-wheeled vehicle began to move, leading the other three trucks in the convoy to the space port.

*So what's he going to do? Do you know his plan?* John thought at Alyssa, then waited expectedly for her voice to appear in his head.

When nothing happened, he glanced at her out of the corner of his eye. The beautiful blonde nodded her head then frowned at him when he wondered why she hadn't replied.

*Oh right, you can read my mind but I can't hear your thoughts?* John reasoned, figuring out the silence.

Another little nod from Alyssa. The truck driver hadn't taken his eyes off the road and was oblivious to the silent conversation happening only inches away from him.

*Okay then, I'll only ask questions with a yes or no answer,* John informed her, before trying to think of what to ask next.

Alyssa nodded slightly, amazed at how well John was adapting to this situation and using it to their tactical advantage.

*Are they going to attack us on the way back?* A tiny head shake from Alyssa.

*Are they going to attack us back at the Invictus?* A little nod from the teenager.

*Immediately?* John asked. Alyssa shook her head slightly.

*Ah, so probably after we finish loading. He's hoping to ambush us when we think the cargo is safe and our guard is down and he's bringing along his 'extra boys' to help him carry out the plan?* John mused to himself.

282

Alyssa nodded her head animatedly before coughing to cover it up. She was very impressed, John managed to put together the whole plan based only on a handful of yes or no answers. The girl desperately wished this mind reading ability worked both ways. She had loads of questions she wanted to ask him, but she had to stay mute... it was so frustrating!

*If he's waiting until we're back at the ship, he's probably after the Invictus too?* John's question was met by another tiny nod from the apprehensive young woman at his side.

John's mind started racing as he began to formulate a plan. *OK, when we get there, you excuse yourself and go and warn Calara, she'll know what she has to do. I'll distract Seb.* He glanced at Alyssa to make sure she had heard his orders.

She nodded firmly, a steely determination in her cerulean eyes.

*Good girl. Don't worry, we'll be fine,* he thought to her, reaching out to take her hand in his and squeezing it gently.

The rest of the journey felt tortuous as they wove their way past dirty dilapidated slums and crawled along through dark, roughly cut tunnels. John was worrying about keeping the girls safe and Alyssa was worrying that he would forget to take care of himself.

All too soon the truck convoy arrived at the spaceport and John spoke briefly to the deck officer and port guards who waved them through. The chunky trucks rolled into the docking bay and then parked against the left-hand wall under the overhanging cargo loading equipment. John and Alyssa stepped out of the cab, just as Seb arrived, riding in the first of two sturdy-looking hover trucks. Alyssa spotted tarpaulins covering some strange lumpy shapes at the top of the hover trucks and worried what they could be. Over a dozen stern-faced men climbed out of the vehicles, but didn't seem to be making any effort to help the miners with the unloading and just loitered around.

"We'll go and open the Cargo Bay for you, while you guys start unloading the trucks," John suggested to the mine owner, who nodded curtly in response.

John and Alyssa walked over to the ship, the hairs on the back of John's neck standing up as though he could feel eyes watching his every move. They approached the airlock of the Invictus and he pressed his palm against the DNA reader. The airlock spiralled open and they stepped through the oval portal.

*Time to move!* John ordered Alyssa, as the airlock started to spiral close behind them. He went through the side door to enter the Cargo Bay and the worried teen darted over to the elevator and hit the call button, tapping her foot impatiently until it arrived. She took the elevator up to the Bridge, hoping to find Calara there, and was relieved when she spotted the brunette sitting at her tactical station.

"We're in trouble!" Alyssa shouted to her from across the bridge, as she dashed over to speak to her friend.

Calara's eyes widened as Alyssa quickly briefed her on the current situation.

"OK, I know what to do," the brunette said reassuringly, activating controls on the Tactical Station.

Alyssa felt confidence and determination from the tiny emotive presence that had reappeared in her mind. Feeling reassured, she spun on her feet and sprinted back to the elevator, determined to help protect John now that she had carried out his orders.

\*\*\*

John opened up the Cargo Bay doors in the hull of the Invictus and watched patiently, as the miners ferried the Tyrenium into the cargo bay using anti-grav loading sleds. He pretended to be intent on the loading operation, but out of the corner of his eye he could see Seb's mercenaries fanning out to take cover. They furtively unshouldered rifles or unholstered pistols whilst ducking behind the storage crates that were scattered around the loading dock.

Finally, the last of the Tyrenium was brought into the cargo bay and John turned to face Seb and his men. All pretences were thrown aside as he saw over a dozen gun barrels aimed in his direction, Seb standing at the back with a heavy pistol in his hand.

"It's over, John!" Seb called out, sounding smug. "Hands in the air and walk out of the ship."

John raised his hands above his head and tried to look surprised and defeated as he walked forward slowly.

"You shouldn't have ripped me off, you little shit," Seb gloated. His eyes narrowed and his voice quivered with rage as he continued, "Yeah, I eventually got word of how much Tyrenium is selling for… fifty times how much you paid me for it!"

"Actually, I got over one hundred times the buying price," John informed him, causing the miner to growl furiously through clenched teeth.

Just at that moment, several things happened at once.

First, the tarpaulins on the backs of the hover trucks were thrown aside, revealing heavy machine guns on pintle mounts that were both trained on John by grinning mercenaries.

At the same time, the door to the elevator in the Invictus swished opened quietly and Alyssa darted down the corridor to stand on the other side of the sealed airlock, her assault rifle held ready.

Unnoticed by all, armoured panels on the hull of the Invictus began to quietly peel aside.

Finally, a ghostly white girl with spiky red hair came sprinting into the Cargo bay, her face showing some relief when she saw John. "The Diablos are after me!" Sparks cried out in alarm, before suddenly realising she had just burst into a tense standoff and screeched to a halt.

Seb lunged towards her, grabbing Sparks in a tight grip as she stood in shock. He placed the blunt nose of his heavy pistol at her temple and yelled, "Give it up, John, or this bitch gets it!"

Moments later, over a dozen red-jacketed gang members came bursting in through the entryway into the hangar. They drew their weapons and pointed them at John and the Mercenaries. "Let her go!" a bulky ganger with a mohawk shouted. "She's Diablos property!"

The mercenaries on the hover trucks spun the heavy machine guns around to point them at the new threat and the tension in the room ratcheted up several notches.

John opened his mouth to speak, but was cut off by a booming female voice being transmitted throughout the dock. "All gang members and mercenaries will leave this docking bay immediately. Refusal will be met with deadly force. You have ten seconds to comply."

Dozens of sets of eyes looked up at the towering hull of the Invictus, suddenly painfully aware of the four turreted Gatling Lasers that had spun up and were now pointed in their direction. An ominous low-pitched whirr began to echo around the docking bay.

"Ten," Calara said, beginning the countdown.

"I'm not kidding John, I'll splatter her brains all over the floor!" Seb shouted, waving his heavy pistol in the air for emphasis, before placing it back against the small girl's head.

"Nine," the Latina continued undaunted.

"Let her go. She's coming with us!" the gang leader shouted, as his men trained their weapons at the mercenaries.

"Eight," Calara intoned.

John tensed the muscles in his legs, getting ready to spring into action.

"Seven," the young woman's voice continued.

Alyssa touched the panel activating the airlock and then hugged the wall closely, staying out of sight. The door spiralled open silently, unnoticed in the tense Mexican standoff.

"Six," Calara declared, her voice echoing around the docking bay.

"Shut that bitch up, John!" Seb bellowed, furious that his carefully laid plans had unravelled so quickly.

"Five," came the booming reply.

"You better do as she says," John called out. "She isn't bluffing!"

"Four." Calara intoned, continuing her relentless countdown.

The mercenaries and gangers were looking increasingly worried now. Staring down a two-meter-long gun barrel will do that to a man.

"Three," the Latina said in a flat emotionless voice.

"Let her go man, she's my property!" the gang leader shouted, the nervous tremor to his voice betraying his fear.

"Two," Calara's countdown continued unabated.

Seb glared across the dock and yelled angrily, "Last chance John, surrender now!"

Alyssa suddenly appeared around the edge of the airlock, her assault rifle at her shoulder.

"One!" the blonde teen sang out, her melodic voice piercing the scene playing out in the room. Her rifle chattered and Seb screamed as his wrist exploded, his severed hand still clutching his pistol as it sailed through the air.

John burst into action, charging directly towards the crippled mine owner who was screaming in pain and holding the bloodied stump of his wrist with his other hand. Sparks had been thrown to the ground and was cowering in fear as the mercenaries with rifles and pistols opened up on John. They weren't expecting him to sprint right past them though, so a fusillade of small arms fire sailed around him harmlessly as he ran flat out towards the mine owner, moving too fast for the surprised mercs to react in time. John barrelled into the critically injured man, shoulder charging him with a ceramic plated pad that sent Seb sprawling, leaving John to bounce off and drop to a crouch next to the frightened redhead.

The low-pitched whir of the Gatling lasers was drowned out as Calara opened up with the Invictus. Staccato blasts of laser fire arced outwards, illuminating the dimly lit room with strobing flashes. The hover trucks were hit by dozens of high energy pulses, the vehicles exploding as the multi-barrelled Gatling lasers chewed through them in seconds.

The Gangers could only stare in terror as the last two Gatling lasers turned in their direction and sprayed the wide doorway with a long continuous burst of laser fire. Most of the Diablos managed to throw themselves to the ground or leap behind storage crates, but two gang members weren't so lucky. One was hit by several laser bolts, each hit searing holes straight through his body and leaving his torso looking like a smouldering Swiss cheese as he toppled over. The other was hit in the shoulder, the laser bolt penetrating clean through and melting the entire shoulder joint. The man's arm fell to the floor, the charred stump glowing with the heat of the impact and he collapsed to his knees in shock, his mouth agape in horror.

"Get behind those crates!" John ordered Sparks, pointing to some sturdy storage containers stacked against the side of the room. The terrified teenager looked up at him wide eyed, before she managed to shake off her fear and started crawling in the direction John had pointed. John attempted to shield the girl, using his armoured body to cover her as she scampered away. Round after round went sailing over his head, but a few hit his arms and back, ricocheting off the tough ceramic plates. He winced as he felt the impacts, one round slammed into his right thigh between ceramic plates and caused him to flinch in pain.

Alyssa's eyes narrowed with anger as she sighted in on the mercenaries shooting at her lover and friend. Her assault rifle chattered in multiple bursts as she took steps to eliminate that danger. The first burst hit a merc who was crouched behind a crate firing his pistol wildly. The three hollow point rounds hit him squarely in the head and his skull exploded as the bullets blasted out the other side.

The second burst hit a merc standing in the open, who had stepped out of cover to try and shoot around his colleagues, his line of sight to John blocked after his reckless charge. Alyssa's shots punched into the mercenary's torso from the side, eviscerating him as the bullets tore through his body and leaving him writhing on the floor in agony.

Her final shot hit a merc in the leg as he tried in vain to conceal himself behind a crate. Two of the bullets hit him in the calf and the last blew out his knee, showering the crate in gore. The man slumped to the ground screaming in pain as he clutched his ruined leg.

The Diablos cowered behind crates as the cargo bay turned into a horrific hellscape. Bright flashes of laser fire kept them pinned down and illuminated the corpses of their brothers who had been cooked by laser fire, ashy clouds of smoke rising from their charred bodies. It was a powerful reminder of what would happen to them if they broke cover, so they wisely ducked down as low as possible.

Sparks finally managed to crawl behind the sturdy storage containers stacked against the rough wall of the docking bay. The containers were pock marked with impacts from the dozens of rounds fired in their direction, but John was glad to see the containers were robust enough to stop the rounds from penetrating. He followed the young woman behind the crates, glad to be out of the line of fire for a moment.

"Are you okay?" He asked the scared girl as she huddled up against the crate, trying to make herself as small as possible.

"Yeah, I didn't get hit," Sparks replied, much to John's relief.

The gunfire from the mercs had gone quiet for a moment, when they were no longer able to shoot at him. After a brief pause, he heard numerous small arms firing again, but this time the rounds weren't headed in his direction. He held his assault rifle at the ready and carefully leaned out behind the crate, to see what the remaining mercenaries were shooting at. He saw they were firing towards his ship's airlock and he heard the distinctive chatter of one of his assault rifles firing back defiantly. John saw the muzzle flash at the airlock door and that sudden flare of light revealed a mane of golden hair.

"Goddamnit!" he swore. *Get down Alyssa!* he shouted in his mind, praying his fearless companion was listening to his thoughts like before.

He was greatly relieved when she immediately disappeared from view. He had the mercs in a good crossfire from his current position and he was able to drop two more with carefully aimed bursts, before the rest of the mercenary team reacted and ducked down low behind cover. Unfortunately for both the mercenaries and the Diablos, the storage crates proved scant protection against the ship mounted Gatling Lasers. These weapons were designed to take out lightly armoured fighters, so a few inches of reinforced plastic provided scant protection against the searing laser bolts.

Calara began to walk laser fire along the defensive positions held by the two hostile groups. Glowing holes were punched through the storage crates before the laser bolts connected with soft flesh, screams of pain announcing every successful strike. Pitiful cries of surrender began to drift up around the loading bay and John contacted Calara using his watch communicator and asked her to cease fire.

"It's over, get out of here!" John shouted loudly to the terrified attackers, their morale truly broken.

The seven remaining Diablos stopped to pick up their fallen brothers and dragged them from the loading bay. The mohawked leader was one of the survivors and he turned to face John before he left.

"This ain't over chief, the Diablos got long memories!" he snarled. When two of the Gatling lasers began to spin up and track him, his bravado disappeared and he fled the docking bay.

John saw the three surviving mercs crawl out of cover and limp away, leaving their fallen behind. He took a quick glance at the abandoned corpses, but he couldn't see Seb anywhere. While he was searching for the treacherous mine owner, he noticed a bloody trail across the grimy

decking. The spatters of blood leading out of the docking bay originated from the point where he had sent Seb sprawling, so John figured he must have crawled away during the heat of combat.

He glanced down at Spark and asked in a kind voice, "Are you okay to walk?"

The shocked girl nodded tentatively and John offered her a strong hand to help her stand up. Adrenalin was fast wearing off and the young woman stood on wobbly legs, reluctant to let go of John's supportive arm. He helped her to walk towards the Invictus' airlock.

Alyssa came dashing over to join them, her face showing her concern. "Are you both okay? Did either of you get hit?"

John gave her a reassuring grin. "I'm going to have a nasty couple of bruises, but other than that, all good!"

"I was so worried!" she gasped, hugging them both.

John held her off for a moment, glancing over his shoulder at the writhing figures still lying in the slaughterhouse behind them. "Let's get inside the ship first. I'm still feeling a bit exposed here."

Alyssa helped Sparks through the airlock on her shaky legs, while John entered the Cargo Bay and pressed the controls that would re-seal the outer hull of the Invictus. He walked briskly over to meet up with the girls in the corridor and they took the elevator up to the Command Deck.

The door swished open quietly and they walked out onto the Bridge. Alyssa watched her friend with amusement as Sparks stood open-mouthed with awe at the technical wonder that was the command deck of the Invictus. The multi-levelled bridge was illuminated with the light blue glow of the holographic tactical images projected into the centre of the room.

Calara stood up from her station when she heard them arrive and rushed over to meet them. "I'm so glad you're all ok!" she said, relief showing clearly on her face when she saw that they weren't injured.

"It's our very own deus-ex machina!" John exclaimed upon seeing Calara and he moved forward to sweep her up in a warm hug. "That was awesome honey, you were amazing!" he said proudly.

The gorgeous Latina beamed up at him, glowing with his praise.

"Thanks for the rescue, you guys," Sparks said in a small voice, clearly intimidated by the massive ship and yet another ravishingly beautiful woman.

"Oh sorry, I'm being rude," John apologised to the girls. "Calara, this is Alyssa's old friend Sparks. Sparks, this is Calara. We're very lucky to have her as the Tactical Officer on the Invictus."

"And she's quite lovely too!" Alyssa said affectionately, wrapping Calara in a hug. "You did a great job today Calara. Thank you so much for saving these two!"

"You're all welcome!" the gorgeous brunette smiled at them, her deep brown eyes warm and friendly.

"Why don't we go to the Briefing Room and we can have a chat," John suggested to the young women gathered around him.

The three teenagers followed as he led them to the as yet unused door on the other side of the Bridge. It led into a sizeable room, with a long meeting table dominating the space, surrounded by plush, comfortable-looking chairs. A long window ran the length of the room, which would no doubt provide spectacular views, but unfortunately all they could see at the moment was the rough-hewn rock of the Docking Bay wall. John

gestured for the girls to sit and once they had moved to take their seats, he sat in the luxurious leather chair at the head of the table.

"Alyssa, why don't you explain to Sparks what you had in mind for her onboard the Invictus?" John prompted gently.

The beautiful blonde nodded and gleefully launched into a long and detailed explanation of her plans for her spiky-haired young friend, shocking the pale teen to the core.

"Now wait a minute, let me just get this straight..." Sparks said, holding up her hand and ticking off each point on her fingers. "You want me to join the crew as Chief Engineer and sail around the galaxy in this monster of a ship. I get an almost unlimited budget to maintain the Invictus and I can work on whatever side-projects I like. I get to hang out with my BFF and I'm going to end up looking like these two goddesses," she said, waving her hand towards Alyssa and Calara.

"And all you want in exchange is for me to dyke out with beautiful and gorgeous here from time to time and have Mr. Handsome blow me up like a balloon whenever he wants?" the redhead asked.

Calara and Alyssa nodded serenely, lovely warm smiles on their perfect faces.

John was a bit startled by her blunt delivery and replied with some hesitation, "That's about the size of it I guess..."

"Well show me where to sign up!" Sparks said with a wide grin.

John chuckled. "Welcome to the team," he said, smiling warmly at the newest addition to his crew.

Alyssa stood and wrapped her old friend in a big hug. "I'm so happy you're coming with us!" she said, overjoyed.

Calara gave the little redhead a hug too. "I'm looking forward to getting to know you," she said with a smile, her voice friendly and welcoming.

"Well I don't know about you girls, but I think I've had quite enough of Karron," John said soberly.

The young women nodded in agreement.

"Alyssa, please take us out of here and plot a course to Olympus Shipyard," he requested, as he rose from his chair and led the group from the briefing room. As he stepped back on to the bridge, he grimaced as he continued, "I'd better speak to the Starport authorities and explain the carnage in the dock. I'll be in my Ready Room; let me know when we're under way."

With that, John strode away, disappearing into his office.

"He's a real take-charge kind of a guy, isn't he?" Sparks commented to Calara, turning to look at the Latina.

"Uh-huh," the gorgeous brunette nodded dreamily, watching John with adoring eyes as he walked into his Ready Room.

\*\*\*

John walked over to his desk, then pressed a button on the built-in console to activate the comm interface. As he sat down, he searched through the list on the local directory until he found the contact details for the starport authority. Swiping across the name, he waited patiently for the call to be answered and unsurprisingly it didn't take long for the call to go through. He was sure news of the shootout in the docking bay must have spread like wildfire throughout the spaceport.

A scruffy-looking man in a crumpled uniform appeared as a holographic image above his desk. "What on Terra do you think you're playing at? Firing off starship weapons in my spaceport!" he blustered, but his stern words were undermined by the hint of fear in his eyes.

"My apologies, Mr. Hammond," John replied calmly, reading the man's name from his callerID. "We were forced to repel boarders. Some locals attempted to steal my ship, so we dealt with them accordingly. I just wanted to advise you of our imminent departure."

"You want to leave?!" the man scoffed incredulously. "No fucking way! I'm impounding your ship, Mr. Blake, until we can get this mess sorted out!"

John produced his ID and slotted it into his desk. "It's Commander Blake actually," he replied, watching the spaceport official's eyes widen as John's rank appeared on his holo-display. "As you can see I have sufficient authority to assert military jurisdiction over Karron if I choose to do so. Perhaps we should begin with a thorough audit of senior staff's financial records?"

The man's white face paled even further and he frantically shook his head. "I'm sure that's not necessary, Commander!" he choked out.

"That's good to hear," John said with a smile. "Now, I'll be departing immediately. Please clean up the mess in Docking Bay Three."

"Yes, Sir! Right away, Sir!" Hammond replied, throwing him a shaky salute, suddenly desperately eager to see John on his way.

\*\*\*

Sparks turned from Calara at her Tactical Station and watched Alyssa dart up the illuminated steps to the Command Podium. Her old friend sat down in the plush Executive Officer's chair and activated a holographic

Sector Map, which sprang into being in the centre of the Bridge. Sparks was curious to see what she was doing and followed the enthusiastic blonde up to her station. She could only stare in amazement at Alyssa's slender fingers dancing confidently across the console, rapidly plotted a course back to Olympus Shipyard, right in the centre of the Terran Federation. A glowing blue line representing her projected flight path appeared on the map, linking from star to star right across several sectors.

"How do you know how to do all that?" Sparks blurted out, gaping at her in shock.

"I had some spare time and John needed a Navigator," Alyssa replied with a shrug, smiling happily as she added the finishing touches to their route back to the core worlds. "Just give me one second..." she requested as she activated the comm interface, raising a delicate finger to her full lips, gesturing for her friend to hold the questions for a moment.

Sounding calm and confident, Alyssa declared, "Karron starport, this is the cruiser Invictus. Requesting clearance to leave Docking Bay Three."

After a brief pause, the communications officer at the starport replied, "Clearance granted Invictus."

Warning lights began to flash in the loading area and a hexagonal patterned force field sprung into being, sealing off the cruiser from the rest of the Docking bay. Shortly afterwards, the force field sealing the outer bay doors winked out of existence and the massive airlock squealed in protest as the doors opened, depressurising the tunnel out into the vacuum of space.

Sparks watched astounded as Alyssa eased the sleek cruiser out of the crudely bored out tunnel and manoeuvred them clear of the asteroid. The beautiful blonde rotated the ship smoothly and then powered up the enormous engines, causing the Invictus to surge forward on its way towards the Nav beacon.

"Say goodbye to Karron, Sparks," Alyssa said to her oldest friend in a quiet voice. "I promise you, the rest of the galaxy has so much more to offer."

The redhead nodded mutely as Alyssa activated the FTL drive and their ship leapt into hyper-warp and away from their old home. Sparks watched the asteroid in the system map and saw Karron grow tiny before disappearing behind them as the Invictus raced away. She was finally leaving the colony where she had spent her entire life.

"To the future," Sparks thought to herself, feeling a bit scared, but daring to hope for the first time.

## Author's Note

This is the opening eBook of a story that has now exceeded 2 million words. I'll be converting all of it to this format in the coming months, but as I'm sure you can imagine that will take a little time!
To continue reading more of John Blake's adventures, you can find my Patreon site at:

https://www.patreon.com/user?u=3814558

There you'll find links to the subsequent chapters as well as art I've commissioned for the girls, spaceships, and weapons that are featured in this story.

Thank you for purchasing this book and supporting my writing.

M Tefler

Printed in Great Britain
by Amazon